A Nose for Hanky Panky

Sharon Love Cook

Neptune Rising Press
900 Cummings Ctr. #404-T
Beverly, MA 01915

Neptune Rising Press

Cover Illustration: Sharon Love Cook
Book Layout and Design: Polgarus Studio

Published in the United States of America

For my parents,
the late Meim & John Love

One

The murder had all the ingredients to create a buzz: attractive professional woman, wealthy Chestnut Hill family, famous (in pharmaceuticals) father, and last but not least, sex. The only missing ingredient was a Kennedy. Thus, I didn't begrudge the media for descending on our town like a flock of seagulls at a clambake. After all, I cover the news, too.

My job as reporter for the *Granite Cove Gazette* takes me many places, most of them not worth visiting twice. I cover events such as the Beautification Society's house tour and the Senior Citizens' Chowder Fest. When we need to fill space, I'll even throw in the latter's bowling scores.

We're a weekly with a staff of four. Until the murder, our biggest story was the salmonella poisoning at the mayor's picnic. Imagine how overwhelmed we were, covering a murder. Not only that, the victim wasn't some brawler from one of the harbor-front bars but a prominent citizen. With her Ivy League degrees and office at the chi chi

Harbour Building, she was the last person you'd expect to end up murdered.

I'd been working at the newspaper for three years since quitting my job teaching high school English. Although writing for a small town paper can be tedious, it beats explaining the difference between simile and metaphor to a bunch of bored teenagers. Today, when folks speak of the "enormous rewards" that come from working with young people, I think, they can have it.

And lately the title "journalist" is applied to anyone owning a steno notebook. Even Beth, our college intern who writes the obits, calls herself a journalist. I, on the other hand, consider myself a reporter reporting on our citizens. Thus, when Dawnette Vicari won Miss Northeast Seafoods, I not only covered the pageant, I included her beauty tips, e.g: a clam shell for exfoliating the skin.

In any event, our staff met the challenge of covering the murder. We worked hard getting that issue out. Even Stew, the part-time sports writer, worked around the clock. For the first time in history we sold every copy of the *Granite Cove Gazette*. Needless to say, there were no bowling scores that week.

As I mentioned, the victim wasn't your average townie. No, she was a paragon who drove the perfect car, a glossy, midnight blue BMW convertible. Its doors sported nautical flag decals meaningful to those who sail. Many times she'd roar past me on Route 128 as I chugged along in my pre-owned Jetta. I'd yell out the window, "Up your exhaust pipe!" Although my words were blown away by the wind, I felt righteous.

Newcomers claim they chose Granite Cove for its proximity to Boston and its cultural offerings, which they ignore unless the Red Sox are in first place. Nonetheless, our town has its attractions, such as a natural harbor and excellent beaches. My favorite, Cape Hedge, is rock strewn and popular with mothers. Yet when the temperature hits ninety, I don't mind a few bloody toes and soccer moms.

Despite its physical beauty, Granite Cove lacks the glamour of other North Shore towns. Twenty years ago and fresh out of college, I blamed the lunkheaded citizens and their preoccupation with high school football and the fishing industry. Today, having lived in an upscale suburb of Saab-driving professionals, I've come to appreciate lunkheads.

Lastly, Granite Cove has its rewards, but you must dig for them, like the clams at Schooner Flats. Stick around long enough and you'll find what you're looking for, providing it's not a Starbucks. Outside of posh Hemlock Point, the town is basically no frills. It's not cozy or trendy. It's a place to leave when you are young, and when you're older, a place to raise a family. Those who leave only to get their butts kicked are welcomed back, no questions asked.

Granite Cove is all that and more. Yet there's one thing we never imagined, not in a million years. It's also a place where people get murdered.

I first heard about the murder on Tuesday, normally a bad day for reporters. No one returns calls on Tuesdays. While you can schedule an interview on Wednesday or later in the week, Tuesdays are black holes for news.

To make matters worse, I had a hot story, by Granite Cove standards, and in order to provide balance, I needed a quote from Mayor Froggett. When I called city hall, Janis Topp, his secretary, put me on extended hold. Time to ruffle some feathers—not one of my strengths, alas.

I called back and mentioned to Janis that my story concerned the mayor's recent purchase of an SUV from Moles Used Motors. Does Mayor Froggett assume the taxpayers don't know that his wife, the former Sandy Moles, is Buster Moles' sister? Isn't that called a conflict of interest?

Janis played it cool. She's had a grudge against me ever since I wrote about the salmonella outbreak at the mayor's picnic. Two senior citizens from the Council on Aging ended up hospitalized. I mentioned that Janis Topp's potato salad was a possible culprit after the public health director cited it. Janis was enraged, as if I'd accused her of attempted seniorcide.

In any case, with a deadline looming I called the city treasurer who informed me that Buster Moles had given the town a break on the SUV's price. According to him, the citizens should be pleased.

My hot story was losing its sizzle. Not that it mattered in the long run. Mayor Froggett ignores negative press. Year after year he's had no opposition for office. As a result, he thinks the citizens will overlook everything, including his toupee and affair with a school crossing guard. As far as Ken Froggett is concerned, giving taxpayers' money to his brother-in-law is good business.

Yet I wouldn't abandon the story. One of these days our readers will become fed up with the shenanigans at city hall. While I don't expect a riot, I'm hoping they'll produce a worthy candidate for the next election or, at the very least, an angry letter to the editor.

In that frame of mind I decided to take a break and visit my dad. After leaving Yvonne a note saying I was going out to price software, I grabbed my bag and headed for the door. Five minutes later I pulled into the parking lot at Stella's Sausage Kitchen.

Stella's is an anomaly. You wouldn't think a sausage joint would prosper in a seacoast town, but it's where the locals and the tourists go. Maybe it's the down-home atmosphere of knotty pine booths and Formica counters. Maybe it's big Stella herself, manning the grill with her giant spatula. Newcomers are intimidated; they don't know that Stella's prickly exterior hides a mushy center.

As usual, the parking lot was crowded. I found a space below the restaurant's landmark, a trio of pink plastic pigs. The giant porkers sit on a riser inside a chain link fence to discourage theft. Last year they were targeted by the high school seniors during Prank Night. Not only are the pigs a tourist attraction, they're a landmark as well. When giving directions to the downtown, folks say, "After you pass the pigs on the left, Main Street will be your third right."

Stella waved her spatula when I walked in. Her hair, the color of scrambled eggs, was frizzled around her broad face. I stood at the end of the take-out line. A new waitress, a young blond woman in a ponytail, zipped back and forth from the counter to the tables in the dining area. Despite the lunch rush, she appeared calm. Before giving her my order, I said, "It looks like you're handling things nicely." I offered my hand. "I'm Rose McNichols, a friend of Stella's."

"Hi, Rose, I'm Brandi." She gave my hand a brief shake. "Stella's given me a chance here. One day at a time I'm paying her back."

"Stella can spot a winner," I said and recited my order: a grilled egg sandwich with sausage, mustard, and Velveeta Cheese. It's my dad's favorite despite Doc Moss's dietary restrictions.

I stepped aside and looked around the room. The lie I'd told Yvonne to escape the office nagged at me, so I decided to put my time to good use. I fished a notebook from my bag and scanned the customers for suitable candidates to interview.

At the end of the counter, two fifty-ish women attached their baked macaroni and cheese as if they'd never heard of Doctor Atkins. I apologized for intruding and introduced myself. Before you could say "bacon bits," I asked their opinion of the mayor's SUV purchase.

One gave a shrug and returned to her plate. Her companion wiped her mouth with a napkin and said, "I hear Buster threw in snow tires and an extended warranty."

I hadn't verified that nugget of information, so I said, "Be that as it may, do you think the mayor should be doing city business with family members?"

She nudged her companion who was ogling a Boston cream pie inside a glass dome. The woman swiveled on her stool to face me. "Honey, it's simple. If the mayor gets a break, the city gets a break."

"I see." I snapped my notebook shut. So much for citizens' outrage.

Back inside the car with the grease-stained bag perched on the console, I drove away from the downtown area. On Route 127, I took a right at the sign for the Granite Cove Senior Life Center. I'd driven fifty yards when I spotted my dad walking on the sidewalk. I pulled over and blasted the horn; he's deaf as a haddock in his left ear. He stooped and peered in at me for the longest time. Then, tucking his cane under his arm, he opened the passenger door and got in.

"I thought you were Mrs. Masucci, my neighbor. She's after me."

"You think everyone's after you, and do I look that old?"

"I left my glasses at home," he said.

The Granite Cove Senior Life Center consists of an administration building and four three-story residence buildings set in a semicircle. This allows the tenants to keep an eye on each other. Recently, when Mrs. Bullock fell on her way to the mail box, three tenants dialed 911. My dad, however, doesn't appreciate that safety aspect. He claims his neighbors aren't looking out for him, they're looking at him. He could be right.

Amazingly enough, the administration building was once Dad's elementary school. Seventy years ago he raced up those thick granite steps carrying a lunch pail. Today that little boy is an old man carrying a cane.

Conditions inside his apartment were worse than usual. Dried oatmeal was stuck like barnacles to the stove top. Coffee grounds speckled the kitchen tiles. The odor of stale laundry hung in the air. I decided to forego using the bathroom. All in all, it was enough to gag a maggot.

"I thought Doris was cleaning today," I said, hanging my jacket on a doorknob.

"She was supposed to," he said. "That's why I went out, to get out of her way."

It was obvious the housekeeper hadn't visited. People like Doris Zack, a home health aide, have enabled my dad to live independently following his stroke.

I found her phone number on a refrigerator magnet and dialed from the kitchen. Doris answered on the first ring: "Hello?"

"This is Rose McNichols. I'm at my father's place—"

"Oh, Rose!" She wailed so loud I had to hold the phone away from my ear. "I should have called him but..." Her voice dropped to a whisper. "The police brought me home."

"The police? Whatever for?"

"This morning I... I found a body."

"What do you mean, Doris? Whose body?"

Dad shouted from the living room, "Is she coming or not?"

I motioned him to be quiet and asked her, "Are you all right?"

"I'm okay now. It's shock. Matter of fact, I only answered the phone 'cause I thought you might be Doc Moss's office. They're sending some pills for my nerves."

"I won't keep you then."

"Hold on a minute, Rose. I might as well tell you, but keep it to yourself. It's not for the newspaper, not yet. What happened was, around seven this morning I'd gone to clean at the Harbour Building, the fancy new place near the park? I've got a couple of private clients that I do early before my agency regulars. One of them's Dr. Klinger, you know, that good-looking head doctor?"

"I know who she is."

"Anyway, I was cleaning her office, and when I went behind the desk... that's when I saw her."

"Saw who?"

"Dr. Klinger. She was lying on the floor in a slip. She was dead all right."

"What! Are you sure?"

"I'm sure. Her hair kind of covered her face, and when I bent closer, I saw blood on the back of her head." Doris wheezed into the phone.

"That's okay. Take it easy. What did you do?"

"I picked up the phone to call the police, and for the life of me, I couldn't remember the number. So I went into Mr. Farley's office—he's right next door—for a phone book. My hands shook so much I couldn't hold it. I told Harold that's it, I'm getting one of those cell phones that the young people have.'"

"You didn't call 911?"

"The police asked me that same question. When Harold had his heart scare, I called 911 right away. I knew it was for home emergencies. I didn't think it was for reporting, you know, dead people."

"I'm sure that's a normal reaction, I said. "You were certain she was dead?"

"I'm sure. Years ago I was helping at the Methodist bean supper. You remember Margaret Stank, the minister's sister-in-law?"

"I'm not sure."

"She was in charge of decorating for the event. But when we got to the church, the tables were bare. No place mats, no centerpieces, nothing. We figured she forgot. Margaret was a little scatterbrained like her sister, but don't quote me. Me and the other ladies pitched in to set the tables. At one point I went into the pantry to get more pickles and found Margaret dead on the floor. They said she had an aneurysm..."

"Doris, you were saying how you couldn't call the police this morning?"

"Right. What happened was, I ran outside. It's early and no one's around, so I went to that little convenience store nearby. A sign on the door said Back in Five Minutes. The kid that works there goes out back for a smoke. I've been meaning to speak to the manager—"

"Yes, Doris, what happened next?" The woman needed a Border Collie to keep her mind on track.

"I went behind the store where the kid's sitting on a milk crate, smoking. I says to him, 'Call the police,' and he says, 'I'm on my break.' Glory be to God, Rose, he's taking a break and hasn't been open more than an hour. That got me mad so I says, 'There's been a murder.' Well, that got his attention. He goes, 'Where?' and I said, 'None of your business. Let me in to use the phone.'"

"And then you called the police?" I asked, prodding her along.

"Not quite. It's a pay phone, and I've only got a dollar bill in my apron pocket, so I tell the kid I need change. He says he can't open the cash register unless I buy something. By that time I'm ready to explode, and you know me, Rose, I'm easy-going. Just ask your dad. He'll tell you how I'm always joking—"

"Doris, did you call the police?" The perp could be setting sail on the Queen Mary by the time Doris finished her story.

"I was getting to that. First I bought some chips so the kid could open the register. Then I called the police. When I got back to the Harbour Building, the cops were already there."

I sighed. "Thank you, Doris. Do you have anyone at home with you?"

"I got Harold. The cops picked him up at the Senior Center. He plays pool there Tuesdays." She chuckled. "He says he almost swallowed his teeth when they walked in, asking for him."

"Did the police identify the body?"

"I suppose they did, but they never said anything to me. Chief Alfano won't tell you if your coat's on fire. Here I was the one who called it in, and he won't let me go back in the building to get my pocketbook and cleaning supplies. Cal Devine ended up giving me a ride home in his cruiser."

Good old Cal. "Would you like me to come over?"

"Thanks, Rose, but I'm better now." She yawned. "I'm going to pull the curtains and lie down awhile. Tell your dad I'll get to his place probably on Thursday. I got some makeup customers to do first."

"Don't worry about that. If it's okay, I'd like to stop by tomorrow morning."

"That's fine," she said. "By the way, there's one thing I forgot."

"What's that?"

"Chief Alfano told me not to say anything 'til they had a chance to notify the family. Keep this under your hat."

"You know me, Doris."

After hanging up I dialed the cell phone of Cal Devine, my favorite cop who also happens to be a former boyfriend. He answered, his voice hushed. "Rosie, why am I not surprised to hear from you?"

"I've been talking to Doris Zack. What's going on?"

"Wait a minute. I'm sitting in the parking lot with twenty cruisers from Rockport to Boston. Let me get out and talk." The sound of a car door slamming was followed by the crunch of gravel. Cal resumed talking, louder now. "Okay, McNichols, what do you want to know? By the way, I figured Doris Zack's silence wouldn't last five minutes. "

"Just tell me what's happening there. Doris mentioned Dr. Klinger."

"You didn't hear it from me, okay? In a nutshell, the victim is Vivian Klinger, a local shrink with an office at the Harbour Building. Apparently she was working latc last night when someone paid a visit and clubbed her."

"My God, I can't believe she's dead."

"She's dead all right. We'll know more after the coroner's report. They're not using Doc Moss for this. They got someone from Boston."

"Was it robbery?"

"Doesn't seem to be. Nothing's out of place and the surrounding offices weren't touched. They're thinking it's a patient with a grudge."

"What was the murder weapon?"

"Blunt instrument, a club, judging from the wound."

"One more thing—"

"Make it quick, honey. The chief's gonna make a statement."

"Was Dr. Klinger sexually assaulted? I understand she was wearing a slip. "

He sighed. "Somebody ought to duct tape Doris Zack's mouth. Yes, she was wearing a slip, but we won't know until the coroner's report."

"Thanks, Cal. I'll call you soon."

"How come you only call when you want information?"

"I'll try to do better. No suspects then?"

"Right now everyone's a suspect, including Doris Zack. After all, she had a key to the office."

"Do me a favor," I said. "Don't tell her."

After hanging up I leaned against the refrigerator and stared off into space. How could Dr. Klinger, of all people, be dead? I had seen her on cable TV two nights ago. The local hospital's mental health unit was promoting the fact that April is Depression Month; the clinic offered free screenings.

Dr. Klinger looked professional and glamorous at the same time. Her dark hair gleamed under the studio lights. She exuded such competence I almost picked up the phone to make a screening appointment. In the end I didn't. I have a pretty good idea what my depression score would reveal, that I'm somewhere between pessimism and despair. Blame it on April, the cruelest month.

Dad interrupted my reverie. "What did Doris say? Is she coming over?"

"Not today, Dad. Maybe Thursday." I decided there was no point in telling him about the murder. He'd hear soon enough.

"They better not charge me for today," he muttered.

I had to get back to the office, pronto. Before leaving, I unwrapped Dad's lunch and set it on the counter. On my way out the door, I made sure his dead bolt lock was securely in place.

Yvonne's bug-eyed stare indicated she'd heard the news. "Rose! I've been trying to get you for an hour. Don't you answer your phone?"

"I left as soon as I heard," I said, making a beeline for my desk. "What do you want me to do?"

"You can start on Dr. Klinger's bio. We've got file photos but nothing recent."

"I took some great shots at that award luncheon. Let me find them." I tossed my pocketbook on the desk and booted up my old Mac.

"I've been getting calls from all over New England. Beth's coming in to help with the phones. They say Dr. Klinger was done in by a deranged patient."

"Who told you that?"

"Insider knowledge. When they find out about her background, this town will be crawling with media." She bit her lip. "We'd better have a staff meeting and decide how we're going to handle this situation."

Yvonne was talking to herself, a sign of nerves. Her editorial experience was in society news. For twenty-five years she covered ladies' teas and fashion shows for a suburban daily that was bought by the same newspaper chain that bought ours. For some perverse reason they appointed her our editor-in-chief. The move was either a promotion or an attempt to force her into retiring.

"A staff meeting sounds good," I said. "Where are Coral and Stew?"

"Coral's taking photos of the Harbour Building. The area is roped off, but she can get some nice exterior shots."

Coral, our free-lance gardening and home columnist, has been with the paper since the days of lead type. When Coral started talking retirement, Yvonne gave me the housekeeping hints column to lighten her load. Basically, what I know about housekeeping could fill a gnat's belly button. This I told Yvonne, who said, "Just have fun with it." I am, and so far the readers haven't caught on.

"Coral's out," I said. "Where's Stew?"

Yvonne didn't answer. She appeared to be in a trance, gazing out the window and scratching her forearms. When she gets nervous, her eczema flares up. I repeated my question.

"Stewart? Oh, he's interviewing the headmaster at Dana Hall, a prep school Dr. Klinger attended."

"That leaves just the two of us for a staff meeting," I pointed out. "How about waiting until tomorrow? This story will be huge. Dr. Klinger came from a very wealthy family. Why don't we put out an early edition?"

Yvonne frowned. "We've never done anything like that before. It might appear crass, as if we're taking advantage of a tragedy."

"Yvonne, the story is bigger than Granite Cove. Dr. Klinger was an icon in this town, and let's not forget she was murdered."

She shut her eyes. "Don't say that word."

"I admit it's shocking, especially for Granite Cove. Nothing like that's ever happened here. Yet we can't relegate it to the police notes. Everyone else will play it up big."

Perhaps my matter-of-fact attitude got through to her. In any case she quit digging at her skin. After a moment's silence she said, "I suppose we could approach it as a tribute to a well-respected citizen." She glanced at me. "Yes, I'm comfortable with that. Now, what did you say you have for photos?"

"Remember when Dr. Klinger was chosen Woman of the Year? I covered the awards luncheon and got some great shots."

"Fine. See what you've got and get started on her bio. In the meantime, I'm waiting for a call from Chief Alfano. He's giving me an exclusive."

At the mention of his name, her cheeks flushed. I knew what kind of exclusive that would be. If Chief Alfano were forbidden to use the word "I" he'd be rendered speechless. "I'm afraid he's in over his head," I said.

"Nonsense. This town doesn't appreciate the man's capabilities."

There was no point in arguing with Yvonne when it came to the chief, but at least she was focused and back on track. Things would hum along, at least until the next derailment.

While Yvonne took phone calls, I looked through files in my desk. The day of the luncheon, I'd taken at least fifteen shots. My demeanor at the time had been professional, my mood sour. Being chosen Woman of the Year by the Professional League is an honor, and while I may snicker at the group's pretensions, every year I hope to be named. This year, not only was I not chosen, I had to work the luncheon. Halfway through the Chicken Piccata, I got up to snap photos. When I returned to my seat, my plate was gone. Not even a lousy doggy bag.

I finally found the CD and after inserting it into the computer, studied the photos. Dr. Klinger looked vibrantly alive. One close-up captured her polished perfection: wide, confident smile and dark, shoulder-length hair with a "signature" silver streak on the left side.

In order to get that picture I'd moved in close, on my knees. Dr. Klinger stood at the podium giving her acceptance speech. She'd removed her suit jacket; under it was a crisp, wrinkle-free blouse. My blouse, on the other hand, was as creased as Granny Clampett's butt, which is why I never take my jacket off in public.

Late that afternoon, Yvonne paced back and forth at the front window. Her espadrilles slip-slapped the tiles, creating an annoying distraction. Not only that, she blocked my view of the town green. There the citizens gathered, their heads bobbing and darting like chickens. No doubt they were clucking about the murder.

"Relax, Yvonne," I told her. "We're not the only news source covering the story."

"I'm well aware of that," she said, pacing. "It's how we handle the subject that worries me. We can't appear vulgar like the tabloids. The nice people in this town won't forget."

There was no point in mentioning that by the time our paper hit the stands, the news would be as outdated as Yvonne's espadrilles. No matter how brilliant our copy, readers will have learned every detail. In fact, they might not bother with our coverage at all. We could blame Dr. Klinger's death on Janis Topp's potato salad, and people might never notice.

"Who did you say Stew was interviewing?" I asked, changing the subject.

"The headmaster at Dana Hall in Wellesley. From what I understand Dr. Klinger was quite an athlete, setting records in swimming and tennis." She paused. "Or was it swimming and fencing?"

"Maybe it was swimming and wrestling," I said.

Yvonne stopped to stare at me. "If that's a joke, it's not amusing."

I ducked my head. "Just trying to ease the mood."

"I'll never understand your sense of humor," she said and resumed pacing while I returned to my photos. The day Yvonne understands my humor is the day I sign on with the Merchant Marines.

It was early evening when I finally pulled into my driveway. I pressed the remote button for the garage door, and nothing happened. Either the batteries were low or the door was broken. Another item needing attention.

Nonetheless, I can't complain. I rent one-half of an old carriage house. Frank, the owner, occupies the other half during the summer. Two years ago he bought a bar in St. Croix, exchanging his Brooks Brothers wing tips for rubber flip-flops. From November to May, while Frank is in the Virgin Islands, I keep an eye on his half of the house.

I make sure the pipes don't freeze, the plants don't die, and the squirrels don't move in. For those caretaking duties I get a rental reduction. It's a sweet deal, especially when you consider the cost of real estate north of Boston. On my salary I can't afford a down payment on a Porta-john.

Chester, my 12-year-old black Lab, greeted me at the door. He ran in circles around me, delirious with pleasure. I rubbed his graying muzzle and wondered what man would give me such a welcome.

After tossing my tote bag on the sofa, I fixed a large vodka and cranberry juice and grabbed a box of Cheez-Its. With that, I collapsed on the antique recliner. Technically, it's not an antique; I doubt that La-Z-Boys were made a hundred years ago.

My furniture is what I call early modern ghetto. It's comfortable, like an old pair of slippers. One of these days I intend to cover everything in a pretty Laura Ashley print. At the same time I wonder, why spend money on thrift shop furniture? Who am I trying to impress? It's unlikely the Granite Cove Beautification Society will include me on their annual house tour. Not only that, if Chester drooled on my expensive custom slipcovers, or Kevin spilled beer, I'd have hysterics. Ambiance, though nice, is not worth the price.

After another vodka and cranberry, I broiled a cheeseburger and tossed a small salad. Instead of watching the news at my tiny kitchen table, I read The Boston Phoenix. I'd had enough local murder for one day. Tomorrow it would be topic number one. As sure as the bluefish will appear in August, murder will be on citizens' minds.

It was close to eight o'clock when I grabbed Chester's leash and headed out for a walk. I didn't need more than a sweater; it was still warm. When we reached the main road, traffic was surprisingly steady. The season's first indication of spring lures the night riders from their beds. Convertibles zoomed past, the music cranked. The cars' occupants weren't teenagers, they were baby boomers tearing up the back roads. While The Rolling Stones blared, they chased down memories of their youth.

Before long I turned into Tally Ho Drive, a new cul-de-sac ringed with pastel-colored McMansions.

Suddenly, Chester came to life, tugging at the leash. Most likely he'd gotten a whiff of outdoor grilling. I unhooked his collar so he could romp. Instead of pursuing the scent of sirloin, he headed for a big white Colonial. There in the center of a gently sloping lawn, he squatted and "did his business."

Oh, crap, I thought, yanking a plastic bag from my pocket. But when I slipped my hand inside, I found a hole the size of a Big Mac. I glanced at the Colonial's big picture window. Two kids lay sprawled in front of a massive TV. The screen was so big you could park cars on the lawn and call it a drive-in.

After making sure we weren't being observed, I attached Chester's leash and dragged him to the sidewalk and down the street, all the while resisting the urge to look back. Normally, I'm a responsible pet owner, picking up after my dog with regularity—no pun intended. I likewise perform acts of good citizenship: returning library books on time, recycling plastic bottles, and buying every flavor of Girls Scout cookies. Thus, my conscience is untroubled.

Back home, I listened to my messages while getting ready for bed. The first was from Betty Ann, wanting to talk about the murder. The next was from Kevin, calling from the Sacred Cod, a local bar where he plays Tuesday nights. Would I join him for a drink, he shouted over the pub's din. Even murder can't keep Kevin Healey from his Guinness.

After deleting the messages, I dialed Doris Zack's number. Harold answered and when I convinced him I wasn't from The National Enquirer, he called Doris to the phone.

"I'm glad it's you, Rose. The news people have been calling here. Harold says turn the phone off, but my sister Shirley had a gallbladder operation three days ago. What if she has complications?"

I told Doris that, gallbladder or no gallbladder, she should unplug her phone. She was a senior citizen and shouldn't be hounded. Not only that, I didn't want anyone getting an exclusive before me. The latter I didn't mention.

I ended by saying I'd drop by around nine the following morning. After hanging up, I made one last call to the newspaper. When Beth the intern answered, I asked why she was working late.

"Yvonne went home to get some sleep,"she said.

"I'm glad to hear it."

"Rose, guess what?" Beth squealed with excitement. "An editor from *USA Today* called. We talked about Granite Cove and before she hung up, I asked if I could send her my resume. She said 'by all means'. Isn't that awesome?"

"Good for you," I said. No flies on Beth. I told her to leave a note for Yvonne saying I'd be in by late morning.

Once settled, I reached underneath my bed and dragged out my seven-year-old laptop I bought on Craig's List. At the time, it never occurred to me that a 1993 laptop would weigh more than a pair of bowling balls. Yet despite its heft, it allows me to write in bed, where I do my best work.

In the late night stillness, the only sound was Chester snoring on the couch. I balanced the laptop on my thighs and with pillows supporting my back, I typed my column. Murder and mayhem may reign in Granite Cove, but readers demand their housekeeping hints.

Auntie Pearl's Helpful Housekeeping Hints

Dear Auntie Pearl:

I recently threw a housewarming party to show off my new condo. I invited family, friends and co-workers. All were impressed with my decorating skills. It was a lovely evening until my cousin Edward arrived, tipsy.

He proceeded to drink all the brandy punch and finish off the pesto dip. Following that, he threw up on the peach shag rug in the living room. Needless to say, it put a damper on the festivities.

I've had the rug cleaned professionally, but the stain remains. Consequently, I sent a bill for the cost of the rug to Edward, who returned it with a nasty note. Now I'm seriously considering small claims court.

My family says I'm not being supportive of Edward, who's going through a difficult divorce. What should I do, Auntie Pearl?

Tormented in Topsfield

Dear Tormented:

Peach shag? In the living room? My dear, what were you thinking, choosing shag for such a high traffic area. It has a tendency to mat and is extremely difficult to clean. Not only that, the color peach shows every stain, as you've discovered.

Try sponging the area with a mixture of equal parts water and white vinegar. Follow with soda water, blotting up the moisture with paper towels. Avoid scrubbing, as this can destroy the rug's fibers.

Let me know how this works. Hope I've helped!

Auntie Pearl

Two

The next morning I was awakened by warm dog breath in my face. The clock read eight-thirty. Holy halibut!

I stumbled into the kitchen to let Chester out. Then I searched the front yard for the newspaper, finding it under the Jetta's rear wheels. With the paper tucked under my arm, I stopped and lifted my face to the sun. For a brief moment I enjoyed the sensation of sunshine on my face, and under my bare feet, warm asphalt.

Inside the kitchen, while yesterday's coffee reheated, I spread the *Boston Compass* across the kitchen table. The murder was on the front page, although below the fold, as they say in newsroom parlance.

Prominent Psychologist Slain in Granite Cove, ran the headline. Beneath that, the subheading: *Daughter of Pharmaceutical Mogul Bludgeoned.* A black-and-white photo of Dr. Klinger in glasses accompanied the story. She looked like a no-nonsense—albeit attractive—academic.

I drank my coffee, my eyes skimming the page. Dr. Klinger's mother, Veronica Kittridge Klinger, was labeled a poet and patron of the arts; her father, Lawrence Klinger, was identified as President and CEO of Klinger Pharmaceuticals.

Background information included degrees from Wellesley in '83 and Harvard in '87, as well as professional affiliations and the prestigious journals in which she'd been published. Even Granite Cove got star treatment; it was referred to as a "summer playground of the rich." That description harkened back to an earlier era when Boston's aristocracy summered at Hemlock Point. According to the old timers, the seasonal residents arrived by train where they were met by chauffeurs. They were then whisked away to their sprawling "cottages" on the Point.

Today it's the new money living at the Point. The former cottages are now Jacuzzied estates from which Mom carpools the kids to Seaside Country Day School. Following that, she heads out to Olde Shores Country Club for a bit of tennis or golf.

The story continued on page five with two photos of the ritzy Harbour Building and Police Chief Victor Alfano. The latter resembled a Basset hound with his deep-set eyes and turned-down mouth. His quote ran under his photo: "Granite Cove is a quiet, close-knit community of people who know and look out for each other."

Except for newcomers like Dr. Klinger, it seems.

Much as I wanted to finish the story, I'd promised Doris Zack an early visit. After a quick shower, I pulled on a cotton jersey and cardigan and a short, black denim skirt. There was no time to search for pantyhose sans holes, so I went bare legged. All the better to feel the balmy air. Spring in New England is like happiness: Enjoy it now—it may be gone tomorrow.

A row of neat, two-family houses lined the Zacks' street, ending in a strip mall. Five years ago, before the mall's arrival, neighborhood kids played street hockey in the road. Today, it's like a speedway.

I banged on the Zacks' front door, the noise of traffic deafening. Harold Zack's impassive gray face peered at me through the screen. "She'll be right down. Come in," he said, swinging open the door.

According to Doris, her husband's "bum" heart was the cause of his early retirement. "Now he sits and watches TV all day," she complains.

I squeezed past his belly to enter a pleasant sun porch. "This is nice. I'll wait here," I said, settling into a white wicker chair. "How's Doris doing?"

"She slept good last night," he said and yawned so wide I could see down his esophagus. With that, his eyes closed and his chin dropped to his chest. When Doris appeared in the doorway, he was snoring. She glared at her dozing husband. "Did you offer Rose any coffee?" she barked.

He opened an eye. "You make some?"

"I told you I made some." She shot me a disgusted look. "They never listen." I laughed and got up, following Doris into the kitchen. "Sit at the table, Rose. I'll bring the cups over."

I sat at a white Formica table and glanced around. The Zacks' kitchen looked like a laboratory. Everything was white and immaculate: appliances, cabinets, and a tile floor. While I can appreciate a tidy room as much as the next person, my motto has always been "Cleanliness is next to impossible."

Doris set a tray on the table. She took a seat across from me. As she poured coffee into white mugs, I asked how she was holding up.

"Truthfully? I never had such a fright. You hear about things like that happening in Lynn or Boston, but never here." She scooped sugar into her cup and pushed the bowl toward me. "Years ago, after my dad's hip surgery, he moved in with Harold and me. One morning I was fixing his eggs while he went into the bathroom." She snapped her fingers. "Like that, he was gone." She shook her head. "So you see, I'm no stranger to death. Still, it gave me a terrible shock, seeing Dr. Klinger on the floor like that." She poured a river of cream into her cup. "Go ahead, Rose. I see you got your pad out. Ask me whatever you want."

"I'll start at the beginning. What's your routine when you're working at the Harbour Building?"

"What I always did was clean Dr. Klinger's office first because she got in early. After that I did Mr. Farley, the lawyer. Their offices have a connecting door, and during the day they keep it closed." She glanced at me. "I only mention it because that's the way the office is set up, not because I thought there was any funny business going on."

"Uh huh."

"They were friends, see? After work, a couple times a week they'd open that door. Mr. Farley would go into her office and they'd have a drink together."

I glanced at her. "How do you know this?"

"Mr. Farley told me it was their ritual. I found out when I went to her office late one afternoon. I'd had the bug and couldn't clean that morning. Her pretty wooden cart was out. It's where she kept the glasses and liquor bottles. In my day they were called hostess carts.

"Dr. Klinger had already gone home. Mr. Farley was still there and spotted me polishing the cart. He said they liked to have a little something at the end of the day, and would I return his mug to his office after washing up." She winked. "I guess he didn't want me getting the wrong idea, thinking he was drinking alone."

"What mug was he talking about?"

"The mugs they drank out of. Hers has Wellesley on it and his says Harvard. After washing the mugs, I polished the cart, swept up the pretzels and nuts and emptied the ice bucket. After vacuuming Dr. Klinger's office, I put Mr. Farley's mug on a shelf in his office."

"Do you clean his office as well?"

"That's right. He used to have one of those companies do it, but tell you the truth, they did a lousy job. They never moved the furniture to vacuum and—"

"So," I interrupted, "they always drank in her office?"

She nodded. "Probably because she's got the view of the harbor from those French doors. That's also where her patients leave when their sessions are over. I guess they don't want folks seeing them leaving a head doctor's office. You know how people talk in this town."

I nodded, making a note to ask Cal about the French doors. "Those two must have been pretty friendly. Did you tell the police about their cocktail hour?"

"I can't remember what I said, I was so shook up. Anyways, it wasn't a secret. It was two friends enjoying each other's company. Folks might think he was sweet on her. His wife Martha is kind of mannish, you know?"

"What do you think, Doris? Were they just friends?"

"Oh, I think so. I've got a nose for hanky panky, and Dr. Klinger's not the type to have an affair."

"What do you mean?"

"Don't get me wrong. She was a good-looking gal and not the kind that goes for women, if you know what I mean. As for Mr. Farley... well, he can leave his slippers under my bed anytime." She laughed and glanced around in case Harold had overheard. "Dr. Klinger, you see, was polite but proper. With her it was always, 'Good morning, Mrs. Zack,' no matter how many times I'd say 'Call me Doris.' You know me, Rose. Just ask your dad. He'll tell you how friendly—"

"Excuse me, Doris, getting back to cocktails, do you have any idea how much they drank?"

"Not a lot. A bottle would last a long time. They drank the good stuff, too, Johnny something."

"Johnny Walker?"

"That's it. A pretty red and gold label. "

I glanced at my watch. It was time to hasten things along. "The police will be looking into Dr. Klinger's patients as possible suspects. Did you ever see them?"

"Not unless I got there late. Most days I was finished by eight thirty."

"On the day you discovered Dr. Klinger's body, you didn't see anyone in the area who may have had an appointment with her?"

She eyed me over the rim of her cup. "Chief asked me that."

"What did you tell him?"

"He asked if I'd seen anyone in the building who might have business with Dr. Klinger. I told him I come to clean, not to poke my nose in people's affairs."

The manner in which Doris clamped her mouth shut aroused my curiosity. "I take it you didn't see anyone suspicious?"

"I wouldn't use that word, 'suspicious.'"

I set my notepad on the table and looked at her. "What word would you use?"

She leaned toward me. "I trust you, Rose. When the chief asked about seeing someone in the building, I wasn't lying. I hadn't. It was later, outside, when I saw someone."

"Someone connected to Dr. Klinger?"

"Uh huh."

"Can you tell me about it?"

She paused for an instant. "Okay, I'll tell you. I was freezing my butt off because the chief wouldn't let me back inside to get my things. That got my dander up. Here I was the one who'd called them, and he's treating me like a vagrant. He's firing questions one after another like a pop gun, making me nervous. Not only that, I was worried about my pocketbook inside. How was I gonna get home with no money?

"That's when I saw the girl, one of Dr. Klinger's early patients. She was riding her bike into the parking lot, but when she saw the police car she turned around and went out, real fast."

"You didn't mention it to the chief?"

"It's none of his business. Besides, if I told him he'd go over to the shelter and hound her like a criminal. I feel sorry for the poor kid."

"She lives at the shelter?"

"Used to. I don't think she does anymore. Ah, that's a sad place—people all jammed in together; cardboard boxes for their things. No place for a pretty young girl."

"You know her?"

"Sure, but like I said, I haven't seen her lately. My church group visits the shelter once a month. We put on bingo games and do cooking groups. One morning in February I saw her outside the

Harbour Building, sitting on the steps. She said she had an appointment with Dr. Klinger. It was cold out, so I told her to come inside and wait."

"She said she was a patient of Dr. Klinger's?"

"Uh huh. When Dr. Klinger found out I'd let her in early, she asked me not to do that. She asked me nicely, but she meant business. That's just the way she was. That woman went by the book, God rest her soul."

"Doris, the police will eventually question this girl along with the other patients. Can you tell me her name?"

Doris laughed. "I was going to, soon's you gave me a chance. Her name's Brandi Slocum. I hear she's been working at Stella's place. The poor kid comes from a hard luck family. Her father, Roger Slocum, used to work at the wharf with my Harold, years back. They called him Fishrack on account of when he got drunk he'd sleep it off on the fish racks. He eventually went out on disability." She tapped her head. "That's where he's disabled."

"I've met Brandi," I said. "She's living at Stella's."

"Stella will keep an eye on her. God knows she can use it. Her family's a tough crowd. The mother ended up at Met State, and the brother's in jail for drugs. Good luck to her is what I say."

I wondered aloud how Dr. Klinger's death would affect the young woman.

"Let's hope she stays on the straight and narrow," Doris said. "I shouldn't be telling tales out of school, but there was talk a while back. You know how folks like to talk in this town; nothing else to do with their time. Anyway, they said she was working as a, you know, prostitute up in Peabody. She wasn't much more than eighteen at the time. What's she now, early twenties?"

I nodded, amazed at Doris's insider information. The National Enquirer has nothing on her. "Where did you hear that?"

"Harold heard them talking down at the wharf. What's worse, they claim that Fishrack, her father, took hush money from the guy running the business."

I remembered not long ago reading about a call girl ring operating out of a house in Peabody. The neighbors were told the occupants were holding house ware parties. They projected a family image. The women drove cars with baby seats and bumper stickers that read, *See You in Church*. It was a clever ruse while it lasted.

"Do you know the name of the man who was behind it?" I asked. Local police claimed they didn't know his identity.

"Some big shot," Doris said. "The cops looked the other way. I heard Fishrack paid him a call one day. The guy took out a wad of bills: all hundreds."

"I gather the Slocums aren't your all-American family," I said.

"Nope. It's hard to believe a pretty girl like that comes from folks like them. I sure hope Dr. Klinger, God rest her soul, was a help to her. If anyone needs a little luck, it's Brandi Slocum."

The Zacks' kitchen clock said eleven when I put away my notes. Doris walked me to the front door. "Tell your dad I'll be over Thursday," she said. "I'm making up for those I missed. The agency pays me for one hour at each apartment, but I'm no clock watcher. I don't leave until the place is spotless."

Doris had her work cut out for her at my dad's. At the same time, I hoped her booster shot hadn't expired. "Is your phone turned on?" I asked.

She grinned. "I never turned it off. And miss all the excitement? The New York Post called. Can you imagine? Maybe I'll be on that TV crime show. In the meantime, I don't want to miss a thing."

En route to the office, I drove by Kevin's house. His Mustang convertible was parked in the driveway and I pulled up behind it. When I rapped on the front door of his duplex, his neighbors' curtains moved. Two widowed sisters and their brother live next door. The three siblings seem happy as clams living together; the years of working and raising children are behind them. A family reunited, they've come full circle.

Kevin, who comes from a big family, scoffs at this observation. I sentimentalize sibling relationships, he says. According to Kevin, his neighbors live together because it's cheaper.

I rapped harder, peering through the gauzy curtains covering the window above his door. From inside, a shadowy form lurched toward me. The door jerked open and Kevin, in a tee shirt and pajama bottoms, squinted at me, his hand raised to the morning sun. "Rosie! I didn't know you were coming over."

I stepped inside, shutting the door behind me. "I hope I'm not interrupting anything," I nodded toward the darkened bedroom.

"Do you think I'd answer the door if I were... entertaining?"

"You dirty dog," I said, jabbing my elbow into his ribs. "Do you think I wouldn't know?" Doris Zack's words rang in my ears: I have a nose for hanky panky.

We stood facing each other in the narrow hallway. Kevin grabbed my wrists and pressed me against the wall. He whispered in my ear, "Vixen, see what you've done? You've given me ideas."

I looked up at him. At six foot three inches tall, Kevin looms over my five foot nine. Although his hair was sticking out in all directions and he clearly needed a shave, Kevin looked cute. He's the type that people call boyish. No doubt he'll look boyish when he's seventy-five. Unfortunately, as the youngest of eight siblings, he sometimes acts like a kid. As I'm four years older, I can feel like Auntie Rose.

"I'd love to stay," I told him, "but I've got to get to the office. There's a murderer on the loose, in case you haven't heard."

"And Rose McNichols, star journalist, is tracking him down, eh?"

"If he or she doesn't find me first."

He leaned back, as if slapped. "Mother of God, Rose. Don't joke like that."

"Sissy." I slipped from his embrace and headed for the kitchen. "Got any juice?"

Kevin followed. In the kitchen he opened the refrigerator. "I've got some Dr. Pepper." He jiggled the bottle. "Still fizzy. You want some?"

"You're the only person over seventeen who drinks Dr. Pepper in the morning," I said, taking a seat at the kitchen table. The surface was covered in crumbs, much like my dad's.

Kevin sat next to me, setting the Dr. Pepper bottle before him. "I'm sorry I don't have coffee. I only drink it with Irish whiskey."

"Never mind. I don't need anything. I stopped to ask if you want to go out with Betty Ann and Tiny next week. I haven't seen them in ages."

Kevin wrinkled his nose. "You know I Iove Betty Ann, but Tiny's a sorehead."

"It'd be a casual night, an early dinner at the Sacred Cod."

"I played there last night. Hey, I called you. Why didn't you come over?" He held my hand as I explained about working late. "You should have come anyway. I got everyone in the place step dancing. I stayed 'til closing." He stretched out his long legs. "My feet hurt because I wore the wrong boots." He looked at me beseechingly. "Honey, do you mind?"

I sighed. "Just for a minute. Then I've got to get back to the office."

He swung his stockinged feet onto my lap. "You give the best foot massage north of the Mystic River."

I kneaded his toes as he winced. Like many kids growing up in South Boston, Kevin took step dancing classes. He became a musician, graduating from Berklee College of Music. Today, as the Mad Irish Fiddler, he entertains all over greater Boston. His gigs take him everywhere, including nursing homes. Consequently, it was at Green Pastures Retirement Home where I met him.

I was visiting my mother, a patient in their stroke rehab clinic. One afternoon, I heard "Danny Boy" coming from the activities room. It was so beautiful, I stopped to peek in the window. Kevin stood before an audience of old people in wheelchairs. He played a violin, his music piercing my heart. When the song ended, the crowd wiped away their tears. The white-haired ladies smiled tenderly at Kevin, as though they wanted to adopt him.

My feelings, however, were not at all maternal...

"How is Betty Ann?" he asked, interrupting my reverie.

"Not so good," I said. "Tiny's thirteen-year-old son from his first marriage is living with them. His mother, Tiny's first wife, is in rehab. She hurt her back at work and became addicted to prescription pain pills." I paused to flex my fingers. "It's tough on Betty Ann. She and Tiny have only been married for two years. Now they have to be role models for the boy."

Kevin, having chugged the bottle of Dr. Pepper, slammed it on the table. "Rose, don't use that language in my house."

"What language?"

"Role model. Geeks talk like that."

"Is that so? For your information, Beth, our intern, calls me a role model."

"If anyone called me that I'd tell them to bug off.'"

I pushed his feet off my lap and stood up. "You're in no danger of that, Kevin Healey."

He jumped up and put his arms around me. "Don't be mad. Let me take you to breakfast."

"It's lunchtime, and I've got to go." I slung my bag over my shoulder. "If I set up a date with Betty Ann and Tiny, can I count on you?"

"How about if I take you and Betty Ann out?"

"No, Tiny's got to come with us."

He yawned and stretched his arms over his head. "You promise to leave if Tiny starts acting like a junior high principal?"

I raised myself up to kiss his cheek. "I promise."

There was nothing to be gained by explaining Tiny's desire to set a good example for his son. Kevin, the boy wonder, wouldn't understand. He'd no more alter his behavior in order to make a good impression than join the Rotarians. My boyfriend's stubbornness can be annoying, but at least he's true to himself.

Yvonne, alone at the office, was the first to speak: "Nice of you to drop by, Rose."

I ignored her sarcasm and headed for my desk. "Did I mention that I have an interview with Spencer Farley?"

"The lawyer? I didn't know you knew him."

"I know him."

She waited for me to elaborate, but I offered nothing more. Minutes later she appeared at my desk, a wad of tissue pressed to her nose.

"Rose?"

I didn't answer right away. Although I sympathize with Yvonne, who's in over her head with the murder, I can't let her take it out on me. She should take it out on Coral, who's accustomed to it.

"Yes?"

Yvonne looked exhausted. The bags under her eyes had bags of their own. Her upswept hairdo, secured by dozens of pins, looked like a mudslide collapsing on her shoulders. All in all, I've seen better looking bag ladies. "Are you busy Thursday night?" she whispered.

"Why?" I asked, sounding suspicious.

"I thought it would be nice if someone from the paper makes an appearance at Dr. Klinger's wake. I'd go myself, but it's the PCA's night off. "

"PCA?"

"Personal care assistant. She helps Mother get ready for bed. Can you go? I'd ask Coral, but she's terrified to leave the house at night, what with this maniac loose."

"Okay, I'll go."

She pressed a damp hand on my shoulder and thanked me in a choked voice. I saw no reason to mention I'd been planning to attend Dr. Klinger's wake anyway. In fact, I wouldn't miss it for all the calamari in Granite Cove.

Late that afternoon I called Betty Ann at work: "Green Pastures Activities Department. Betty Ann Zagrobski speaking."

"It's me," I said. "I'm sorry I haven't called."

"I was beginning to think you were victim number two. I almost called Cal Devine at the police station."

"Don't do that. I've been bugging Cal enough as it is."

"I don't think Cal minds you bugging him at all. By the way, did you hear he's separated from Marcie?"

"What? Since when?"

"You are so in the dark, buddy. See what happens when you neglect your friends?"

"I'll make it up to you. How would you like to go to a wake with me on Thursday night?"

"Best offer I've had all week," she said. "Whose?"

"Dr. Klinger. Who else? Yvonne asked me to go and represent the Gazette."

"I thought Dr. Klinger was Jewish."

"Her father is. Her mother's Episcopalian."

"Kiddo, with their money they can call themselves Wampanoag Indians and no one would care. Where's the wake being held?"

"Frost Funeral Home. Please go. I hate attending those things alone."

"Okay, I'll go. I need a break from Jonah. My life is so depressing that a wake actually sounds good. Pick me up?"

"Around six-thirty. Thanks, Betty Ann."

I switched my computer to sleep mode and approached Yvonne. "I've got to leave for my interview with Mr. Farley." She looked up with a smile so big, I added, "And I'd like to visit my dad beforehand. He needs help now and then."

She held up a hand. "Say no more. I'm a caregiver and I understand. Now remember, don't ask Mr. Farley any touchy questions. The poor man's had a terrible scare, what with his office being next door to the crime site."

"I thought I'd grill him on his whereabouts the night of the murder."

Yvonne's eyes bulged until she realized I was joking. "You're such a card, Rose. Now I won't belabor the point, but keep in mind that Martha Farley advertises with this newspaper, and it's quite a substantial account."

"You don't have to remind me. Who can miss her ads?"

"Those ads pay our salaries," she said.

"In that case, I won't tell Spencer that his wife's nickname in high school was Leather Legs."

Yvonne pursed her lips. "Certainly not. Martha Farley is a force in this town."

I was halfway to the door when she called, "Remember, Rose, you'll catch more bees with honey than with vinegar."

Dad's TV was so loud, I heard it when I got off the elevator at his floor. When I pounded on his door I got no response. He'd probably removed his hearing aid. I knelt on the floor and searched my pocketbook for his door key. Then I realized I'd left it in my glove compartment. On a whim, I turned the doorknob and the door swung open. He was dozing on his recliner.

"Dad, it's a beautiful day. What are you doing inside?" As soon as the words left my mouth I got a sense of deja vu. I remembered, years ago, Dad standing in the doorway of my bedroom and asking the same question.

He blinked at me. "Guess I fell asleep. I went out earlier to the community center. They had pea soup today. Not much ham, but it's only two dollars and fifty cents."

"I've got a little time this afternoon. If you want to go to the drug store, get dressed."

He struggled to his feet. "I am dressed."

I gave him the once-over. His flannel shirt hung out of khaki pants that bagged in the seat. Why do old men wear such baggy-ass pants? Although I don't make a point of checking out their butts, it's a fact of life: When you reach seventy-five, your ass disappears.

I refrained from mentioning the pea soup stains on his shirt. I didn't want to be overbearing. When I nag him, it's for important issues, like leaving his door unlocked with a murderer loose, or for picking his nose in public.

At the drug store, he scurried off with his list while I browsed the vitamins and herbs section. I settled on ginkgo biloba and fish oil capsules. The latter nourishes the skin, the former the memory. I need all the help I can get in both departments. Although our long winters are rough on the complexion, they are devastating to the spirit. And when it comes to memory, lately my brain is like a sieve. Whatever I pour in seeps out. No doubt I've got too much on my mind, such as deconstructing a murder.

Dad met me at the front of the store. I noticed his shopping basket held three different brands of laxatives including something called Natural Nan's Potion. As we stood in line, I debated mentioning Doc Moss's warning regarding laxative dependency.

In the end (no pun intended), I chose to remain silent. My father enjoys discovering new brands of laxatives the way teenage girls love finding new shades of nail polish. Thus in the greater scheme of things, being a seventy-five-year-old laxative junky is not the worst thing in the world.

Three

The police car in the parking lot of the Harbour Building was a grim reminder of recent events. Likewise, the white van from Cable 5 Live, a local station. I pulled into the space next to it. Two technicians were loading camera equipment into the back. Miranda Trowt, news reporter and minor celebrity, sat in the front talking on her phone.

My presence must have interrupted a private conversation. She glared at me and rolled up her window. Had she glanced my way I'd have stuck my tongue out.

After locking the car, I approached the building. It was impressive looking. Dark, glossy ivy covered the rust colored brick front. Black lacquered shutters bracketing each window gleamed in the late afternoon sun. The place looked like the alumni building of a prestigious college.

Inside the lobby was cordoned off with rope and an attached sign: *No Admittance Per Order of State Police.* A security guard sat near the entrance, a clipboard balanced on his knee. He asked for my name and destination.

"Rose McNichols to see Attorney Spencer Farley."

He checked my name off, picked up a phone and punched in a number. After muttering something unintelligible, he hung up. "Mr. Farley's office is straight down that hall, room one-sixty." Having said that, he leaned over to release the catch on the rope with a gruff warning to stay in the designated area.

My footsteps echoed as I passed a waterfall in the center of the cavernous lobby. The sound of rushing water cascading over granite boulders was soothing. Lush tropical plants around the perimeter grew tall under the skylights above. I wouldn't have been surprised to hear the screech of a macaw in a palm tree.

Before knocking on Spencer's door, I glanced at the adjacent office. It was semi-obscured by a tangle of yellow police tape and signs warning: *Absolutely No Admittance*. I leaned over to read the small ebony plaque in the center of the door: *Vivian F. Klinger, Ph.D.*

Just as I lifted my hand to knock, Spencer Farley swung the door open. "Rose, come in, please," he said, stepping back. He wore a dark pinstripe suit. That and the thick silver hair gave him the appearance of an ambassador from central casting. The lines etching his forehead, however, spoke of recent troubles.

I stepped into a sunny reception area, incongruous considering the nearby crime scene. The decor was genteel—prints of tall ships in gilded frames hanging on pale walls. The furniture was dark wood, solid.

"I apologize for the security. I can't do much about it," he said.

"Will they be here very long?"

"I hope not. Thank God the media have cleared out."

I didn't remind him that the *Granite Cove Gazette* is considered the media. Despite our bowling scores and housekeeping hints, we cover the news. "Have many tenants in the building stayed away?"

"A few on this floor. They should be back by tomorrow."

While we talked, he led me into a spacious adjoining office, the walls of which were covered with framed photos of Spencer schmoozing with various Beacon Hill pols. "Have a seat," he said, indicating a velvet wing back chair. As I plunked myself down on the elegant upholstery, he sat behind a desk the size of a dory. Giving me an appraising glance, he said, "You're looking good, Rose."

I thanked him, discreetly tugging at my skirt. As I retrieved my notebook, he leaned forward, his elbows on the desk. "Do you mind if I ask you a personal question?"

"Of course not. I'm grateful you're seeing me at such a time."

He shook his head, dismissing my comment. "Your dad and I go way back. All through high school I worked at my father's marine shop. Russ McNichols was a steady customer."

"He appreciated your help in selling the house after my mother died."

"In that case it's mutual admiration," he said. "Now, about that question: How come a good-looking girl like you isn't married?"

"I don't know. Just lucky, I guess."

It's my stock answer to a question that's asked fairly often by men Spencer Farley's age. Yet hearing him utter the cliché was disappointing. Spencer Farley's got a reputation for being cool and savvy. He is the proverbial local-boy-makes-good.

A former Granite Cove townie, he now lives at Hemlock Point, straddling two worlds. Yet he hasn't forgotten his roots. He attends high school football games and has breakfast at Stella's with the regulars. Likewise, he's married to the former Martha Muldoon, another local who does everything in her power to conceal the fact.

"Not only are you attractive, you're bright," he said, chuckling at my response. "Now, how can I help you?"

I sat up straighter. "As I mentioned earlier on the phone, I'm doing a profile on Dr. Klinger for the paper. I may also submit a longer version to *Back Bay Living*, the Boston magazine. While I was gathering information it became obvious that her story goes beyond Granite Cove. Not just the tragedy, her life. First I have to interview those who knew her professionally and personally. You had the neighboring office, so I'd appreciate your input."

He leaned back in his swivel chair. Behind him a floor-to-ceiling bookcase bulged with old leather-bound volumes. It was the kind of backdrop often faked in cheesy photographs designed to lend their subjects an air of professionalism.

"I really don't know what I can tell you outside of what I've already told the police. You're aware that lawyers are a tight-lipped breed. Not only that, there's a murder investigation going on. Chief Alfano hasn't said anything officially, but I imagine I'm a suspect, having been the last to see Vivian. "

"I understand, Mr. Farley. You can't discuss the details of the crime, nor would I want you to. I'm merely aiming to create a picture of Vivian Klinger, not only the professional person but the woman. She impacted the lives of many people in this town. You knew her not only professionally but as a friend."

"Vivian was a private person. I doubt you'll find anyone in Granite Cove who knew her intimately. She never mentioned a steady boyfriend, yet she was always going to functions at the Museum of Fine Arts or the Wang. Later you might try contacting her parents, although I got the impression things were strained between Vivian and her dad."

"I see."

He lapsed into silence, and the only sound was the measured ticking of a ship captain's clock in the corner. Then he looked at me. "Just between the two of us, I am devastated by this crime. I keep going over it in my head. If I'd stayed late that night, she might still be alive." He looked down at his hands. "I guess it's what psychologists call survivor's guilt."

I nodded and waited. Finally, he spoke. "She had the adjoining office for two years. During the past six months, we'd become close. I was fond of her. I'll be honest—Vivian was an attractive woman, though ten years my junior."

Fifteen, I scribbled in my notebook.

"But that's what it was, a friendship. I imagine the local busybodies were clucking their tongues. People in this town thrive on gossip." He leaned back again, staring at the ceiling. "You could say I played a mentor's role in Vivian's life. She was ambitious, both professionally and socially. When she arrived here five years ago, she needed someone who knew the inner workings of Granite Cove. I introduced her to various groups, the Chamber of Commerce, the Women's Professional League. I took her to City Hall, introduced her to Ken Froggett and some others. Martha and I sponsored her membership at the country club."

I interrupted, asking, "Mr. Farley, do you think her ambition was directed toward building a psychotherapy practice?"

"Good question and one I used to wonder about. Her practice was small, which she seemed to prefer. Enough to pay the rent, she used to joke. My opinion? Vivian had her eye on the big picture. She was a bright, capable woman who wanted to make a name for herself, eventually on the national level."

"How do you know that?"

"Let me give you an example, off the record. One afternoon I was in her office when she got a phone call from that TV gal, you know, Oprah."

I dropped my pen. "Oprah Winfrey called?"

"Not Oprah herself, her people did. At the time Vivian was involved in the violence against women movement." He pursed his lips. "Ironic, isn't it? She was working to draft a bill that would protect women facing abuse."

"I understand Dr. Klinger was also planning a run for state rep."

"Yes, I heard that," he said.

"I also heard that Bunny Alfano, the police chief's brother, is running for that seat."

"You could be right."

"Do you know of any animosity between Dr. Klinger and Bunny Alfano?"

He shook his head. "I can't comment. You see, Bunny's a former client."

"Can you tell me off the record why Bunny Alfano needed your services?"

He rolled his eyes. "Rose, you know I can't do that."

"And you know I can look it up at the courthouse."

He smiled. "You're spunky, like your dad." He glanced at his watch, my cue.

"Can I ask one more question, Mr. Farley?"

"Only if you call me Spencer."

"Will do. I understand that you and Dr. Klinger had cocktails together after work."

"What did I say about small towns?" He shrugged. "It was no secret. We got together in her office a couple times a week, schedules permitting. We'd have a drink and discuss whatever happened to be on our minds. I certainly needed the break. As any lawyer will attest, the practice of law can be draining." He gripped the arms of his chair, ready to rise. "Is there anything else, Rose?"

"Your opinion: Who do you think killed Dr. Klinger?"

He scratched his chin. "Originally I thought it was an addict, someone lurking outside who assumed Vivian was an MD with drugs in her office. Now I'm leaning toward the police suspect. He's a bad apple, a former local guy who hangs around the park next door, drinking. Matter of fact, I caught him once right outside her window. I can't say more. Chief Alfano hopes to make an arrest soon."

I nodded and made a note to ask Cal. "You don't think it was one of Dr. Klinger's patients, someone with a grudge?"

He shrugged. "She never mentioned her patients as I never mention my clients." Now he looked pointedly at his watch.

Taking my cue, I got up. We walked to the door. Hanging above the light switch was a photo of a younger Spencer and Martha Farley in a sailboat. Next to them, wearing movie star sunglasses, was none other than Ted Kennedy. The two men were seated while Martha stood over them, gripping the lines. Her tanned thighs looked as sturdy—and wide—as the ship's mast.

At the entrance, Spencer turned to me. We were inches apart and his lime cologne smelled delicious. "You know, Rose, you're in a position to do a little digging on your own. Our state boys are thorough, but you're a local gal. You know this town." He winked. "I'll bet there's little that gets by you."

I thanked him, saying I'd take it under advisement. As I retraced my route through the lobby, my legs felt wobbly, as though I'd just stepped off a sailboat. Was it the compliment or the cologne?

Back in the parking lot, I attempted to sort my notes. My thoughts, however, kept returning to Spencer's parting suggestion about investigating the murder. The man must be psychic. How did he know I'd become obsessed with the case? Not only the murder, but the victim, Vivian Klinger, a woman too perfect for mere mortals.

The fact that we were the same age was the only thing we had in common. I certainly didn't identify with her aristocratic background. In that area we were polar opposites. Was it envy because she'd been chosen Woman of the Year while I was again overlooked? Was I jealous of her self-assurance, her impeccable grooming?

Yes to all of the above. And let's not forget the stacks of Nancy Drew mysteries I devoured as a kid. They turned me into an amateur sleuth who studied yellowed shopping receipts found in gutters, looking for clues.

Despite my tenuous reasons, I had to accept the fact that once the story went to press, that ended my involvement so far as the *Granite Cove Gazette* was concerned. Yvonne would not devote another inch of newsprint to murder, not with the Beautification Society's annual window box contest coming up. Whether the crime was solved mattered little, not when there were flower boxes to judge. If I wanted to keep my job, I had better dance to her tune.

The moving finger writs, and having writ, moves on.

As I drove out of the parking lot, a big bronze Mercedes caught my eye. Its license plate was SPENCE. One thing you can say about Granite Cove's most successful attorney: he doesn't hide his light under a clam bucket.

I spotted Cal Devine on Main Street, hunched over his parking ticket pad. I pulled into a space diagonally across the street and watched him slap a ticket on the windshield of a white Lexus SUV. Despite the chill, Cal wore the department's summer uniform: khaki shorts and knee socks. He's one of the few guys on the force who looks great in them. Likewise, back in high school playing defense for the Granite Cove Lobstermen, he filled the uniform nicely. His wide shoulders, slim waist and hips inspired the cheerleaders, as well as female spectators of all ages.

Almost twenty years later he's still a hunk, though he pretends otherwise. How can a guy not be affected when high school girls slip him their phone numbers? This happened during Senior Week when Cal delivered the annual safety lecture: no alcohol, no drugs, no fires on the beach. Oh, the irony of Officer Devine warning the kids about acts he once enthusiastically committed.

I lowered my window and whistled. He looked up and crossed the street to kneel next to my window. "I felt eyes devouring me. What's up, Rosie?"

"You've been holding out on me. I understand the chief has a suspect."

"Give me twenty-four hours, and I'll tell you more." He removed his cap and ran a hand through his hair. "I'm really beat."

Remembering Betty Ann's remark, I said, "I'm sorry to hear you and Marcie are separated. I thought you two were pretty tight."

"Tight? Try welded. Marcie's a control freak. Lately, she's got a stranglehold." Cal's wife is old school Italian. Unlike me at eighteen, Marcie Ventimiglia knew what she wanted from life. Thus, when I broke up with Cal and subsequently fled Granite Cove, she moved in like a shark smelling blood. One year later, Marcie Devine gave birth to the first of three sons.

Time passed. I returned home to help when Mom got sick. One night, fearing my mother was having a stroke, we went to the emergency room; Marcie Devine, RN, was on duty. She took Mom's vital signs and within minutes inserted an IV line, at the same time hooking her up to monitors. She was professional and efficient, her manner impersonal. As far as Marcie was concerned, I was the one that got away in her husband's life. People like that never forget.

"Where are you living?" I asked.

"Home Suite Homes, off 128. I've been there a couple weeks."

"What about your kids?"

"I pick them up after school every day. I've been honest. I tell them their mother and I are having problems right now. I hate hurting my kids, but I can't live with Marcie the way things are now."

"What's it about?"

He shook his head. "It's a long story. You see, Marcie's dad died when she was twelve. He was at the wharf loading his truck when a freak storm blew in. Lightning killed him. Just recently, when Tyler, our oldest, turned twelve, Marcie began having nightmares about her father. She's convinced history will repeat itself, and something bad will happen to me. Now she's pressuring me to quit the force."

"Has she talked to anyone about this?"

"Yeah, she was seeing Dr. Klinger."

"Oh."

"If Marcie was nervous before, she's frantic now with a murderer loose. She expects me to check in every hour. If I don't, she calls around looking for me."

"How does she expect you to earn a living if you quit the force?"

He smirked. "She's got it all planned. That woman could run the universe. Her brother Sal is involved in real estate in Alabama. Ever meet Sal? A born salesman. He and a couple investors are putting together a development called Lagoon Estates. They hope to lure the Baby Boomers. For six hundred thousand dollars, you get two and a half bathrooms, a wine cellar, and a putting green."

I laughed. "What's your function, wrestling 'gators?"

"I'd be head of security, keeping out the Bible salesmen. It's a gated community. Marcie says we'll be nice and safe down there."

I looked at him. "What do you think?"

He paused. "Tell you the truth? At first I thought it was totally insane, but the more I think about it, the more I'm liking the idea."

"Cal Devine! I've known you since fifth grade. Even then you wanted to be a cop."

"Things change, Rose. When my dad was on the force he dealt with saloon brawls and lobster poachers. Today, we've got punks in this town who've seen too many Quentin Tarantino movies. They want to fight. I'm getting it from all sides. Even Stella's on my ass about those damn pigs. She's threatened to sue the town if the kids steal one during Senior Week."

"Can't the chief deal with her?"

He shook his head. "The chief's scared of Stella. That leaves me, who graduated second at the police academy, guarding plastic pigs."

"Cal, it sounds like you need a vacation. Why don't you and Marcie find a nice sunny beach and chill out for a week? It's been a long winter. Everyone's feeling the stress."

"Marcie would never leave the kids. She's afraid something will happen." He shrugged. "Maybe I'm burned out. That might explain my attitude. Fifteen years ago my mother pinned this badge on my chest. I've loved every minute of being a cop. Except lately something's changed, and I can't figure it out."

"This doesn't sound like my former partner in crime." I leaned out the window. "Remember prank night our senior year? The statue of Homer Frost? Whose idea was it to paint the horse's butt maroon and blue?"

He smiled. "Who sat on my shoulders holding the paint cans?"

"It was a two-person job."

"Did I ever tell you how much I liked having you up there?"

We smiled at each other, remembering that night. I said softly, "If you move down South, who will remember your secrets?"

His mood changed, and he scowled. "What's so special about being buried in the town you were born in?"

Cal needed more help than I could give in a quick conversation. "Promise you won't do anything hasty without talking to me first. Give yourself time. Things have a way of working out."

He got to his feet, brushing off his knees. "Fine, but Marcie's not the patient type. She's threatening to see Spencer Farley unless I make a commitment."

I turned the key in the ignition. "Trust me, Marcie won't let you get away."

Quick as a minnow, he leaned in and kissed me, whispering, "I let you get away. Biggest mistake of my life."

I tried to keep my voice steady. "Let me know about that suspect, will you?"

He pulled the ticket pad from his pocket. "Sure thing, and you know where to find me." With that, he sprinted across the street.

I shifted into drive and soon merged with the Main Street traffic, my face burning. Did Cal seriously think I'd visit him at Home Suite Homes? I'd be putting my life in jeopardy. Marcie Ventimiglia Devine might appear a contemporary woman, but she's old school. They go straight for the jugular.

Because I was preoccupied, I didn't notice the man with the peculiar gait on the sidewalk. He balanced a case of beer on his shoulder. With each step his right leg swung in an arc, creating a pronounced limp. Yet he looked jaunty. His tangled, copper-colored hair and ruddy high cheekbones gave him the appearance of a Ralph Lauren model if you ignored the matted sheepskin vest flapping in the breeze and the threadbare jeans

The man looked familiar. I followed him with my eyes until *whump!* I banged into the car ahead of me. It had stopped at the light while I hadn't. The driver glared into his rear view mirror, blasting the horn and at the same time giving me the finger. I waited for him to pull over. He didn't. Fortunately, I'd hit a clunker. When the light turned green, the car continued on its way. I turned my attention back to the road.

Thursday evening at six, I pulled up in front of the Zagrobskis' house. It was an olive ranch with a rooftop satellite dish the size of a beach umbrella. The thing looked capable of picking up transmissions beamed from Jupiter.

Betty Ann's husband Tiny and his son Jonah were throwing a football around in the front yard. The contrast between them was striking. Tiny was broad, his arms and neck straining his tee shirt. Jonah, on the other hand, was a wraith. His legs in cutoffs looked like pipe cleaners speckled with insect bites.

The football spiraled through the air. Jonah lurched toward it, but at the last minute he covered his head. The ball bounced off his back into the bushes.

"Go on, son, throw it back!"

The boy scowled at his dad and began kicking the azalea bushes in his search for the errant football. I lowered my window. "You two look good," I lied.

Tiny approached the car. "Jonah's coming along. We haven't spent much time together these past years, so I'm playing catch-up."

"How's it going?"

"It's going," he said. "The kid's been living with Judy. She's not the best role model for a young teen."

Though I didn't know Judy personally, I'd heard plenty from Betty Ann about Tiny's wacky first wife. "Is Betty Ann ready?"

"Last time I checked she was trying on shoes. I said, 'Babe, who's gonna look at your feet at a wake?'"

At that moment, Betty Ann appeared at the side door wearing a long, flowered caftan. She looked like a Samoan fortune teller. Like her husband, B.A. is large, the type people call big boned.

She stopped a few feet from my car and said, "Be honest, Rose, do these shoes look too slutty for a wake?"

I studied the open-toed, high-heeled sandals and the lavender toenails. "Absolutely, which is why you should wear them."

She climbed into the front seat. "Good. I wear sneakers all day at work. My feet need to breathe."

"Ladies, guys don't look at feet," Tiny said.

"Tiny, we're going to a wake, not a bar. I just want to look appropriate." She smoothed her dress over her knees.

He leaned into the window and kissed her, a long one. When he spoke, his voice was husky. "You look better than appropriate, babe. You look hot. Now behave yourself tonight."

I laughed and drove away, glancing at the rear view mirror. Tiny stood watching us while Jonah was still kicking the bushes. "Tiny acts like a newlywed," I said. "He's crazy about you."

"I'm crazy about him, too. Unfortunately, having Jonah in the house has put a strain on our relationship."

"How much longer will he be with you?"

"We'll know more after the results of Judy's tests are in."

"She'll probably be discharged soon. Insurance companies don't pay for lengthy rehabs anymore."

"It's not just drug rehab, it's her back injury. That's how she became addicted to pain pills. She ruptured a disc moving a computer at work. They're saying that after rehab, she might need back surgery." Betty Ann let out a sigh. "Such is my life."

"Is Jonah getting... any better?"

"The kid's a classic manipulator. He's got Tiny feeling sorry for him. Last night, for instance, we were in bed. Finally, we were alone. As we were getting cozy, there was a strange noise outside the door. It sounded like a sick warthog.

"Tiny got up and opened the door. Guess what? It was Jonah curled up on the floor and blubbering that he was scared, he wanted daddy to come in his room 'til he fell asleep." She stopped and rifled through her oversized pocketbook.

"So? What happened?"

"So Tiny and Jonah went off down the hall, hand in hand. The little weasel turned and gave me a triumphant look. I would have slapped his face, had he been close. I should have flipped him the bird. He's turning me into a first class bitch."

"Not you," I said. "I don't believe it."

"Believe it. All day at work I deal with Alzheimer's patients. Yesterday, Mrs. Smedlie threw a box of Depends at the nun who comes in to say the rosary. Twenty minutes later someone drove a wheelchair over Mr. Masucci's catheter tube; urine squirting all over the place.

"Things like that I can handle. Yet I'm totally incapable of dealing with a thirteen-year-old. Call me paranoid, but that kid is out to wreck my marriage. He's evil."

"Have you talked to Tiny about how you feel?"

"Tiny feels guilty for not playing a bigger role in Jonah's life. He thinks his son is an innocent victim of Judy's bad mothering."

As she talked, Betty Ann continued to grope inside her pocketbook. Finally, I said, "What in the world are you looking for?"

"My nicotine gum. I think I left it at home. I won't survive the night without it."

"B.A., you're quitting smoking? That's terrific."

She turned to me, grim faced. "I'm trying to quit because I can't smoke in the house anymore. It's little Jonah. The court says he can't be exposed to secondhand smoke."

I patted her hand. "Things will work out. Tiny loves you."

"I know he does, but sometimes love just isn't enough."

Auntie Pearl's Helpful Housekeeping Hints

Dear Auntie Pearl:

Occasionally, I stay overnight with my mother, who lives in a senior retirement community. One night, when I got up to use the bathroom, I heard strange noises coming from her bedroom. When I checked, I found Mother's fourteen-year-old cat drinking from the glass that holds her dentures.

The next morning, when I informed Mother, she wasn't the least bit concerned. Should I contact her doctor about this health hazard?

Signed,
Flustered in Foxboro

Dear Flustered:

I consulted Dr. Emil Fetlocke, a highly regarded veterinarian. He said your mother's cat is in no danger from drinking this solution as it is basically a mild, well-diluted cleanser. However, you ought to convince your mother to put out a bowl of fresh water, allowing the cat access throughout the night.

Pleasant dreams!
Auntie Pearl

Four

The Frost Funeral Home is the birthplace of Homer Frost, the town's founder. Over the years the Georgian mansion has served as headquarters for various organizations, such as the Colonial Dames and the Visiting Nurses. Five years ago when the historic building was declared a fire hazard and thus facing demolition, funeral director Henry Koski stepped in with an offer to purchase.

This turn of events resulted in protests by civic groups who envisioned the house as a museum "luring tourists to the downtown," they postulated in a flurry of letters to the Gazette. And while everyone agreed that a museum was an appropriate use for the property, one obstacle stood in the way: money to make it happen.

Finally, when an out-of-town developer (represented by Spencer Farley, no less) submitted a proposal to convert the mansion into high end condos, the town fathers decided that a funeral home might not be such a bad thing after all. Later, in a nod to the civic groups, Mr. Koski restored the building's original name—with unfortunate results. The Frost Funeral Home became the butt of many jokes, such as: "Drop in for a cool one at Frosty's."

The parking lot was full, as well as the spaces lining the street. We finally found a spot two blocks away. Betty Ann hurriedly applied lipstick before getting out. She said, "I feel funny going in there. I've got a thing about death."

"You work in a nursing home. Aren't you used to it by now?"

"That's different. When someone dies at Green Pastures, you're aware it happened, but you never come face to face with it. Two men in black suits show up carrying a collapsible gurney. No one looks at them. No one talks to them. It's like they're invisible. Upstairs, they zip the deceased into a body bag, load it on the gurney and then take the service elevator down. Poof, they're gone."

"Don't you ever attend the wakes?" Rose asked.

She shook her head. "The administrator has a policy. If you go to one, you must go to all of them. Otherwise, you're showing favoritism."

"That's a pretty heavy-handed policy," I said.

"I suppose it is, but no one's fighting it."

We stood on the curb across the street from the funeral home. Cars crawled past us, rubbernecks gawking at the long line snaking out the side door and onto the driveway. Eying the crowd, Betty Ann said, "I'll bet most of them are nothing but curiosity seekers."

I didn't mention that we, too, belonged in that category. Although I was representing the newspaper, I would have attended anyway. Furthermore, it was only natural that the wake of a murder victim whose death had sexual overtones would attract sensation seekers. Although Dr. Klinger's life had been one of respectability and prestige, her death had become tabloid fodder. Consider, for instance, the headline in a recent Boston Herald, which read *The Corpse in the Freudian Slip*.

Finally, we crossed the street and got at the end of the line. Before long we were joined by the Zacks, who stood behind us. Doris wore a popsicle-orange pantsuit and matching lipstick while Harold wore a cardigan sweater.

"I hope I don't fall to pieces when I see her," Doris whispered to me.

"You do, and I'm leaving," Harold said.

"You think the casket will be open?" Betty Ann asked me.

Overhearing the question, Doris piped up. "Absolutely. My friend Loretta does the hair for all the Frost wakes." She turned to me. "Rose, you remember Loretta. She was lunch monitor at the high school. After a nervous breakdown, she went back to school and got her hairdressing license."

"Uh huh," I said, having no idea who Doris was talking about.

She continued. "Loretta said the Klinger family wanted the casket closed, until they saw what a nice job she did." She lowered her voice. "She used hairpieces to cover, you know, in the back."

Harold shook his head. "Nice work if you can get it."

Instead of being put off, Betty Ann appeared intrigued with Doris's insider information. She said, "When my sister was in nursing school, she worked nights at St. Elizabeth's Hospital preparing the deceased for the undertaker. It was better than babysitting, she said."

Doris nodded approvingly. "Smart girl."

As the crowd moved forward, a buzz stirred the air. People cast eager glances at the side door through which the line disappeared. Chief Alfano, wearing a dark uniform covered with medals, stood on one side. Mayor Froggett, wearing a dark gray suit, was opposite. His salt-and-pepper toupee was combed in a style similar to Mad Magazine's Alfred E. Neuman.

As we inched closer to the door, I nudged Betty Ann. "Get ready. We're almost there." Moments later we reached the three steps leading to the side door. After a nod from Chief Alfano, we ascended and stood poised at the entrance.

Inside, the reception area had been enlarged, its partitions removed to accommodate the crowd. Fifteen feet from the entrance a receiving line of three people stood under a dim chandelier. Doris tugged at the sleeve of my blazer. "Those two at the front are her folks. I don't know who the bald guy is at the end."

Mr. Koski, the funeral director, appeared and like a maitre 'd asked, "Two?" With a sweeping motion of his hand he indicated the receiving line. We nodded our thanks and approached.

The first person in the trio, a short, trim man, offered his hand. "I'm Lawrence Klinger. Thank you for coming." Deep grooves gave his face the appearance of a Tiki god. "This is my wife Veronica." He passed us off to an elegant woman on his right.

She was taller than her husband, the dark silk dress emphasizing her body's sharp angles. I shook her cold, limp hand and smiled into empty gray eyes. "I'm Rose McNichols, Mrs. Klinger. I write for the *Granite Cove Gazette*. I'm very sorry for your loss."

I introduced Betty Ann, who added, "We were very fond of your daughter."

Up until that point she'd shown not a flicker of interest. Now she widened her eyes and asked, "And how did you know Vivian?" Her glance said she suspected we bought our underwear at Goodwill.

"The Women's Professional League," I blurted out.

"I see." She looked off into the distance as though willing us away.

"We'd better be going," Betty Ann said, nudging me. Unfortunately, to my left was a wall of people. They had gone through the receiving line and were reluctant to move on and miss something. Consequently, they prevented us from advancing. Since we were temporarily stuck, I decided to bite the bullet and speak to Mrs. Klinger. I doubted I'd get another chance. Leaning toward her, I said, "I wonder if sometime in the future we could talk. I'm doing a story on Dr. Klinger and her impact on our community. "I reached into my pocket and removed a business card which I pressed into her lifeless hand. It fluttered to the floor. Betty Ann caught my eye and shrugged.

The awkward moment did not go unnoticed. The last member of the receiving line, a distinguished-looking man in a natty pinstripe suit, bent his tall frame and said, "I'm Doctor Bingham. I'm with the family. It's awfully good of you ladies to come out tonight." Mrs. Klinger, roused from her reverie, now stared downward and muttered something unintelligible. Dr. Bingham moved to wrap a protective arm around her. "What's that, Veronica?"

"Why do they glow like that?" she said, her voice shrill. We followed her gaze. In the dim chandelier's light, Betty Ann's toenails shone a fluorescent mauve. Seconds passed as we stared, entranced.

"It's the polish," Betty Ann explained. "It must glow in the dark." She glared at me. "Let's move on, Rose, and give other people a chance to pay their respects."

"Yes, let's."

I surveyed the mass with dismay. At that point I was ready to get down on all fours and crawl through the legs of those blocking our escape. As it turned out, Lawrence Klinger was also suffering. He'd gotten stuck with Doris Zack, who was detailing the programs offered by the Granite Cove Elder Services.

Desperate, he spotted Mr. Koski and snapped his fingers. The funeral director, unaccustomed to being snapped at, nonetheless approached. The two men had a brief discussion after which Mr. Koski strode away. Seconds later he returned with Chief Alfano, briskly rolling up his sleeves. Together the pair herded the crowd into an adjacent room.

Betty Ann and I, swept along with the crowd, found ourselves in the center of the room. People pressed against us on all sides. It was like being at a huge cocktail party, minus the drinks. Betty Ann smoothed the skirt of her dress. "Thank God we got away. That woman is the most arrogant person I've ever met."

"She's in a state of shock. Imagine how you'd feel if your only child was killed."

"I don't have a child," she said peevishly.

"Don't be a nitpicker. By the way, who's the doctor with the British accent?"

Betty Ann rolled her eyes. "You mean you don't recognize Chandler Bingham? According to *Back Bay Living*, he's the most exclusive psychiatrist in Boston. All of Louisburg Square goes to him."

"I don't hang in those circles," I said. "He looks like Prince Philip, the Queen's husband. Is he related to the Klingers?'"

"I doubt it. I suppose he's here to keep an eye on Veronica. She doesn't seem too tightly wrapped."

"Imagine that, the Klingers travel with their own doctor."

"I have to wait four weeks for an appointment with mine," she said, raising herself on tiptoe and scanning the room. "I wonder where the food is."

"Betty Ann, this is a wake, not a luau."

"I'm not expecting prime rib. Cheese and crackers, maybe wine."

I was about to respond when I heard Spencer Farley's voice over the crowd. I turned. He was huddled with his wife Martha and a short, bronzed man in a canary yellow sports coat. I motioned to B.A. and whispered, "Don't turn around. The Farleys are behind us. Who's the guy dressed like Big Bird?"

Despite my words of caution, she turned to gape. "That's Bunny Alfano, the police chief's brother. Jeez, Rose, for a journalist you don't know much."

B.A. takes pride in her celebrity acumen. She's followed the goings-on of the rich and famous since high school, where she was president of the New England chapter of the Joan Collins Fan Club.

"I know him, I just don't recognize him," I said. "It's the nose. It used to be bigger, like the chief's."

"He's probably had some work done. Bunny winters in Palm Beach. Can you believe he's running for office? Do you know who his opponent is... was?"

"Of course. Vivian Klinger."

Despite our attempt to keep a low profile, Spencer Farley spotted us. It's hard to conceal Betty Ann, who's six feet and has a voice to match. He maneuvered through the crowd until he reached our side. His mood was somber. "Hello, Betty Ann, Rose. Good to see you both."

As we shook hands, Bunny and Martha joined us, the latter reluctantly. She wore a navy double-breasted coat dress that made her look like a high-ranking prison official. Her long face indicated she'd rather be shucking oysters with her teeth than socializing with us. Like royalty, Martha Farley never speaks first. Thus, I flashed a phony smile and also remained silent.

Bunny Alfano was another story. A short, barrel-chested man, he gazed up at me in wonder. "So you're Rose McNichols. Do you know how much I enjoy your stories in the *Granite Cove Gazette*?"

I smiled modestly as he pumped my hand, his grin bigger and whiter than Dawnette Vicari's, the local beauty queen. The man's enthusiasm was a stark contrast to his brother, who's never been known to smile.

Yet despite his cheerful countenance, I'd heard stories about Chief Alfano's corrupt brother. Bunny certainly looked the part. The gaudy jacket, gold chains and perennial tan shouted Atlantic City off-season. Yet, though I was prepared to dislike the man and what he stood for, it's hard to diss someone who acts like I'm the greatest thing since tortilla wraps. Sadly, it's one of my biggest character flaws. When someone sucks up, I'm a sucker for it.

He continued shaking my hand. "I'd love you to interview me as soon as I get my campaign up and running." He lowered his voice. "After a period of respect for the deceased, of course."

"Of course," I said, attempting to extricate my hand from Bunny's grip.

Betty Ann saved me by announcing, "Rose, it's time we paid our respects in the mourning chapel."

I yanked my hand loose. "You folks will excuse us?"

Bunny pouted while Martha looked relieved. Spencer nodded benevolently. "You two go right ahead. We'll follow later."

"What's the rush?" I asked, catching up to B.A., who plowed through the crowd.

She spun around and jabbed a finger in my chest. "Listen, McNichols, I like wakes about as much as I like Martha Farley. When I have to deal with both at the same time, I get nauseous. Furthermore, how can you be civil to that man? Don't you know what he and Martha are up to? They plan to build villas at Settler's Dunes. Villas!"

"They can't. That's town land."

"That's what everyone thinks. Now I hear that all these years it's been held in a trust by the Frost family. The last remaining member has the option to sell. Guess what? It turns out he's broke."

Betty Ann's words were preposterous and at the same time plausible. "If that were so, the Gazette would be covering it."

"Really? When Bunny Alfano is involved, people don't intrude. It's bad for their health. Now can we please go home?"

"Shh. We said we're going to the mourning chapel, remember?"

"So what? Tell them I left my glasses at home. It's dark in there. I might trip over a body."

"Betty Ann, it would be rude to walk out now after saying we're going inside. What if they're watching?" As if on cue, we turned and spotted Bunny grinning and waving from across the room. "See? We can't sneak out now."

"Yes we can. I'm not like you, Rose. I don't have a compulsion to be nice to phonies."

Her remark touched a sore spot. It's true I crave approval from the guardians of good taste, but at the same time I enjoy shocking them. This dichotomy, the yin and yang of my character, is most likely genetic. From my dad I inherited a feisty iconoclasm, and from my mother, a dread of calling attention to oneself. After all, her family motto was Die, but don't let the neighbors know.

In any event, B.A. was attracting attention. I took her arm as if she were a cranky child in need of humoring. With that, I led her to the double doors of the chapel. "You can stay here, or you can go inside with me," I explained. "In either case, I'm going in to pay my respects."

She patted me on the head. "You're cute when you show spunk." She reached over my head to swing open the door. "I might as well go with you. Just make sure I don't trip over any short people in the dark."

The stillness of the chapel seemed a world away from the milling crowd outside. The narrow room with its rows of upholstered benches was lit with candles and recessed lighting. A long burgundy runner led to an altar where a gleaming white coffin sat surrounded by flowers.

A prayer bench positioned before the coffin was occupied by two women I recognized as members of the Women's Professional League. Betty Ann and I slowly approached. The runner's thick pile and the soft music issuing from hidden speakers muffled our steps. We stopped a few feet away to wait our turn.

One of the women spoke up. "The suit is Armani. I saw it in a window on Newbury Street."

"My dear, you're mistaken. It's Prada, their fall collection. Shall I check the label?"

"Don't be vulgar. What do you think of the blouse, that big bow?"

"It's not as ghastly as the white casket. Don't these people know the rules? Coffins and limos should always be one color: black."

"The father probably picked it out. It just goes to show, money can't buy class. By the way, do you know what Mr. Klinger manufactures?"

"No, what?"

"Condoms."

"Get out! Vivian claimed they made synthetic home care products."

"Well, she wasn't lying."

When Betty Ann coughed, the two women turned, surprised to see us standing behind them. After making hasty signs of the cross, they rose.

Their heads lowered, they walked past us and out the door.

"Nice Catholic girls," Betty Ann muttered as we took their place at the prayer bench. Before us, the body of Dr. Klinger reclined in tufted satin splendor. She was dressed in a charcoal suit with velvet trim. The dark hair, as glossy as the inside of a mussel shell, fanned the pillow. Her complexion was as pale as the silk bow tied under her chin. A beam of recessed light softly illuminated her features. Lifelike and serene, she seemed to be merely napping.

The effect, coupled with the heavy perfume of the flowers, was unsettling. I felt the room spin and ducked my head. "You okay?" Betty Ann whispered. When I didn't respond, she got me to my feet. "What's wrong? You're paler than death. "

"I feel dizzy... nauseous."

Now it was Betty Ann's turn to lead. Gripping my arm, she assisted me down the aisle and out the doors. After scanning the room, she guided me to a chair near the window. "Sit for a minute," she said.

I glanced out the window. On the porch, a woman in a short knit dress was smoking a cigarette. A mass of champagne-colored hair tumbled down her back. Every time she brought the cigarette to her lips her hem rose six inches. The woman was definitely not a local.

"Who's that?" I asked.

Betty Ann fumbled in her bag for her glasses. Peering outside, she said, "Aha!" like a birder spotting a rare Baltic gull. "That's Pamela Bingham, Dr. Bingham's third wife."

Once again I was impressed with my friend's celebrity savvy. "You should write a gossip column."

"I enjoy following celebs. I'll never make the team, but I like to know the players."

We stared at the glamorous stranger whose high-heeled boots and sexy dress were incongruous at a funeral parlor. "*Back Bay Living* did a feature on the Binghams," Betty Ann said. "They have a priceless collection of ancient Mayan death masks at their Louisburg Square brownstone."

"Really?" I said. "Maybe *Back Bay Living* would be interested in my collection of ancient hotel ash trays."

She laughed. "Kiddo, don't be jealous. You're worth a dozen Pamela Binghams. Besides, she's definitely not society. He met her while skiing in Aspen. She was a cocktail waitress at his hotel." She took in the long tanned legs of our subject. "But you've gotta admit, Pamela Bingham is a perfect example of a trophy wife."

I studied the retro go-go hair and sniffed. "The trophy's a little tarnished. She needs a root job."

"I don't think Dr. Bingham pays much attention to her roots," she said.

Fascinated, we watched her toss the cigarette into the bushes and withdraw a compact from a tiny purse. Turning her back to the light, she peered into the mirror. This action caused her hem to rise so high, her leopard print panties were visible to one and all.

While this ritual was taking place, Mr. Koski was performing his own ritual, moving from window to window to lower the shades. When he reached a window overlooking the porch, he glanced outside and spotted Pamela Bingham's backside. Consequently, he lost his grip on the shade. The resulting whap caused everyone to jump.

Precisely at that moment, a disheveled Lawrence Klinger rushed into the room. He ran to the chapel doors and flung them open, disappearing inside. He was soon followed by a grim-faced Dr. Bingham.

Betty Ann was first to reach the doors. As she peered inside, I joined her. Together we watched enrapt as Lawrence Klinger caromed the length of the runner. He threw himself upon the casket and cried, "Vivian, darling, forgive me!"

As we watched, a raspy voice behind us demanded, "What's going on?"

We turned to see a short, squat woman with a bulldog face glaring at us. A crowd had formed around her. She reached for the door as Betty Ann turned to block her. Her hands on hips, Betty Ann said, "It's a personal matter, folks. Let's give the family some privacy."

This did not go over well. The bulldog woman moved closer, her upturned face inches from Betty Ann's chest. "I saw you gawking at them. Now move aside."

When Betty Ann failed to move, the woman snaked her hand around her and yanked the door knob. The door flew open with a klunk, hitting the back of Betty Ann's head. Immediately the crowd surged past, stopping to gape at the spectacle of Lawrence Klinger prostrated upon the coffin while Dr. Bingham hovered nearby.

"Are you okay?" I asked a stunned Betty Ann. Her answer was blotted out by a shrill scream arising from the reception area. The bulldog woman and her gang, hearing this, reacted like a pack of dogs. They turned en masse and charged out the door, knocking Betty Ann's head once again.

"Are you okay?" I repeated, pulling her away from the chapel entrance.

"I think so." She shook her head to clear it. "Let's see what's going on."

We rushed to the reception area where Veronica Klinger lay sprawled on the rug. Her thin legs in smoke-colored hose looked as substantial as chop sticks.

"Call 911!" somebody shouted.

"I'll get Dr. Bingham," I told B. A., and raced back to the chapel. On the way I passed a flustered Mr. Koski, muttering to himself.

Inside the chapel, Mr. Klinger was now on his feet. Dr. Bingham, his arm around the man, led him away from the coffin. In the stillness, my voice rang out: "Dr. Bingham, you'd better come. It's Mrs. Klinger. She's fainted."

He stopped and stared. Then he half-dragged his companion to a nearby bench where he sat him down and whispered something in his ear. Taking a moment to straighten his tie, Dr. Bingham then strode to the door. When he passed, he was so close I could count the beads of sweat dotting his bald head.

That night, Boston's most exclusive psychiatrist was earning his fees.

Five

Yvonne's voice rang out in the office: "Rose, I've got you the most delicious story. You'll adore it."

"What is it?" I've discovered that the things Yvonne adores are usually pretty lame.

"Are you familiar with the Phippses of Hemlock Point?"

"Last time I was at Hemlock Point I was trick or treating. They called the cops on me."

"Seriously."

"I am serious. They're paranoid out there. How threatening is a twelve-year-old dressed like Cindi Lauper?"

"Now listen. You must have heard of Lester and Myrna Phipps of the Miles O' Tiles chain? Their stores are all over the country."

"I've seen the stores. Who hasn't? I can't say I know the owners."

"Then you're in for a treat. I've just learned that their dog won Best of Breed at the Westchester Dog Show. Isn't that fabulous? Mrs. Phipps said she wouldn't mind if we did a story on him."

"What about Coral? She loves rubbing elbows with the Hemlock Point crowd."

Coral's got the Boston Flower Show, unless you'd rather switch with her."

"No, that's fine. I'll stick with dogs. "Fighting big city traffic and huge crowds just to stare at flowers was too painful to contemplate. "What breed, by the way?"

"I'm not sure." She stuck a pink Post-it on my desk. "Here's Mrs. Phipps' private number. Be sure to call soon. We don't want her changing her mind." She was halfway to her desk when she turned. "I forgot to ask about the wake."

"It was absolutely packed."

"But you were able to pay your respects to the family?"

"I did, prior to Mrs. Klinger passing out in the middle of the room."

"She didn't! What happened?"

"The EMTs took her away. This morning I called Mr. Koski for information. He said Mrs. Klinger is doing okay. Apparently, she was on a new medication and hadn't eaten the entire day. They think that's what caused it."

"That poor woman," Yvonne said. "Imagine having to endure your child's wake."

"Imagine not eating all day." I turned back to my computer monitor but couldn't concentrate. It was a good time to broach the subject. Yvonne and I were alone. Furthermore, I'd done her a favor by attending the wake; she owed me one. "Yvonne, can I ask you something?"

"Why, of course."

"Are you aware of the controversy surrounding Settler's Dunes? It seems everyone's talking about it. Now they're pressuring the city council to hold a hearing."

"Well, of course I've heard. What a silly question."

"In that case, why haven't we written anything about it?"

She gave me a look of exasperation. "For one thing, we've been too busy covering a murder. Everything's taken a back seat to that, in case you're not aware."

"I realize that. We're also moving on, news wise. I'm covering dog stories, Coral's doing flower shows, and Stew's interviewing the graduating high school jocks. Meanwhile, Settlers Dunes is a major issue, one that impacts our village in a big way.

"All these years we assumed Granite Cove owned the land. Instead, it's been in a family trust held by the Frosts. Recently an unknown fact has come to light: The last remaining family member has the right to sell the land."

"I'm familiar with the history, Rose. I might not be a native, but I do stay informed."

I ignored the sarcasm. "His name is Dwayne Frost. Those in the know say he's considering selling. Do you realize what this means? It's like you discover the people you've been calling Mom and Pop aren't really your parents."

"Come now, isn't that a bit dramatic?"

"Not really. Settlers Dunes is where the town's earliest residents located. They built their fish shacks right on the beach. It's where my friends and I learned to swim." It is also where the teenagers go to make out, smoke pot and drink beer, but I didn't see any point in mentioning that.

"Again, I might not be a local, but I'm aware of Settlers Dunes' significance."

"Are you aware that every few years when the tide washes the sand away you can see the foundation lines of those early houses? Some people think it should be protected as an historic landmark."

"That's typical of this town," Yvonne said. "Everyone has an opinion, yet nobody's willing to follow through on it."

"The Colonial Dames want the town to buy the property."

Her laugh was shrill. "This town couldn't afford a new roof for the Homer Frost House. How on earth can they buy five acres of oceanfront property?"

"It seems Martha Farley and Bunny Alfano aren't worried about raising the money. Those two are tight as clams at low tide. I wonder what bank they're snuggling up to."

"That's none of our business. At the moment it's nothing but rumors. For all we know this Dwayne Frost has no intention of selling. Think of it—his ancestors created a trust to benefit the town. What civic minded person would undo all that goodwill?"

She waved a hand dismissivly. "Don't be so impetuous, Rose. When and if the town holds a hearing, we'll cover it. In the meantime, I'm not going to lose my head just because a bunch of busybodies are overreacting to gossip."

I felt my cheeks burn. That happens when I get my wrist slapped, unseemly at age thirty-nine. "Forgive me," I said, "I forget that Martha Farley's real estate business is our biggest advertiser."

"That's a cheap shot, and it is not the reason."

I pressed on. "Is it because Bunny is Chief Alfano's brother?"

She sighed. "I'll have you know that Victor Alfano hasn't spoken more than ten words to his brother in as many years. Now, my dear, I've got work to do, and I'm sure you do as well. I will not discuss Settlers Dunes at this point."

"Okay." I waited in silence, knowing that eventually Yvonne would feel guilty for chastising me. Finally, she spoke:

"You're a young, single woman, Rose. Keep in mind that I'm a widow who's responsible for my eighty-five-year-old mother. If anything happened to me, she would be shuttled off to some... home." Her voice wavered. She reached for a tissue and blew her nose. Muffled sobbing followed.

Now it was I who felt guilty. On the other hand, Yvonne can be a convincing actress when it suits her. She's been involved in community theater for decades. In fact, she hangs a framed review on the wall of a 1979 performance of *A Streetcar Named Desire*, where she played Stella. Although I was curious to learn what was behind her reluctance to tackle the Settlers Dunes issue, I decided to back off for the time being.

"I'm sorry."

It was a good opportunity to pay a visit to Stella's Sausage Kitchen. My objective was two-fold: to interview Stella about a potential pig-napping and to talk to Brandi, the new waitress. The young woman had been on my mind ever since my conversation with Doris Zack.

I arrived after the lunch crowd had cleared out and thus had no trouble finding a parking spot. At Stella's, I never worry about locking my car due to the fact that the cops eat there. As I got out of the Jetta, I glanced up at the trio of pigs inside a chain link enclosure. The pink plastic haunches gleamed in the sun while their big, cartoonish eyes gave them a look of sweet innocence. I took out my camera and climbed the rise to snap a couple of shots.

Inside the restaurant, Stella was hunched over the cash register counting receipts. She gave me a nod, saying, "Be with you in a sec."

I jumped up on a stool near a couple of men wearing Granite Cove Ice Company uniforms. They were polishing off plates of fried calamari. Otherwise, the place was empty of diners.

I swiveled around to check out the bulletin board above the coat rack. The board's surface was covered with photos of Stella's customers under the banner Our Regular Hogs. I scanned the familiar faces of those scarfing down sausage, eggs, and sweet fried dough. Needless to say, Attorney Spencer Farley was not among the so-called hogs.

Stella slammed the cash register drawer shut. "What can I do for you, Rose?"

"I was hoping to do a story on the pigs, and if Brandi's around, I'd like to talk to her as well."

Stella shook her head. "The poor kid took the doctor's death awful hard. She was so broke up, I made her go inside and lie down. I guess talking to Dr. Klinger had helped Brandi some. Just between you and me, I never put much stock in airing dirty laundry to a stranger. Where I come from, you take your problems right to the source, our Savior Jesus Christ. You don't need a third party to tell your business to."

When I nodded, she went on. "I suppose it's different for kids today. They grow up knowing all about psychology." She rapped her knuckles on the counter. "Now you sit down here, and we'll talk. You want a Coke? Coffee? How about a root beer float?"

"You know, I haven't had a root beer float since high school. I didn't know they still made them."

She chuckled. "They don't, but I do. Gimme a minute."

I moved down the row of stools and climbed on one at the end of the counter. I watched Stella put ice cream, syrup and seltzer into an old-fashioned metal container that in our part of the country is called a frappe cup. After a steady blast from the soda nozzle, she stuck a straw inside and placed the container in front of me.

The first sip of vanilla and root beer transported me back to the Tick-Tock, a downtown luncheonette patronized by generations of high school kids until the fast food chains arrived. "I'm spoiled for life, Stella."

"That's on me." She untied her apron. "I got a few minutes before I get going on my American Chop Suey. What do you want to know?"

"I need a little background on those pigs of yours for the story. I took some great pictures outside. The light was perfect."

"Good. While you're at it, make sure you write down what's gonna happen if anyone lays a hand on my pigs. I put up with it last year. It was supposed to be a big joke, one of my pigs turning up at the wharf wearing a cap and gown. The high school kids had their fun. This year's different. If they need to pull a prank, let 'em go back to spray painting the horse's hiney on that statue in the park."

"The Homer Frost statue," I said. "I'm afraid that's old school." I took out my notepad. "You said the pigs came from Ohio, is that right?"

"Uh huh. Wintersville, Ohio."

"How did you happen to acquire them? Were they in your family?"

"Nah. My family sold farm equipment, secondhand. See, what happened was about three years ago I was driving down to visit my brother in Wheeling, West Virginia. It was late spring, and I was pushing it 'cause I didn't want to be driving on those roads after dark. Going through Wintersville, I passed an old amusement park all boarded up, kinda seedy looking. A sign out front said they were closed for good. I didn't pay much attention. I was watching the road. At that hour there's muskrats that'll run right out in front of you.

"I'd just about passed the amusement park when out of the corner of my eye, I saw the pigs. The sun was setting at the time. They were all lit up and glowing like."

She pursed her lips. "This is gonna sound strange coming from me. I'm not the type who's impulsive. That's why I can't explain. It's like someone took control of my steering wheel. I pulled over to the side of the road to get a better look at the pigs.

"They were behind a rusted metal fence. I walked over to the entrance, but it was all locked up. On the sign there was a phone number that I copied down. Then I drove off.

"The next day I called that number from my brother's house. I talked to someone who gave me another phone number. The man who answered said yes, he owned the pigs. When I asked if they were for sale, he hemmed and hawed. I figured he was surprised someone was interested in them. He gave me a load of bull crap about some company that owns a miniature golf place that might buy them.

"I knew he was blowing smoke up my wazoo, so I said give me a call when you know for sure. Then I hung up.

"That night I said a prayer. Those pigs had got to me the minute I laid eyes on them. You might say they were the children I never had because God had other plans for me. Two days later the guy called, said he'll sell me the pigs. My brother Gene thought I'd gone off the deep end, buying three plastic pigs, each weighing at least a hundred pounds. I spent the rest of my vacation calling movers to haul them back to New England. "

"Where were you living at the time?" I asked.

"I was living in Kingston, New Hampshire, and running a food concession at a race track nearby. I wasn't making much money. Folks at a race track don't want meatballs, sausage and peppers. They want beer. The concession's lease was coming up for renewal, and I didn't know what to do.

"While I was trying to make up my mind, a friend called. She had two tickets for a whale watch cruise out of Portsmouth and asked me to go. I thought a day on the water would take my mind off things." She rolled her eyes. "I learned the hard way that me and boats don't mix.

"We weren't out on the sea an hour before it started raining hard, so we all went down below. That was worse, the rocking and tipping. I was about to lose my lunch 'til someone told me to go up on deck, keep my eyes on the horizon.

"I wasn't alone up there. Another passenger was at the railing puking his guts out. I told him to move over and I joined him. After awhile we were starting to feel a little better. We got to talking, us two survivors in a storm. He said he was from Boston's North Shore and had a little restaurant in Granite Cove he was thinking about selling. He and his wife wanted to move to Florida to be near the grandkids.

"I told him my situation, how I was thinking of giving up my concession at the race track. He said why not come to Granite Cove and check out his place. The people there don't want fancy food, he said. If you can cook, you can make a living.

"Long story short: I drove down and looked this place over. "She leaned on the counter and gazed around the room. "I knew me and my pigs had found our new home."

"That's beautiful, Stella. Sounds like you were destined to come here."

She straightened. "You understand how I feel about my place. Wish I could say the same about Mayor Froggett and Chief Alfano. I warned them I'd take matters in my own hands if I had to. That's the way we do it back in West Virginia."

"What did they say?"

"They said 'talk to your lawyer,' so I did. I asked Mr. Farley why I couldn't get my fence electrified to keep the little buggers out. He said I'd be liable if anyone got hurt."

She slammed a fist on the counter and I jumped. "Doesn't that frost my ass! Some high school punk trespasses on my property, and I end up getting sued."

"I'm sorry, Stella. We're a litigious society."

"Cal Devine said I could lose my business if I set out traps. Honest, I'd pitch a tent outside if I knew what night they were gonna pull their idiot prank."

"Probably the kids won't even come here. Seems to me they'd be foolish to try it again, knowing you're watching. Besides, you've got the police keeping an eye on the place. Not only that, I'll write a story that'll make them think twice."

"Fair enough," she said. "Sorry for getting so excited. You want to talk to Brandi now?"

When I nodded, she moved to the end of the counter. Hands on hips, she leaned back and yelled "Brand!" in a voice so loud it made my ears tingle. The two men at the counter were either deaf or accustomed to it. They didn't even look up.

Moments later Brandi appeared in jeans and a blue flannel shirt. "I was feeding the chickens," she said. "Hi, Rose. What's up?"

"Can we talk for a minute?"

She glanced at Stella, who said, "Don't worry about it. Take all the time you need."

"Let's sit over here," she said, moving to a table on the other side of the room near a window. She pulled out a chair. "It's more private."

I sat opposite her. Brandi's pale eyes were pink rimmed, as if she'd been crying. Her blue shirt accentuated her eyes and blonde hair, the latter secured with a wide barrette. Brandi had an elegant simplicity, a marked contrast to Pamela Bingham's flashy looks. Yet despite her origins, Brandi was the true aristocrat. "Did you go to Dr. Klinger's wake?" I asked.

She nodded and wiped her eyes with a tissue. "I'm handling it better today. Did Stella tell you I'd been seeing Dr. Klinger?"

"Not only Stella, Doris Zack told me—privately, of course. She saw you in the parking lot the morning Dr. Klinger's body was discovered."

Brandi lowered her gaze. "Did she tell the police that?"

"She didn't think it was any of their business." I paused, uncertain how to phrase it. "Why did you suddenly leave the parking lot?"

She shrugged. "Obviously, your dealings with the police are different from mine. They've hounded my family for years. It goes back to when my dad was in grade school. Apparently, he used to beat up Chief Alfano. They were the same age.

"I don't know how much is true, but Alfano's had a grudge against us. He harasses my brother, always pulling him over and searching his truck for drugs. The last time he found a joint, not even a half inch, in the ash tray. My brother didn't even know it was there. Because he was already on probation, Butchie got a year at Middleton Jail. He's there now." She glanced at me. "That's why I run when I see the cops."

"Uh huh. I can understand that. Right now I don't want to talk about the police. I want to talk about a story I'm doing on Dr. Klinger. It's not just the newspaper coverage, it's something bigger. I've gotten the attention of *Back Bay Living*, a very good periodical.

"As a result, I don't want to do a typical laudatory piece. I want something more. How could this accomplished woman wind up dead? Granted, we live in a society where violence is common, but that doesn't explain her abrupt end." I glanced at her. "I can't seem to close the book on this, Brandi. I keep waiting for the next chapter."

She nodded, subdued. "I know what you mean. Dr. Klinger was so sure of herself. Even though she came from money, she understood what women like me go through. She had a way of listening. It was like you were being heard for the first time." She covered her face with her hands and said, "What'll happen to me now?"

I pulled napkins from the metal dispenser and pressed them into her hand. Soon she let out a sigh and looked at me. Her eyes, washed by tears, were the color of the sea in June.

"Are you okay now?" I asked.

She nodded. "When I first heard about the murder, I wanted to get drunk or high. If I hadn't been living with Stella, I probably would have done that."

"I'm glad you didn't," I said. "How did you meet Dr. Klinger, if you don't mind talking about it?"

"I don't mind." She gave me a weak smile. "It's good therapy. I met Dr. Klinger after I was arrested. It was last winter. I was in Boston in an alcoholic blackout. I don't remember a thing. I'd been drinking for a couple days, staying with a guy in the North End. According to the police report, I went into Shreve, Crump & Low and attempted to steal a diamond ring." She smiled again. "I've got class when I'm drunk.

"Because it wasn't my first arrest, I was looking at spending time at Framingham Women's Prison. The judge at my arraignment mentioned a new program for women under twenty-five. Instead of doing time, those who qualify take part in therapy, vocational training or tutoring for the GED.

"Through that program I met Dr. Klinger, my therapist. She was the first person who took me seriously. Before therapy, I was always filled with fear. I couldn't even go into the grocery store without having a drink. She focused on my strengths, wanting to know why I allowed men to use me, to treat me badly."

"Like your father?"

She nodded. "I found the courage to move out of his house. When he threatened me, Dr. Klinger helped me get a restraining order against him."

"How did he react to that?"

"He hated losing control over me. My dad's an alcoholic, a sick man. One night he called Dr. Klinger and said she'd better watch out or she'd end up as crab bait."

"What did she do?"

"She reported it to the police, and they brought him in, gave him a warning. The cops know he's basically harmless. He's got emphysema and can't walk to the mailbox without his oxygen. But it made me see that I had to move out, even if it meant living in a shelter."

I put my notepad away. "Brandi, we'll talk later when you feel stronger."

"I'm getting better. I'm learning to trust. I've got Stella, the mom I never had."

I smiled. "I have a hunch you're going to make it. You're stronger than you know."

Her expression was wistful. "That's what Dr. Klinger used to tell me." She pushed her chair back and stood up. "I'd better go. Stella claims she doesn't need my help at the moment, but I know she does."

"I'll come by in a couple of days. In the meantime, here's my number." I handed her a card. "You're sure you'll be okay?"

She nodded. "When I didn't get drunk after Dr. Klinger's death, it wasn't just because of Stella. I had another reason for staying sober. Fact is, if I got drunk I wouldn't find out who killed Dr. Klinger. Believe me, Rose, I intend to find out."

"Maybe I can help you," I found myself saying.

I was pulling out of the parking lot when a police cruiser, Cal Devine at the wheel, pulled in next to me. I lowered my window. "How are things going?"

"The same. Listen, I bought the fixings for a meat loaf. Do you want to come over tonight and sample some? I'll get a nice Chianti."

I stared, my mind blank. My answer was lame: "I'm giving Chester a flea bath."

"Great. I lose out to a dog. By the way, I have some information that just came back from the medical examiner's office. Dr. Klinger wasn't a victim of sexual assault, and blood work showed she was taking birth control pills and had diazepam in her system."

"Dia—what?"

"Commonly known as Valium. It was a big dose, forty milligrams. "

"Valium? Why would Dr. Klinger need tranquilizers?"

"Maybe she was nervous about someone stalking her." He got out of the car.

"Do you know if she was being stalked?"

"Chief's got a suspect. I can't say anything right now."

I knew better than to press him. "Going in for coffee?" I asked.

"Nope. I've gotta tell Stella the department's official plan for protecting her pigs."

"Those pigs mean the world to her," Cal.

He leaned down and rested his elbows on my open window, his face inches from mine. "I am so aware of that. On the other hand, I got into police work to help people, not three little pigs."

I smiled. "That's why you're everyone's favorite cop. You're so versatile."

"Tell that to the guys at the station. You wouldn't believe the ragging I'm getting."

"Don't get so distracted you forget to track down the murderer," I said.

"Pretend to track down the murderer. Everyone knows if the perp isn't caught within twenty-four hours, the trail gets so cold you can skate on it."

"You won't give up, will you, Cal?"

He leaned in closer and in a low voice said, "I never give up when I really want something."

I looked into his gray-green eyes. Suddenly it was very warm in the car. "Gotta get back to the office," I whispered, turning to look out the rear window. Shifting into reverse, I backed the car up. Cal watched me drive away.

After I regained my composure, I thought about my conversation with Brandi. While I sensed her determination, I didn't know how well she'd hold up in the long run. She had a record of poverty, crime and abuse. Although she appeared strong, she was young and in early recovery.

And what of Dr. Klinger, the mystery woman, a blank screen upon whom others had projected their images? My image had been based on assumption, not personal knowledge. Because she grew up in tony Chestnut Hill and attended exclusive schools, she was therefore elitist, a snob. Wasn't I guilty of the same close-minded assumptions nurtured by many typical Granite Cove-ers?

Conversely, Brandi, someone who'd grown up with nothing, didn't begrudge Dr. Klinger's privileged background, so why should I? And just because I wouldn't have chosen her as my therapist doesn't mean she wasn't a crackerjack shrink. One had only to look at Brandi's transformation to know that.

My resistance to engaging Dr. Klinger's services revolved around my personal quirks. Take the issue of grooming, for instance. Because I am someone who, in a pinch, sprays cooking oil on her shoes, one could assume I'm not fastidious. Vivian Klinger, meanwhile, was always immaculately groomed. Finding herself in a shelter following a nuclear disaster, she would never resort to cooking oil for a quick shine.

"Hello?"

"Mrs. Klinger? This is Rose McNichols from the *Granite Cove Gazette*. I spoke to you at the wake."

"Oh, yes, the reporter."

"Exactly. I hope you're feeling a little better?"

"I am."

"Good. You indicated you'd be willing to talk to me about the piece I'm writing for *Back Bay Living*. I was hoping we could set up an appointment."

"I don't remember agreeing to that."

"Well, you didn't rule it out, and I know you'd want your daughter portrayed as accurately as possible. She was an invaluable member—"

"Yes, Ms. Nicholson."

"Uh, McNichols. Rose McNichols."

"At the moment I'm in the middle of editing a poetry journal. My writing group elected me editor, no doubt to keep me occupied during this time."

"I'm sorry to bother you."

"Everyone says that, yet bother they do."

"Did you receive the *Granite Cove Gazette* story I sent you?"

"I must have. I'm sure it's on my desk somewhere."

"That piece was limited by the necessity of making it local for our readers. What I'm working on is something bigger, something that deals with professional city women and their difficult rise to the top. Dr. Klinger had associations all over Boston. Her roots were in Wellesley, Harvard, Mass General—"

"Ms. Nicholson, I'm aware of my daughter's resume."

"Then you'll understand my need to talk to those who knew her best in order to balance the picture and provide a personal glimpse—"

"How about Wednesday at two? Come for tea."

"Oh? Yes. Yes I will, Mrs. Klinger."

Auntie Pearl's Helpful Housekeeping Hints

Dear Auntie Pearl:

My boyfriend Roland is a rugged type guy who plays handball. Ours is a solid relationship; lately, we've discussed marriage. Roland and I are so compatible, yet there's a minor problem I can't seem to overlook...

I've discovered he's been taking my pantyhose from the laundry hamper. This has happened on four occasions. For some reason I can't bring myself to mention it. Outside of this tiny flaw, Roland is so right for me. Nonetheless, I can't stop wondering what he's doing with my pantyhose.

Signed,
Baffled in Boxford

Dear Baffled:

It's no mystery to me what Roland is doing with your pantyhose. I'm willing to wager he's discovered they make excellent ties for tomato plants. Simply cut them off below the crotch and then in 10" lengths. The nylon strips secure the plants firmly to the stakes with a flexibility that allows for growth. Furthermore, the ties can be used year after year.

Instead of being wary, you should be grateful for such an industrious young man. Come August, he might even whip up a tasty batch of gazpacho. Hola!

Signed,
Auntie Pearl

Auntie Pearl's Helpful Housekeeping Hints!

Six

Myrna Phipps' s directions to her house were as flighty as the lady herself:

"Then you'll come to a mailbox with a lovely clematis vine around the base." It's easier to find clams at high tide than a Hemlock Point address. For one thing, the streets are unnamed. I guess it illustrates the old saying, if you have to ask...

Still it was unnerving to navigate the main thoroughfare, a dusty, bumpy road that meandered past hidden driveways where great estates were tucked away. I was careful not to turn in at the wrong entrance. The sight of a battered lime green Jetta would not be reassuring in that high rent district. It was a world far removed from downtown Granite Cove. I rolled down the window. Even the air smelled expensive.

Finally, I was rewarded when the aforementioned mailbox appeared. Next to it sat a short wooden sign that bore the nam Marbella. I turned into the narrow lane, maneuvering around the protruding shrubs lining the driveway. Upon reaching the end, the Phipps' house appeared. It was a sprawling stucco affair nestled among wild beach roses and scrub pine and overlooking an expanse of sea and sky. Striped awnings shaded the windows and terrace while the bright cherry tiles on the roof bespoke the home of a tile mogul.

At the front door a maid escorted me to what I assumed was the library, judging by the rows of old books lining the floor-to-ceiling shelves. Myrna Phipps sat on a settee near a marble fireplace.

"There you are, Miss McNichols. Come in, please." Mrs. Phipps looked like the society lady in The Three Stooges. Her silver hair was worn in an upsweep and secured with combs. Her chest was like an upholstered shelf. To complete the overall impression, she carried a lacquered fan.

After the greetings were out of the way, she instructed the maid to "fetch Raul from his nappy." Then she led me to a broad window at the end of the room. Outside, a wide lawn ended at a thin crescent of sandy beach and beyond that, the ocean. It was a bewitching view. I stared longingly, careful not to press my nose against the glass.

She hugged herself. "The ocean looks chilly today, doesn't it?"

"If I lived here (and if my aunt had balls she'd be my uncle, I thought to myself), I'd be in the water every day."

"My husband and I rarely swim nowadays. The water's not as nice as when I was a girl."

While few things in life are as nice as they once were, having a private beach was a reasonable compensation. I sighed, reluctant to turn away from the view.

While we waited, Mrs. Phipps and I made small talk, something I loathe. I told her about the paper's circulation, the publisher, and my duties as reporter. All the while I was wondering what happened to the maid.

Just as I was launching into an account of the Seniors' Summer Picnic, minus any mention of the Salmonella, Mrs. Phipps patted my arm and got to her feet. "I'm going up to see what's keeping Raul. The little fellow sometimes gets cross when he awakens. He's apt to nip." She gestured to a tall glassed-in case against the far wall. "While I'm gone, take a peek at Raul's awards. I'll be right back."

I took her suggestion and checked out the various ribbons and engraved silver trophies inside the wooden case. As I was putting on my glasses to read an inscription, Mrs. Phipps returned. "We're back," she called.

I turned and sucked in my breath. In her arms Mrs. Phipps carried the weirdest looking creature I've ever seen. It was small, shriveled, gray and hairless with big sad eyes and ears that stuck out like inverted ice cream cones. I hoped my face didn't register the shock I felt. And to think the dog was worth thousands, thanks to its peerless, yet hairless, lineage.

"Let's sit here and get acquainted, shall we?" she said, lowering herself onto a sofa near the window. "We'll take a moment to get used to each other first." She patted the cushion next to her. "Sit here. You can pet Raul, but don't try to kiss him."

Kissing Raul, who resembled a large rodent, was the last thing I had in mind. At the same time I didn't want to offend Mrs. Phipps, patron saint of Yvonne. Thus I hesitantly touched the clammy skin, repressing a shudder. "He's darling," I lied, peering into the dog's yellow eyes, "but his skin feels a little cold."

She cuddled him closer. "Hairless breeds are cold-blooded. Do you notice how warm this room is?"

Did I notice? It was so warm the candles were in danger of melting.

She continued, "Raul sleeps in a climate controlled room where the temperature never drops below seventy-five degrees. His little heart must work overtime providing heat for his body. That's one reason why Lester and I drive to Florida every winter. We can't risk taking him on a plane. Even in first class the temperature can drop." She kissed the top of his wrinkled head. "Besides, it's nice and cozy in the car." She touched her nose to his wet, black snout. "Raul loves Palm Beach, don't you, peaches?"

Raul, in response, regarded her morosely.

After recovering from my initial shock, I dug out my notebook and began the interview, asking questions concerning the dog's lineage. Mrs. Phipps said they went to Bristol, England, to get Raul. I made a feeble joke. "You mean, you didn't drive?"

She took the question seriously. "We'd planned to fly back, but Lady Higganbottom, who owns the kennel, discouraged us. She said the pressurized cabin in a plane could result in ear infections in a wee pup. Fortunately, we were able to book passage on the QE II. Lady Higganbottom also mentioned that Raul's first few days with his new owners are a time of bonding. We shouldn't be separated for even a minute.

"On the ship, we didn't want to expose him to the passengers in the dining room, so we took our meals in our stateroom." In a confidential tone she added, "One must commit oneself."

"He must be a very contented dog," I said, examining the tiny mutt whose skin was the color of wet clay. It isn't fair, I thought. Why didn't the Phippses adopt me? I never get ear infections or require climate control.

Instead of agreeing that Raul was indeed contented, Mrs. Phipps pressed him closer. I was afraid the thing would suffocate, but he didn't protest. In fact, Raul was strangely passive. "At least he's not noisy," I said, "like some small breeds."

When Mrs. Phipps spoke, her voice wavered. "This is off the record, Miss McNichols. Raul, you see, is clinically depressed."

Surprised, I murmured an apology as she continued. "I became aware of the change in him about three weeks ago. He became listless. When Lester came home from the office, Raul didn't run to the door and do his little dance."

"Dance?" I asked.

With that she sat up and bounced on the sofa, wrists bent and hands flapping up and down. "Yip! Yip! Yip!" she barked in a high-pitched tone. It was a good imitation of a dancing Hairless Peruvian.

She continued. "As the days passed, Raul got worse. He started to tinkle on the legs of the furniture. Finally, when he did toity in Lester's slippers, we made an appointment at the Angell Memorial Hospital in Boston. Their doctors gave Raul a thorough examination and said the problem wasn't physical, it was behavioral.

"We wondered how this could be. We've treated Raul like our own child. We didn't know where to turn until someone suggested Dr. Klinger. At that point we'd seen so many specialists—"

"Excuse me, Mrs. Phipps. You contacted Dr. Klinger?"

"For a consultation." She placed a hand on my arm. "Please don't mention any of this in your story."

"Of course I won't. I asked because I'm surprised to learn that Dr. Klinger treated dogs."

"She didn't actually engage in therapy. She observed what she called the family dynamic to determine if there was anything in our interactions that was upsetting Raul."

"And did Dr. Klinger learn anything?"

"Before she died—so tragic, that was—she'd told us that a sudden change in Raul's environment was likely responsible. The only change I could think of was the decorating job in the solarium. We had new wallpaper and slipcovers made. Yet after we returned the room to its original state, Raul still remained depressed." She gazed sadly at the sleeping dog.

"Excuse me, Mrs. Phipps. Do you mean to say you had the solarium decorated and then you had it undecorated, changed back to the original state?"

She nodded, the loose skin under her eyes quivering. "It didn't help. The poor baby still moped pitifully."

I couldn't help staring. "Mrs. Phipps, you really love that dog."

"Oh, we do."

I studied Raul, who now resembled a sleeping cactus plant. "Let me ask you, as Raul's caregiver, what is your gut feeling?"

She looked startled. "What do you mean?"

"It's like the bond among family members. You know when something's wrong."

She averted her eyes. "Odd that you should mention that. I do have a hunch, but I haven't mentioned it to Lester. Although my husband is a high-powered businessman, he's also extremely tenderhearted. If I told him about my hunch, he'd feel terribly guilty."

"Guilty about what?"

She sighed. "About a month ago, Lester attended a tile convention in Texas. When he got back we had a dinner party, inviting some of our oldest friends. As a matter of fact, we had cocktails right here in the library.

"After an hour or so, Lester excused himself and went upstairs. When he returned, he was wearing a ten-gallon cowboy hat he'd brought back from his trip. It was quite amusing, and everyone laughed at the sight. Raul, who was sleeping under that chair, woke up. When he saw Lester in that hat, he froze. It was eerie. Little Raul seemed to turn to stone. Of course, Lester immediately removed the hat and we continued with the party. Yet from that moment Raul developed a haunted look."

"Did you mention this to Dr. Klinger?"

"I did without telling my husband. Dr. Klinger seemed to agree that it could have been traumatic for Raul to awaken and see Daddy, I mean Lester, looking so strange. Raul is sensitive. He comes from an old, aristocratic line. Dr. Klinger said he may also have a fear of men in hats. Many breeds do."

"Now that you have your suspicions, what are you going to do?"

She rested her cheek on top of Raul's head. A tear slid from her eye. "I don't know, Miss McNichols, I just don't know... "

Lunchtime found me picking alfalfa sprouts from my computer keyboard. I'd bought a veggie wrap from Mega Mug, a downtown hole in the wall whose only attraction is its proximity to the office. As I grappled with the soggy, loose wrap, bits of mushroom, tomato, peppers and sprouts rained down.

Seeing my dilemma, Stewart asked, "Shall I hose you off?"

I chucked the remainder in the wastebasket. "That's the last time I go to Mega Mug for anything but coffee."

"You should bring something from home," he said. "I brought a thermos of lentil soup that saved me four dollars."

"Maybe in my next lifetime I will."

"Just trying to be helpful," he said in a prissy tone.

I wiped wet, sticky hands on the restaurant's thin napkins. They shredded on contact. "Don't mind me, Stew. I'm just mad I went back there after swearing I'd never step foot in that place again. I always expect it to improve, but it never does. Now they hired some pea-brained kid who's not too tightly wrapped himself."

"Young people have to get work experience somewhere," he said, chidingly.

An appropriate response from a trust fund recipient who's never worked full-time in his life. "I wish they'd get some experience in manners," I said. "Nothing major, just a simple thank you. And while I'm on the subject, do these kids have something against smiling? Is that not a cool thing to do?"

Stew chuckled. "You're showing your age, Rose."

Immediately, I reached in the wastebasket for my discarded sandwich to throw at Stewart's head. While I was doing this my phone rang, thus sparing him. It was Betty Ann. "What are you doing right now?" she asked. No greeting, no preliminaries.

"Picking sprouts from my keyboard. What's up?"

"Can you come over here? I'm at work, and I need to see you." She sounded like she was talking through clenched teeth.

"I can kill two birds with one stone. I was planning to interview one of your residents, Mabel Snodgrass. She'll be one hundred one years old at the end of the week, and—"

"I'll see you then."

"Fine," I said, although she'd hung up. I grabbed my bag and said to Stewart's back, "Tell Yvonne I'll be at Green Pastures Nursing Home if she needs to reach me."

"I heard. You're meeting Betty Ann and interviewing a hundred-and-one-year-old lady. Do me a favor. Let me know if there are any good-looking nurses over there."

"You thinking of settling down?" I sized up the thin, greasy hair, the loafers bound with duct tape.

He shrugged. "Providing she's good-looking and can discuss the issues without sounding like a bimbo."

"I'll let you know," I promised. Stewart should add another requirement in his search for the perfect woman: embalmed. No living, breathing woman would last two days with Stew. Although he's got an encyclopedic knowledge of sports, he's totally lacking in social skills.

I found a parking space in the visitors' section under the big white sign reading: Green Pastures Nursing & Retirement Home. Printed in italics below that was their motto, *where dreams come true*. Betty Ann is fond of adding, "if you dream of being drugged, diapered, and permanently detained." Although she loves working with the elderly, B.A. laments the modern nursing home. Often, usually after her third drink, she launches into her dream of someday running her own establishment.

"I'll buy a big old house and put in tile floors so we won't have to worry about spills. We'll have a couple of cats, maybe a dog. And instead of vegetating in front of the TV all day, the residents will be outside in the garden, picking vegetables. We'll raise our own crops. Nothing will be processed or precooked. Some can help inside doing housework. It will be like a family where everyone has chores.

"At the end of the day they'll be so tired they won't need sleeping pills. In fact, they won't need half the medications the average patient takes."

"You know what?" I said. "My dad will be the first person to sign up for your nursing home."

She smiles, though before the night is through her optimism fades. "Who am I kidding? I wouldn't last a week in the business. The nitpickers in public health, the license boards, will descend with a checklist. Have I recorded the residents' urine output? Their daily weight? Their blood pressure?

"The state will ask where's the elevator. Public Health will check the refrigerator, cupboards and bathrooms. One wet mop and I'll be written up for violations I never heard of." Eventually, she becomes wistful. "I could create such a wonderful environment, but in the end the fussbudgets would win."

I paused outside the door with its black lacquered sign: Betty Ann Zagrobski, Director of Activities. Through the tiny window I spotted her two assistants setting up tables stacked with bingo cards. I stuck my head in the doorway. "Is your boss around?"

"She's in the break room having lunch," the younger woman said.

Where else? I thought, heading down the long hallway whose ambiance, if that's the appropriate word for linoleum tiles and institutional green walls, was a marked contrast to the residents' public areas. There they had embossed wallpaper, chandeliers, and pastel carpeting; all the better to spill upon. As a result, Green Pastures Nursing Home exuded all the warmth of a suburban hotel while its rates doubled those of The Ritz.

I found Betty Ann hunched over a submarine sandwich that dripped oil. At a nearby table, a group of nurses' aides carried on a lively conversation in Spanish. They seemed to be the only people in the place having fun. I approached and stood over Betty Ann. "What's that smell?"

"Rosie, you scared me. What smell?"

I pointed to the oversized sandwich. "I smelled it all the way down the hall."

"It's probably oregano. Stella makes the best fried eggplant subs." She picked up a plastic knife. "Let me give you half. It's loaded with fiber."

"No, thanks. Fiber is all my dad talks about." I sat down. "Why are old people so bowel obsessed?"

"Don't knock it. Bowels are my bread and butter."

I winced. "Please. Not at lunch."

"Aren't you hungry?"

I got up and surveyed the stainless steel vending machines bordering the room. Finally, I inserted coins into a slot. An ice cream sandwich, smaller than the one depicted in the display, fell into the trough. I removed the wrapper and bit into a frozen disk that resembled, and tasted like, a hockey puck.

At the table, I said, "You seem in better spirits than you sounded on the phone."

"Probably because I've had lunch." With her fork she scooped up the remaining bits of minced green peppers and onions from the paper plate. "But eventually, I have to face the music."

"Which is?"

She glanced at her watch. "Which is cigarette time. Every day after lunch around this time, I look forward to a smoke. There's a group that gathers outside the storage shed. One guy's from the laundry department, a couple are from nursing, and one's from accounting. Every day, rain or shine, we gather to smoke." She glanced at the window. Her lips quivered. "They're probably there now wondering what's keeping me."

"Betty Ann, this time is different. This time you called me because you want to change. Isn't that right?"

She nodded dully. "Calling you, I reinforced the commitment I made to Tiny. Instead of smoking, I said I'd walk after lunch." She crumpled her napkin, tossing it on the table. "But you know the saying, the road to hell is paved with good intentions."

I licked the last of the ice cream sandwich from my fingers and jumped up. "In that case, I think we'd better start walking."

Betty Ann sighed and slowly got to her feet while I gathered up the trash and threw it into a corner barrel. When I returned to the table, she was staring fixedly at a man sitting across the room. "Betty Ann?" When she didn't respond, I followed her gaze and spotted the pack of Marlboros in the breast pocket of his olive uniform. I placed my hand on her arm. "Is that your brand?"

"Right now, everything's my brand," she said.

"Come on," I said, leading her away. Like a zombie she followed me out of the room. We stood at the door overlooking the parking lot. I turned to her. "Which way do you want to go?"

"You see over there to the left?" She pointed beyond a row of vans. "Behind those dogwoods, that's where the shed is. They'll be there now, waiting." She inhaled deeply. "Holy crap, I can smell the smoke."

"Then we'll go this way," I said, taking her arm and heading to the right. Before long we were off the nursing home property and in the middle of a suburban neighborhood. It was a new subdivision of brightly colored Victorian style houses. We followed a freshly paved sidewalk bordered in granite.

If I had assumed that B.A. would trudge along dispiritedly, I was wrong. She soon picked up speed, swinging her arms forcefully. Seconds later she broke away, silently striding ahead. I didn't attempt to keep up, figuring she wanted to work out her frustrations. When she increased her speed, going so fast I feared she'd walk right out of her shoes, I called, "Betty Ann, wait!"

Head down, arms pumping, B.A. charged down the street like King Kong on a rampage. Eventually she slowed, allowing me to catch up. We fell into an easy stride. I patted her back. "Just think, you're out walking while those poor souls are back at the shed barbecuing their lungs."

"Today's only one victory. The war rages on."

"What do you mean?"

"I'm saying I know better. When the craving hits, you don't care about promises. You forget everything. You'll even pick up a butt from the street, yellow with dog pee."

"You wouldn't do that."

"I would, if I hadn't had a cigarette in awhile." She closed her eyes. "It would be the finest smoke of my life."

Her face had such a look of rapture, I had to get her mind off the subject. "Guess who I'll be interviewing on Wednesday?"

"Who?"

"Veronica Klinger. I'm invited to Chestnut Hill for tea."

"Lucky you, tea with the dragon lady. Be careful she doesn't poison you."

"By the way, how well did you know Dr. Klinger?"

"Not much. She came to the nursing home from time to time for psych evals."

"What's that about?"

"When someone starts acting gaga, the director needs an evaluation from a shrink. It's standard procedure even if the resident is ninety-eight years old. Everything is documented at a nursing home. You get a pimple on your butt, it goes in your chart."

"But isn't it natural at ninety-eight to get a little... spacey?"

"Not necessarily. In any case, they have to rule out physical causes first. If that checks out okay, you need a psych eval. The shrink comes in, asks a few questions like 'Who's the President?' and then sends a bill for three hundred fifty dollars."

"So Dr. Klinger did your evaluations?"

"Uh huh. She had a way of addressing the residents as if they were school kids and she was the teacher. You know how she enunciated every word? 'Can you tell me what holiday we celebrate in July?' "

It was a pretty good imitation. "Did the residents respond to her?"

"Most were so happy to have company, they'd welcome Jeffrey Dalmer. By the way, I don't approve of how Mr. Guskin, our Administrator, is handling the murder. He's decided to not tell the residents. He's cut out any references in the newspapers."

"If it's any consolation, Chief Alfano is releasing the name of a suspect. It's some vagrant who was hanging out at the park. Apparently, Spencer Farley caught him once outside Dr. Klinger's office."

"Humph. That's no vagrant. Don't you know who they're talking about?" She flashed me a Cheshire Cat smile.

I stopped in the middle of the sidewalk. "Betty Ann, do you know something about the murder that I don't?"

"Hah! You should pay me for all the juicy tidbits I provide."

"How about I buy you a drink instead? Now tell me right now."

"Don't get your undies in a twist. Do you remember Rusty Favazza?"

"From high school? The football player?"

"The same. That so-called vagrant is none other than Granite Cove's boy hero."

The image of the limping man carrying a case of beer on his shoulder suddenly flashed in my mind. "I think I saw him walking on Main Street." I gave her a brief description.

"That's Rusty."

"Unbelievable."

It was hard to connect the disheveled stranger to the former handsome high school athlete. Back then, Rusty Favazza was our version of the New England Patriots' Tom Brady. His performance with the Granite Cove Lobstermen resulted in a full scholarship to Boston College. Rusty was a god, idolized by everyone. "How in the world is Rusty connected with Dr. Klinger?"

"Before he got kicked out of BC, Rusty met her at a frat party. At the time she was a student at Wellesley, a couple of years younger. If you recall, Rusty was used to women throwing themselves at him. When beautiful, brainy Vivian gave him a chilly reception, I imagine he was intrigued."

"Maybe I should have given him a chilly reception," I said. "He never noticed me anyway." A skinny sophomore, I tutored in the high school writing lab where Rusty was sent for help with his English essays. I secretly swooned over him, the high cheekbones, the curly copper hair. Not only was Rusty gorgeous, he had a sense of humor, unlike many jocks, and never took himself seriously. When sports writers labeled him "New England's best high school quarterback," he shrugged. Football, he told everyone, was his ticket out of Granite Cove.

"Basically, Rusty was out of his league," she continued. "Vivian was Chestnut Hill, and he was the housing project. Yet it was a definite case of opposites attracting." She gave me a sly look. "I hear they had a sizzling affair."

I stared in disbelief. "Dr. Klinger and Rusty Favazza? Get out! Where are you getting this information anyway?"

"Tiny has been moonlighting a couple nights a week at the Sacred Cod where Rusty's a regular. Tiny's become his confessor."

The funky wharfside restaurant is known for its generous drinks and fresh seafood right off the boats. "Rusty's a regular?" I asked.

"When his disability checks hold out."

"How is he disabled?"

"Fractured pelvis from working on a tuna boat in California. During a storm, the mast split and fell on him."

"Poor guy," I said. "Still, I still can't imagine Vivian Klinger and Rusty Favazza getting together. Talk about polar opposites."

"She wasn't a Ph.D. back then. She was a sheltered college student living at home. I don't have to remind you about his effect on women."

"Everyone had a crush on Rusty," I said. "Remember Ms. Snelson, the guidance counselor who drove him to Maine to tour Bowdoin? What a scandal when it got out they'd stayed at a motel."

"Uh huh. Rusty claimed he'd slept in the car."

"Right. Come to think of it, I wonder what Rusty saw in Dr. Klinger. She couldn't have been what you'd call a fun date."

Betty Ann shrugged. "It was probably one set of glands calling to another."

"Is that why she eventually settled here?"

"To rekindle an old romance with an alcoholic ex-con? Is that what you mean?"

"Rusty's an ex-con?" I stopped and stared

"According to Tiny, who gets it from the source, the sword fishing was just a cover for drug smuggling. Rusty did two years in prison."

"Sounds like he's been on a slippery slope." I thought about high school heroes and the pressure they face to live up to the public's expectations. We demand much, and when they fall, we take it personally. "If all that is true, why in the world did he come back?"

"He claims he ran out of choices. He got out of prison and didn't want to go back to the life, so he came home. He was living at the shelter downtown until his disability checks from California got transferred to Massachusetts."

"But it's so weird that Dr. Klinger ended up here in Rusty's home town."

"Rusty introduced her to Granite Cove. One day they borrowed her old man's sailboat and headed down the coast. When they sailed into Granite Cove harbor, she fell in love with the place, said she wanted to live here someday. Perhaps her vision included Rusty as well. Who knows? Her old man had other plans for her that didn't include marriage to a wharf rat."

We came to the end of the sidewalk, finding ourselves confronted by a busy thoroughfare. I looked at Betty Ann. "Are you ready to go back? We can cross here and continue our walk. I've got a few more minutes."

"I'm ready to go back."

We turned and retraced our route. When we got within sight of Green Pastures, I said, "Are you okay? What about tonight if you crave a smoke? What will you do?"

"I've got a video program I watch. It's all about replacing negative conditioners with positive conditioners."

"You mean like reaching for a candy bar instead of a cigarette?"

She laughed. "Don't I wish. No, it's basically what we just did. Since I associate lunch with smoking, I substituted a positive conditioner: walking. Right now it's a piss-poor substitute as far as I'm concerned, but the program claims I'll actually come to prefer the positive." She kicked a rock at her feet. "If only I had a better reward in store."

"Are you kidding? How about a healthy heart?"

"I'm not talking about the health aspect. I'm talking about something else."

"No more dog breath?" I asked.

She shook her head. "Let's say I quit for good. Guess what my reward will be?"

"You tell me."

"Jonah. When Tiny tells the court our home is free of secondhand smoke, there's a good chance we'll be awarded custody of Jonah." She closed her eyes. "Does that sound like a win-win situation?"

I tried to come up with something encouraging to offset the bleak picture she painted. Yet I could not, because my attention was drawn elsewhere. In a remote region of my mind, associations were forming. They'd been set in motion when Betty Ann discussed negative and positive conditioning. Although my brainstorm needed time to percolate, I felt I was onto something.

I had stumbled upon a solution to Raul Phipps' neurosis.

Seven

"Egads! What in the name of God...?" Yvonne's face registered dismay as she examined a stack of photos recently delivered by the lab. "Are these yours, Rose?"

Without turning from my monitor, I said, "Are you referring to Mabel Snodgrass's birthday party?"

"No, this looks like some kind of dog, if I had to guess."

"Oh, then that must be Raul."

"What kind of dog is it?"

"He's a miniature Hairless Peruvian. Worth a fortune."

"If he appeared at my door in a blizzard, I'd throw water on him."

"Even if you knew his owners were Mr. and Mrs. Phipps of the Miles O' Tiles fortune?"

"Oh, that's who he is." She held the photo at arm's length. "I'm sure he's got his positive qualities. It's like abstract art. Seen with an uneducated eye, it appears bizarre. Yet when you develop an appreciation, a whole world opens up. I imagine it's the same for exotic dog breeds. Mr. and Mrs. Phipps no doubt discern qualities that the average person cannot fathom."

"He's been going toity in Mr. Phipps's shoes," I said.

She sighed, placing the photos on my desk. "I suppose he's got his reasons."

"He may. In the meantime, I think I've found a solution to the problem."

"Good. I'm glad you've gotten over your obsession with murder."

I flashed a goody-girl smile and at the same time felt a twinge of guilt. My interview with Veronica Klinger would take place during working hours. Yvonne would not approve. Yet, how many nights had I worked at home past midnight doing the housekeeping hints column?

I picked up a photo of Raul from the pile, a close up. He resembled the mutant from the movie It's Alive! His puckered skin was the color of a wet slug. I shuffled through the stack until I found the one of Mrs. Phipps cradling a sleeping Raul and beaming with maternal pride. "How about this to accompany my story?" I held the picture up.

Yvonne slipped on her glasses and peered at it. "We'll put it on the front page. I'm sure Mrs. Phipps will be pleased."

"When people see Raul, they'll say, 'What in hell is that?'"

"In that case it's your job to educate them," she said, patting my shoulder.

The night was cold and misting when I took Chester for a walk. With my collar turned up and an umbrella tucked under my arm I set out, dodging puddles. I wished I'd worn gloves. The cold numbed my fingers.

Dark clouds skittered across a faint, ghostly moon. All in all, it was the dreariest of landscapes. Spring in New England is like that. It will break your heart. One day you're wearing cutoffs, the next day you're scraping ice off your windshield. A stretch of good weather—three days is considered an undeserved blessing—convinces us that spring has arrived. Then it snows—heavily. You'd think we'd wise up, but we never do. Hope for spring springs eternal.

On the walk home I heard the phone ringing before I opened the door. Normally I don't answer at night, unless I'm expecting a call from my dad. He's suspicious of answering machines and won't leave messages. I decided to answer:

"Hello?"

"Ah, just the girl I want."

My first impulse was to tell the caller that at age thirty-nine I was hardly a girl. Likewise, my dad can't get it right. He calls women girls. If they're pushy, they're called calls dames. In any case, it was no time for a lesson in political correctness; my feet were wet. "What can I do for you?"

"You could pay me the honor of having lunch with me tomorrow."

The voice oozed warmth; I recognized the caller. "Hello, Mr. Alfano. Thanks, but I'm pretty busy around lunch time."

"You career gals are always busy. Don't you have any fun?"

"You know how it is, stories breaking out all over town."

"And you have such a unique way of writing about them."

Bunny Alfano was doing what he did best, slinging the BS. Of course the man had his reasons. He faced an election and needed positive publicity. Yet I was intrigued. Bunny, with his pseudo innocence, had the inside story on Settlers Dunes as well as certain people in high places. The guy had the goods on everyone. If I played to his vanity, I might get him to spill those goods. Although it wouldn't be following the highest journalistic standards, it reflected Yvonne's policy regarding our advertisers: tit for tat.

"Want to meet at Stella's?" I asked.

He chuckled. "I hope you're joking. My brother likes that hash joint, but I'm fussy."

"I mention it because it's convenient."

"Listen, darlin,' forget convenient. How does the dining room at the Olde Shores Country Club sound? I've got a private table. Meet me there at noon, okay?" "Sounds good to me."

"Now I'm a happy man. By the way, don't forget your camera."

"I never do."

The next morning I rummaged in my closet, searching for something suitable to wear to the venerable Olde Shores Country Club. Although I had no idea what the landed gentry wore to lunch, I doubted it was denim or mini.

Settling on a navy skirt and tailored silk shirt, I turned in front of the mirror, Chester stretched out at my feet. "What do you think? I asked. He lifted his head, regarded me solemnly and went back to sleep. Just as I thought.

Before leaving, I phoned the office. Fortunately, Yvonne didn't pick up. I left a message at her extension saying I was going to re-shoot Mabel Snodgrass's birthday party. It wasn't a lie. In all my photos Mabel appeared to be in a coma. Her family had mistakenly held the party during nap time. When Mabel periodically awakened, I hurriedly snapped pictures. Not surprisingly, few came out good. Mabel looked not only old, but mummified.

Before hanging up, I hastily added that I'd also be seeing Bunny Alfano. "We don't have a file photo of him, so I'll take care of it."

The drive along the coast was so beautiful I felt like weeping. The sea sparkled like a field of diamonds under a pale yellow sun. It was one of those rare days when the smell of the ocean is so strong you can taste it. Passing the giant rocks overlooking Thatcher's Island, I had an urge to stop the car, kick off my shoes and climb those ancient, sun-warmed boulders worn smooth by centuries of crashing waves.

As I neared Hemlock Point, the houses got bigger and farther apart. I passed the narrow, dirt road leading into Settlers Dunes, almost missing the new, unfamiliar sign stuck in the sand outside the entrance. I stopped and backed up to get a look.

Dark blue lettering stood out against a white background: *Coming Soon: Cormorant Cove, Oceanfront Villas of Unparalleled Elegance!* In the corner of the sign was the ubiquitous trademark: Ask Martha!

I floored the gas pedal and peeled out, tires screeching and spinning in the sand. Of all the ballsy maneuvers, this was in a class of its own. This time Martha Farley had outdone herself. Her so-called development, whether legal or not, required a devious mind coupled with a steely assurance.

Obviously, she wasn't working alone. Most likely Bunny was behind the scenes, clearing the way when opposition reared its head. It would be interesting to find out who was supplying the upfront money...

Thinking about Martha Farley had destroyed my pleasure in the beautiful day. Were she a true business woman, perhaps I wouldn't be so harsh. But Martha was a phony who'd undergone a major transformation. Not only had she acquired a proper boarding school accent since high school—she had been three years ahead of me at Granite Cove High—but a sense of entitlement as well.

This in spite of the fact that our backgrounds were similar. We both came from poor-but-respectable families. However, the former Martha Muldoon had bagged Spencer Farley. The union had opened doors, allowing her to create Ask Martha!, a real estate business that catered to Hemlock Point's rich and famous. Every week I'm forced to see her mug smirking at me from ads in the Gazette, touting the latest multi-million dollar estate for sale.

That's why when my dad sold the homestead, he got an out-of-town realtor, although Spencer Farley checked the paperwork. My childhood home sold for two hundred seventy-five thousand dollars, a tidy sum in the mid '90s. Meanwhile, Martha's clients pay that for a poolside cabana.

I glanced at the speedometer and lifted my foot from the accelerator. My thoughts were spinning like gerbils in a cage. Brooding about Martha was definitely bad for the nerves.

Before long I approached the entrance to Olde Shores Country Club. The rambling wooden building looked timeless in the soft spring light. Flowering azalea and tulip beds provided color against sea-weathered gray shingles. On the wraparound porch, a row of empty rocking chairs moved in the breeze as if propelled by ghosts. Farther off in the background, the ocean reflected the robin's egg blue of the sky.

I found an inconspicuous parking spot under a drooping bridal wreath. After getting out of the car, I looked around at the manicured grounds bordering the brilliant green of a fairway. It brought to mind the saying, It's what God would have created if he'd had the money.

I followed a walkway made of crushed shells that led to the entrance. Along the way, several low, discreet signs pointed in various directions to destinations such as the Ladies Locker Room, the Pro Shop, and Pool. Another indicated the 19th Hole, no doubt the members' most popular destination.

I climbed the broad wooden steps of the front porch and opened the main door to the lobby. Inside, portraits of stern-faced Yankees in heavy gold frames regarded me with disdain, as if suspecting an interloper. A large Oriental rug in faded reds and blues covered the wooden floor. At the far end of the room, a wide window offered a view of the rolling golf course and ocean beyond.

As I checked my reflection in a mirror, a lavender-haired woman approached. A name tag worn over her left breast read Mrs. Procter: Dining Room Manager. "Can I help you?" she asked. Her tone suggested she could not.

"I'm meeting a member, Mr. Alfano."

Before she could respond, a loud, gravely "Rosie!" rang out. Mrs. Proctor and I both turned in the direction of the voice, a sound more appropriate for a barroom than a staid country club.

Bunny, seated at a table near a window, waved a white dinner napkin. If Mrs. Proctor disapproved of his boorishness, she gave no indication. She led me through the large dining room, passing tables of well-dressed members who spoke in murmurs.

When we reached his table, Bunny jumped up and kissed my cheek. He wore a blueberry-blue sports jacket over salmon colored pants. The top buttons of his shirt were open, revealing enough chest hair to stuff a small pillow. Mrs. Proctor scurried off.

"Is this place the balls, or what?" He pointed out the window. "That's the ninth tee and behind those hedges, the tennis courts." He waited while I murmured my appreciation and then said, "Let's order a drink. Ever been here before?"

"Years ago." I didn't add that I'd been with my dad in his truck, making a delivery of lobsters to the club's kitchen. "How long have you been a member?"

"About six months."

We took our seats. "I understand they have a long waiting list." I'd done my homework researching the club.

He winked. "Waiting's for losers."

At that moment Mrs. Proctor appeared. She handed out menus and announced that our waiter would be with us shortly. When she left, I asked, "What do you mean about losers?'" What I really wanted to know was how Bunny got in at all. In that room of old New England blue bloods, he stuck out like Barbara Bush at a Harley Davidson convention.

He grinned at me over the top of his menu. "One thing you should know about Bunny Alfano, he makes things happen." He indicated my shoulder bag hanging from my chair. "Get your pen and pad out. That's a good quote."

While I dutifully scribbled away, a waiter arrived to take our drink order. Bunny wanted a Southern Comfort Manhattan while I requested iced tea. "Get a real drink," he insisted. "Live a little. I'm paying."

"I've got to go back to work, Bunny."

"Don't worry about it. Didn't I tell you Yvonne and I go way back? Never mind"—He whipped a cell phone from his pocket—"Lemme call her."

I clamped a hand on his arm. "No need of that. I guess I'll have a Johnny Walker Black." What the hell. How often do I lunch at Olde Shores Country Club? Even with Bunny Alfano as my tablemate, it was a far cry from Mega Mug. When we were alone, I asked, "What were you saying about that waiting list?"

He winked at me. "This is not for publication. You see, in order to join this club you need a member to sponsor you, to put your name up for membership." He shrugged, glancing around the room. "I didn't know anyone. Bunch of stiffs here, as you can see. What I did was, I looked at the list of members and had them checked out. My source found someone who was into the ponies big time."

"The ponies?"

"The race track, honey. He was losing his shirt. Anyway, he and I had a little talk. After that, he put my name up for membership."

"Is that ethical?"

"What do you think this place is, the Supreme Court? Stuff like that goes on all the time, 'cept nobody talks about it. So then my name goes to the nominating committee. This is where things get sticky. If some guy's got a beef against you, he can prevent you from getting in."

"Did that happen?" I asked.

He grinned. "It pays to have friends in high places. They can find out some interesting stuff." His glance swept the room. "Looking at these old buzzards. You wouldn't believe the jams they get into, whether it's broads or business."

"Your friends in high places," I said, "does that mean your brother, Chief Alfano?"

He made a face. "My brother's small potatoes. Besides, he wouldn't tell me if my coat was on fire."

Our drinks arrived. I raised my glass. "Here's to your membership."

"Thanks," he said. "I'll stick around 'til I get bored."

A few minutes later, the waiter appeared to take our food order. "The tenderloin de boeuf looks very good, Mr. Alfano," he said.

"Lemme have that," Bunny said. "Rose, order anything you like. Get the twin lobsters. Hell, get the triplets."

I ordered filet of sole. When the waiter departed, I asked, "Do you come here for dinner with your wife?"

"When she's around. We've got a place at the Jersey Shore, close to her relatives. My wife's not crazy about Granite Cove. She likes to shop." He shrugged. "I grew up here. It's in my blood. Roots, you know?"

Bunny's defense of our town made me view him in a warmer light. If only I could bring the conversation around to Settlers Dunes, perhaps I could get through to him.

I didn't have long to wait. He suddenly put his drink down and nearly lunged across the table, eyes bulging. "Will you check out the gams on her?"

"What gams?" I turned to see the object of his fascination. Seated on the other side of the room were Martha Farley and Pamela Bingham. The latter's short, tight skirt exposed sleek, tanned legs. Her hair, worn in a French twist, was as bright as her diamond encrusted Rolex. I glanced at Bunny. "Which are you ogling, Martha or Pamela?"

He took a gulp of his drink and smacked his lips. "Mrs. Bingham is one fine package. I'll have to introduce myself."

I was somewhat chastened, losing my date's interest to another woman so early into our "date." However, I got over it. l slipped on my glasses, not to view the so-called gams—which I'd already observed at the Frost Funeral Parlor—but to check out the bottle their white jacketed waiter was pouring.

Not surprisingly, it was Dom Perignon Champagne. The stuff went for a hundred and fifty dollars at The Liquor Chest downtown. When I turn forty, I've promised myself a bottle. "Hmm, I wonder why Pamela is lunching with Martha. "

He shrugged. "I suppose ol' Martha is pushing her Settlers Dunes project."

I coughed and almost sprayed my drink over the table. "Funny you should mention that, Bunny. I've been meaning to ask. You see, I've always assumed that Settlers Dunes was town land. It seems I'm wrong. On the other hand, Martha Farley's name certainly isn't on the deed."

He signaled the waiter for another round of drinks. "You're right it's not town land. According to Ken Froggett, it's tied up in a trust held by the Frost family. They've had it a helluva long time. The last surviving family member decides what to do with the land—sell it, or deed it to the town."

"It all comes down to one surviving family member?"

"Uh huh. Name's Dwayne Frost. He lives on Bimini, in the Bahamas. He's a wild man, been married four times." He grinned. "Me, I've only had three wives. No, Dwayne's not one of them Puritans, like his ancestors. You ever see Homer Frost's portrait at City Hall? Looks like he's been sucking lemons all his life. Dwayne is one crazy bastard, that's for sure."

"You met him? When?" Our second drinks arrived. I moved mine aside as Bunny took a big gulp of his.

"Not long ago. Spencer Farley invited him up for a round of golf. Turns out Dwayne doesn't play golf. He didn't want to go sightseeing, either, or visit his ancestor's house or see the statue in the park. You know the one with ol' Homer on horseback, the statue all the kids like to spray paint? All Dwayne wanted to do was hang out at The Sacred Cod bar. He was there every night."

"What's the point of his visit to Granite Cove?" I asked.

He paused. "A bunch of people thought it would be a good idea to meet the last member of the Frost family, to take him around, show him the town."

"Would these people be trying to influence him?"

"Let's say they were showing respect for Homer Frost's great-great-grandson." "He tapped my hand. "Nothing illegal about that, darlin'."

I was halfway through the filet of sole, when Pamela Bingham got up from the table, grabbed her purse, and headed somewhat unsteadily for the door. I got to my feet and said, "Bunny, I've got to use the ladies'."

He pointed to the entrance. "Little girls' room is right across the hall."

Fortunately, we were alone in the pink floral bathroom. Before ducking into a nearby stall, I glanced at Pamela. She leaned over a sink, staring into a mirror. When I came out, I moved to an adjacent sink and turned on the faucet. In my best impersonation of a Hemlock Point accent, I said, "That's a marvelous (mawv-lus) tan, Pamela. Where did you get it?"

She didn't seem surprised that I knew her name. A celebrity herself, she was accustomed to being recognized. "Anguilla. It's gorgeous there."

"Uh huh. This time of year, my husband and I head to Antigua for Race Week. He adores sailing." I squirted liquid soap into my hands. "I see you're lunching with Martha Farley. Old friend, is she?"

Drunk on her image, and what smelled like gin, she didn't take her eyes from the mirror. "Just met her," she said and removed a slim gold cylinder from her purse. Stepping back, she unbuttoned her suit jacket, revealing that she wore nothing underneath, not even a bra. She depressed the cylinder and sprayed perfume on her breasts.

The scent was an intoxicating blend of citrus and spice with earthy undertones. Had I not been impersonating a blue blood, I'd have asked for a spritz. Instead, I lowered my gaze and scrubbed my hands in an effort to avoid staring at her breasts. It was like trying to ignore the Hood blimp passing overhead.

"I suppose Martha's trying to interest you in her villas?" I asked, casually.

This time she glanced at me, green eyes rimmed in pink. "She showed me the architect's drawings. They're fabulous." Having spritzed herself, she removed a pack of Marlboro Lights from her bag. Ignoring the discreet sign on the wall that asked us to "kindly refrain from smoking," she lit a cigarette.

"What a coincidence," I said. "I had my heart set on one of the villas, too."

"So, what happened?" She leaned against the sink and blew smoke over my head.

I sighed. "I'm afraid I know what can happen in August."

She frowned and shook her head slightly. "What happens in August?"

"You know, the black tide?"

"What black tide?"

"I forget you're not from around here. Black tide is what the locals call it. There's a scientific name for that particular algae. No one knows exactly what causes it or why it's been appearing off Settlers Dunes for the past few summers." I dried my hands on one of the embossed paper towels stacked on a side table. "Personally, I blame George Bush: global warming."

She stared unsteadily as her mind slowly absorbed my words. "Wait, wait, you're saying there's some kinda algae in the water? What's so bad about that?"

"It's probably not harmful, though you wouldn't dare swim in it. The black tide is known for its pungent odor."

"Pungent?"

I laughed. "They should call it the stinky tide. It only lasts a month or so. If you stay inside with the windows closed, it shouldn't be a problem." I gave my hair a final pat. "I don't know why it's chosen Settlers Dunes every summer... Maybe this year it won't return." I looked at her. "Are you sure Martha didn't mention it? "

"Shit!" She stabbed her cigarette in the sink and marched to the door, her heels clacking on the tiles.

"Ah, Pamela... "

Too late to warn her she was unbuttoned. Given her agitated frame of mind, she probably wouldn't have listened. Instead she flung open the ladies' room door and disappeared outside. I scurried to catch up, opening the door a crack to peek out. It was a sight that would be remembered by all present on that day. Pamela Bingham, her suit jacket flapping, marched bare-breasted through the dining room. She headed straight for Martha Farley, leaving a sea of startled faces in her wake.

Adding to the calamity, the smoke detector in the ladies' room set off a loud, pulsating alarm. Pandemonium ensued. Silver-haired diners, scrambling to rise, clutched at tablecloths. Chairs, dishes and glassware crashed to the floor. Amid the shrieks, Mrs. Proctor raced from table to table, vainly attempting to restore order. Soon the whine of approaching fire trucks added to the din.

Dodging the fleeing members, I managed to reach our table. "Did you see her?" Bunny said above the noise. "That was worth the annual dues." He appeared amused by the ruckus until a police car's siren sounded outside. "Let's get outta here," he said, grabbing my hand.

I followed him out the exit and down a hallway to the kitchen's swinging doors. It was vacant; the dining room commotion had attracted everyone. We made our way past enormous stainless steel refrigerators to a rear door that opened onto a back porch. Wooden steps led to a concrete walkway. A sign at the bottom pointed to the Pro Shop, a tin-roofed building where a row of shiny golf carts were lined up. The area also appeared to be deserted.

Beyond the pro shop we approached a woodsy setting. Bunny stopped. "How about taking my picture here?"

I glanced around. The light was good, filtered through the branches. "Why don't you stand under that tree?" While I got my camera ready, Bunny ran a comb through his slicked-back hair. Then he leaned against the tree, his gold chain flashing in the tangle of chest hair. I hesitated. "Want to button your shirt up a little?"

"I'm not the formal type," he said. "Besides, the gals love this look."

"Whatever you say." I adjusted the lens and snapped away.

It was late afternoon when I returned to the office. I had a headache from the brouhaha at the Club. I was also late and wary of Yvonne's disapproval. But I needn't have worried. Instead of a scowl, I was treated to a big smile when I walked in.

"I just got through speaking to Mrs. Phipps," she said. "She was so excited."

I sat down and kicked off my pumps. "Why is that?"

"Why? Because you've saved the day at the Phippses' household."

"I have?"

"Don't be so modest. That advice you gave her about Raul's problem? It's pure genius. She told me how listless and depressed he'd been, how they were frightened he wouldn't survive."

"So my advice really worked?"

"It turned the situation around completely. How did you ever come up with that solution?"

I shrugged. "It made sense to repeat the trauma, the negative conditioner. In this case it was a cowboy hat that offended. Reintroduce it until the sight became commonplace. I suggested Mr. Phipps wear the hat day and night. In other words, repeat the negative conditioner."

"At first poor little Raul nearly had a seizure," Yvonne remarked. "Mrs. Phipps said he hid under the sofa and wouldn't come out. Yet Mr. Phipps refused to take the hat off. The next morning, he wore the cowboy hat at breakfast and again at night when he came home. On the third day the miracle happened. Little Raul timidly entered their bedroom where Mr. Phipps was reading the newspapers. Raul stared at him for the longest time. Then they discovered he'd fallen asleep at the end of their bed." Yvonne reached for a tissue and dabbed her eyes. "When Mrs. Phipps told me that story I almost cried buckets."

"I'm glad everything's back to normal," I said.

"It is, except for one teeny problem."

"What's that?"

"Apparently Mr. Phipps must wear the hat *all* the time. When he tried taking it off, Raul became hysterical. So, for now he keeps it on. They feel it's a small price to pay to have Raul healthy again." She gazed at me, misty eyed. "You've made such a difference in that couple's life, Rose."

"Glad to help." I felt so proud I thought my buttons would burst. The sight, however, would be nothing compared to Pamela Bingham's show stopper.

"Dearie me," she said, "I forgot to mention the exciting part. Mrs. Phipps is so pleased with how everything turned out, she's throwing a party."

"Are you saying I'm invited?" I asked.

"Silly girl, you're the guest of honor. It's Friday at seven. Cocktails and buffet on the verandah. Doesn't that sound enchanting?"

"Are you invited?" I asked.

She sighed. "I could never leave Mother for an entire evening. In any case, the point is to introduce you to her friends. They also celebrate Raul's recovery."

Spending Friday night with a bunch of Hemlock Point fossils did not sound enchanting. Truthfully, I'd rather scrub toilets at Fenway Park. "That's awfully nice of Mrs. Phipps, but really, I don't—"

"She mentioned donating a substantial amount to the local animal shelter in our name."

"Our name?"

"The newspaper's name. Do you know what this means? Now the shelter can build that outdoor dog run they've always wanted. Rose, the Gazette can't buy publicity like that. "

"Fine, but can I at least bring a date?"

She laughed. "You're expected to bring a guest."

"Good. Kevin will get a kick out of it."

"Kevin?" Yvonne looked aghast, as if I'd mentioned Charlie Manson. "Mrs. Phipps distinctly said it would be black tie. "

"Don't worry, Yvonne. Kevin will be presentable."

She gave me a worried look. "It's an open bar as well."

I got the message. "Don't worry, he won't disgrace our reputation."

She turned away. "That's the farthest thing from my mind."

Auntie Pearl's Helpful Housekeeping Hints

Dear Auntie Pearl:

I'm caught in a dilemma that's tearing my family apart. It all started during the annual Fourth of July celebration at my parents' lakeside cottage. My sister and I and our children attended, along with my parents' friends and neighbors.

After an afternoon of swimming and boating, it was time for the cookout. While I was getting my cucumber salad from the refrigerator, I heard strange noises coming from the bathroom downstairs. Thinking it was my grandmother in need of assistance, I opened the door. Auntie Pearl, I almost fainted when I saw my brother-in-law groping the neighbor's eighteen-year-old daughter. Somehow, I managed to grab my bowl and rush outside.

Later that night when I told my husband what I'd witnessed, he advised me to forget the incident. Yet I cannot get the image of that shirtless, sweaty man from my mind. Although I'd never deliberately hurt my sister, I think she should know the father of her children is a pervert. At the very least my parents should be informed.

Please advise, Auntie Pearl.

In a Quandary in Quincy

Dear Quandary:

While reading your letter, one thought came to mind: I'll bet those cucumbers weren't properly dried before you added the dressing. So many cookouts are ruined when the hostess serves wilted, soggy cucumber salad. Needless to say, Auntie Pearl has the solution to this problem.

First, peel and thinly slice the cucumbers. Lay them flat on paper towels, and sprinkle with salt. After they've "sweated," cover with another paper towel, replacing as necessary. When the cucumbers are suitably dry, toss with the dressing. It will now properly adhere. And by the way, it is not sugar that wilts cucumber salad or cole slaw, it's the vinegar. Thus, add the dressing at the last minute.

Follow these steps, and your cookout will be a smashing success. You might even put your brother-in-law in charge of salads. Give him something to do besides getting into mischief!

Signed,
Auntie Pearl

Eight

On my way home I stopped at the Liquor Chest, rewarding myself for solving the Mystery of the Hairless Peruvian. When I stepped inside, I couldn't believe my luck. Rusty Favazza was heading for the check-out with a case of beer.

I grabbed a bottle of Johnny Walker from the back shelves and stood behind him. He pulled crumpled bills from his wallet, one by one. As he hoisted the beer onto his shoulder, I tapped his arm. "Rusty, are you carrying that home?"

Bleary eyes came alive with recognition. "Rose McNichols, I'll be damned. How ya doin'?"

"Good. Want a ride home?"

"I can walk. No problem."

I wasn't going to let the opportunity pass. Pointing to the parking lot visible through the screen door, I said, "You see that lime green Jetta? Climb in, the door's unlocked. There are a couple things I'd like to ask you. You'd be doing me a favor."

"I won't argue with a lady," Rusty said, winking. His bad leg thumped as he crossed the old wooden floor.

I handed the white-haired clerk my credit card, ignoring his stare. He rang up my order and handed the card back, saying, "I hope you know what you're doing, miss. That one's known to be a troublemaker."

I smiled. "Surely you're mistaken."

Rusty had the passenger door open. He sat with his legs outside the car, sipping a beer and smoking a cigarette. "Smoke bother you?' he asked.

"It's fine. Just roll down the window." I settled my bottle on the floor in the back.

"What did you buy?" he asked.

"Scotch."

"Uh huh. What kind?"

"Johnny Walker."

He shook his head. "You always were a classy broad."

I started the car. "I'm afraid it's champagne taste on a beer pocketbook. You know my background. Mom was a schoolteacher and Dad sold fish."

He adjusted his seat, pushing it back to make room for his legs. "I wasn't talking about money."

I swung onto Harbor Road, passing deserted lots where the rusted skeletons of old boats lay partially hidden by tall weeds. The surrounding chain link fence was pitted with debris, including plastic shopping bags and shards of Styrofoam coffee cups.

The future of this dormant section of wharf was forever being debated. Politicians, environmentalists and developers all had differing opinions of its use. The old-timers wanted to hold out in the event the fishing industry regained its vigor. Meanwhile, the developers, citing the success of the Harbour Building, pushed for a restaurant, shop and condominium complex. Others called for more surveys. Not surprisingly, the issue was deadlocked. At the same time, the interest rates, like the weeds taking over the lot, grew higher.

Rusty took a last swallow of beer and crushed the can. "I'm serious about what I said. Even in high school you had class. You wouldn't go out with someone like me."

Rusty obviously had had a few beers to make such a statement. In high school I was seriously flat-chested, flat-haired and flat-footed. It wasn't until I reached my twenties that I started receiving male attention. Cal Devine, however, had been smitten since fifth grade.

"Modesty doesn't suit you, Rusty. Weren't you voted best looking and best athlete in your class?"

"You forgot class flirt," he said, flipping the empty into the back seat.

I glanced at him. Up close, the cheeks that appeared so ruddy were in fact a crosshatching of broken blood vessels. The copper-colored hair was streaked with silver. His smile, nonetheless, revealed teeth as white as an anchorman's.

He leaned his head against the seat and closed his eyes. "This is nice of you."

"I'm going in the same direction."

"I'll be putting my truck on the road soon's I get my license back."

"How'd you lose it?"

"DUI," he said, reaching into the back seat and grabbing another beer. "Some ass wipe from Hemlock Point had parked his Jaguar on Main Street. When he opened the door, he didn't even look around, just swung it wide open. You know how narrow Main Street is with cars parked on both sides. I clipped his door, and he called the cops. I got outta there fast."

"What happened?"

"I wasn't fast enough. They got me for DUI, causing property damage and leaving the scene of an accident. They tried to get me for resisting arrest and lewd behavior, but my lawyer got them to drop it."

I had to ask: "Lewd behavior?"

He nodded. "What happened was, I'd pulled over to take a whizz. I carry one of those plastic urinals in my truck because of my leg I can't just hop out anytime I gotta take a leak.

"Anyway, the cops pulled up behind me, yelling for me to get out of the truck. I was still taking a leak. What was I supposed to do, climb out with my pants around my knees? They called it resisting arrest. Peeing in my truck was lewd behavior. My lawyer hired a disabilities lawyer from Boston. He got me out of that one."

"Who represented you?"

"Spencer Farley, Mister Granite Cove himself."

"He's a good lawyer."

He shrugged. "He told the judge a sob story about my family, said we were as poor as a one-armed oyster shucker. He talked about my football scholarship, my injuries, all that crap. The judge was looking at me like I was Tiny Tim. I thought he was gonna start bawling."

"Sounds like Spencer did a good job."

"He got the court to reduce the charge to second offense DUI even though it was my third. I didn't do time, but the Registry pulled my license for a year. Bastards."

"I doubt that Spencer or anyone can influence the Registry of Motor Vehicles."

"That's what he said. Yet before we went to court, he promised I wouldn't lose my license. All the time he was blowing smoke up my wazoo. He let out a wild laugh. "I got even, though."

"What did you do?" I reluctantly asked.

"When I got his bill, I wrapped the check in fish guts and sent it to him." Rusty laughed again, pounding the dashboard with his fist.

I chuckled at the thought of Rusty's smelly check arriving at Spencer Farley's elegant law office. "Did you hear from him?"

"Nah. Next time I saw him was at the park. I sometimes go there to chill out. They got a kiddy pond stocked with big orange carp. I saw Farley outside his office, getting into his big Mercedes. I yelled something. Okay, I might have been a little wasted. He reported me for vagrancy, like he owns the park. He's a phony."

As we got closer to his house, Rusty directed me through the narrow streets that wound around the wharf. "Pull into that parking lot," he said, pointing.

The lot was full of potholes and broken asphalt. I parked in a space that overlooked the harbor. "Home sweet home," Rusty said, indicating a ramshackle house perched near the wharf. The old Victorian had seen better days. The windows were a hodgepodge of Plexiglas and plywood. On the front porch, a sagging sofa kept company with a pair of aluminum beach chairs whose plastic webbing flapped in the breeze.

"Come in for a drink?" he asked, his hand on the door.

"Thanks, but it's late. I have to walk my dog."

"That's okay. If I had a choice, I wouldn't go inside there either."

"That's not what—" Rusty clamped a hand over my mouth, cutting off my words. In the light from a lone street lamp, his eyes were dark, unreadable. "Don't pretend, Rose, and don't lie to me. The house is a shit hole. You know it and I know it."

He took his hand away and I let out my breath. "Okay, it's a shit hole. Are you planning on staying?"

"For now, yes. My girlfriend gets after me to move. She wants me to go to the disabilities office and sign up for housing, get a nice clean place. No roaches, no drunks passed out in the halls."

"What's wrong with that?"

"I'd have some social worker on my ass all the time. Here I'm my own man. I come and go as I please. No one calls the cops if you party too loud, and if you run out of booze, you can knock on any door. Someone will help you out."

He drank from the can, wiping his mouth on his sleeve. "That's not to say that during the next hurricane the house won't fall in the water. C'est la vie," he said, tossing the empty out the window. The resulting *ping* echoed across the water.

"When you mentioned that girlfriend, you weren't by any chance referring to Brandi Slocum?" I asked.

"You know Brandi?"

"Sure. She works at Stella's."

"Stella's a hard ass, but she's good to Brandi."

"How do you know Brandi?" I asked him.

"After I moved back here, I was broke. I had to live at the shelter 'til my disability checks got transferred from California. In the meantime, the Commonwealth of Massachusetts didn't give a rat's ass."

"That's where you met Brandi? In the shelter?"

He nodded "I didn't put the moves on her because she's just a kid."

"I understand Brandi's trying to reform you."

"Yeah. She quit drinking, drugs. Now she's a missionary, trying to convert me." He laughed. "She even dragged me to a couple AA meetings. I only went to keep the scumbags from hitting on her." He flicked his cigarette out the window. "I gotta go," he muttered, reaching for the door.

"Rusty, wait. I want to talk to you about Vivian Klinger."

But he was already half out the door, his lower body performing a complicated maneuver. His right leg lifted his left. At the same time, he pivoted and in one fluid motion was standing outside, looking at me through the window.

"Thanks, Rose."

"Wait." I reached behind the seat and grabbed the bottle of scotch. Setting it on my lap, I slowly slid the bag away. Light glinted on the thick, dark glass. The cap made a crackling sound when I twisted it open. Soon the acrid, smoky aroma of fine scotch filled the car. "Care for a drink?"

He got in and closed the door.

The night of the Phipps's party was mild with a gentle breeze off the ocean. When I arrived at Kevin's house, he was outside socializing with his neighbors. The foursome sat on lawn chairs and drank from paper cups. Kevin got up when I pulled into the driveway. He looked handsome in a dark suit, although the yellow bow tie was a bit much. Kevin is not the bow tie type. "Don't you have a tie?" I said, getting out of the car.

"It's Walter's." He patted the tie. "Makes me look debonair, like George Clooney, don't you think?"

I stepped back and gave him the once over. Not wanting to appear difficult in front of his neighbors, I said, "It'll do. Besides, the Phippses know you're a musician. They expect you to be a little... outré."

"Then I won't shock them when I relieve myself in the sink?"

"Just remember that everything you do reflects upon the newspaper. Yvonne will hear about it. She hears about everything."

The two gray-haired sisters laughed at this exchange. Clara said, "Kevin will be the best looking man at the party. If I were thirty years younger, I'd be after him myself."

"You mean forty years," Ruth said, draining her glass.

Walter got to his feet. "Rose, let me pour you a glass of my dandelion wine. We had the best crop in '98."

I told Walter we were running late. "The invitation says seven o'clock."

"Society arrives late. People expect it," Kevin said, handing Walter his empty glass.

"This is an older crowd," I said. "It'll probably be an early evening." I refrained from adding, "I hope."

"You young people enjoy yourselves," Walter said, turning to Kevin. "Keep your eye on this lovely gal. You're bound to have competition."

"I won't let anyone move in on her," Kevin said.

As we walked to the car, Ruth called, "You make a handsome couple."

Kevin turned and bowed. "If Rose plays her cards right, tonight could be her lucky night."

"Whoopee for me," I said, climbing behind the wheel.

Once again I found myself on scenic Shore Road. As we approached Settlers Dunes, I slowed down. "Check out the new sign." Ahead was a dusty Mercedes station wagon blocking the Dunes' entrance road. As I slowly passed, Martha Farley suddenly emerged from behind the car, her sweaty brow creased with irritation.

Startled, I stepped on the gas, causing the Jetta's tires to fishtail in the sandy road. I gripped the steering wheel as Kevin lowered his window and yelled, "Maaaartha!"

"Cut it out!" I glanced in the rear mirror. Martha stood in the road, glaring at us.

"Relax, I'm just having a little fun," Kevin said.

"You call that fun? I'll have you know Martha Farley is the newspaper's biggest account. Yvonne would not be happy to discover we're harassing her."

"We weren't harassing her, babe, I was. By the way, what's that sign, Cormorant Cove, all about? I've been to Settlers Dunes thousands of times and never once saw a cormorant."

"Of course you haven't. The name's a fake, just like the woman who thought it up. Martha wants to build high-end condos—excuse me, villas—on land that's not hers and is not for sale."

"That's a Donald Trump maneuver," Kevin said. "Before he got rich, he had nothing. But he was clever. He rented a bunch of heavy equipment and showed potential buyers the site for a proposed luxury building. At the time he couldn't afford a wheelbarrow, but the buyers didn't know that. They looked around, saw the construction equipment, liked his pitch, his *chutzpah,* and bought his vision. Before long, the vision became a reality."

"Donald Trump has charisma," I said. "Martha is annoying." I fretted anew. "I hope she didn't recognize me and pull her ads. I'll be out of a job."

"If you get fired, don't worry. You can join my act."

"And sing? My dog has a better voice."

"You won't have to sing, babe. Just wear a bikini and shake a tambourine. You'll be sensational."

"Kevin, can we not talk about it right now?"

We stopped at the Hemlock Point gate house where a security guard, after scanning a list of names, waved us through. Kevin whistled. "I feel like a celebrity. What did you do to deserve this treatment?"

I told him how I'd applied Betty Ann's quit-smoking conditioning program to Raul's situation. "But instead of stressing the positive, I suggested they enforce the negative. By repeating the trauma, the negative conditioner, it would eventually become commonplace"

"I don't get it," Kevin said.

"When Mr. Phipps first put on the cowboy hat, the sight traumatized Raul. I suggested he repeat this by wearing the hat all the time, and that's what he did. Predictably, Raul nearly had a seizure seeing that hat again. But on the third day, according to Mrs. Phipps, a miracle happened. The dog rolled over and fell asleep under their bed."

"So everything's back to normal?"

"Yes, though there's one tiny problem. Apparently, Mr. Phipps has to wear the hat all the time. In any event, they consider it a small price to have Raul his old self again."

"You're a smart lady," Kevin said, kissing my cheek and placing a hand on my knee.

"Maybe I've got a second career as a dog analyst."

I slowed down as the road became bumpy. Hidden behind the hemlock and scrub pine were turn-of-the-century estates set far apart. Before long we came upon Marbella, the Phipps's property. I followed the winding driveway now lined with flowering dogwood. At the end, a uniformed cop motioned us to a clearing where a dozen vehicles were parked.

I pulled into a space flanked by a Jaguar on one side and a cream-colored Rolls Royce on the other. The latter's occupants, a silver-haired couple in evening dress, cast a worried glance as they exited their car. The woman's tiara glittered in the waning light.

"We scared them," Kevin whispered. "Look, he's hiding his wallet."

"Keep your voice down," I said. "Remember, this isn't the Sacred Cod."

"Right you are. I don't see many tiaras at the Cod."

The regal pair swept past us to the walkway, the man holding his companion's elbow. We couldn't take our eyes off of them. "I'll bet he didn't rent that tux," Kevin whispered.

"Probably not," I said and adjusted the car mirror to check my makeup. The plum eye shadow nicely matched my dress. I turned to Kevin. "Well, here goes. You ready?"

We stepped out of the car. Kevin extended his arm. "Madame?" Together we followed a flagstone path that led across a wide lawn to the big stucco house. Faint notes from a piano drifted out into the night. As we neared the entrance, Kevin asked, "Is that them?"

I looked up to see Mr. and Mrs. Phipps standing in the lighted doorway. Myrna Phipps wore a floor-length aqua dress with a long front panel that hung over one shoulder, giving her the appearance of a Roman general. Her powdered bosom was stuffed into a low neckline; the effect was like two loaves of fresh baked bread. In one hand she held a champagne glass, in the other, Raul. Squashed between the billowy breasts, the dog gave us a piteous look.

"Holy crap," Kevin whispered. "That's the dog?"

"That's the one."

Spotting us, Mrs. Phipps cried, "Rose, how divine to see you!" She turned to the man standing next to her. "Lester, this is Rose McNichols, the girl who saved our darling's life."

Mr. Phipps, incongruous in a tuxedo and white Stetson, lifted me off my feet in a hug even though he was four inches shorter. When I introduced Kevin, our host pumped his hand and slapped his back. "This party's a tribute to your young lady," he enthused.

Myrna Phipps chimed in. "Rose, we've made a nice donation to the animal shelter in the newspaper's name."

"That's wonderful," I said, "But really—"

Lester Phipps waved away my protests. "You two kids run along and get some champagne. Have fun."

It was an excellent suggestion. "We'll do that," I said, but when I yanked on Kevin's arm, he didn't budge. Myrna Phipps stood before him on tiptoe, gazing up into his face.

"Rose never mentioned she was bringing such a devilishly handsome man," she gushed, straightening Kevin's tie.

"Oh, didn't I?" I said. "Kevin, let's go and let our hosts greet their guests." With a final pat on his cheek, Myrna released him, allowing me to drag him away.

Inside the house we headed down a long, arched hallway, a thick Persian runner muffling our steps. Stopping before a heavy gold mirror, Kevin smoothed his hair, staring at his reflection. "Devilishly handsome, huh? I think she likes me."

"Because you're the only man here under seventy-five," I snapped. Catching sight of my sour expression in the mirror, I told myself to let it go.

The fact that women of all ages flirt with Kevin is not his fault. There's something about him that causes proper ladies to become brazen. Maybe his boyish looks make them feel safe. Whatever the reason, it's annoying.

We reached a large, high-ceilinged room where white-haired guests in evening clothes stood in clusters, chatting and drinking champagne served by uniformed waiters. Out on the terrace, a pianist played show tunes from an earlier era.

"Night of the Living Dead," Kevin said, glancing around. He lifted two glasses of champagne from a passing tray and when a waiter approached with a platter of shrimp, he speared three with a toothpick. "How can I go back to Roach Motels after this?" he said, sighing.

"You wouldn't have bugs if you didn't leave food around," I said, still irritated by Mrs. Phipps's fawning.

"Hey, everybody's gotta eat."

Before we could move into the room, our hostess descended upon us. "There you are! I'm going to steal Rose for a moment, Kevin. My friends want to meet our guest of honor."

I waved at him as she led me to a gaggle of older women seated in a corner of the room. After the introductions, I found myself entertaining them with newspaper stories, at the same time refraining from mentioning the murder. They seemed fascinated, most likely due to good breeding, and so I held court. After a while my throat became parched. It was time for a drink. Not only that, I'd spotted Spencer Farley standing near the terrace.

I excused myself to the group, departed, and approached him. "You look very distinguished tonight, Spencer."

"And you are a rose among thorns, if you'll forgive the pun," he said, chuckling.

"You're too kind," I said. "Where's Martha?"

"She's out talking plans for that project of hers at the Dunes."

"As a matter of fact, I wanted to ask you about that project."

He leaned toward me and said, "Go right ahead." I smelled his lime cologne and on his breath, something stronger than champagne.

"A lot of people assumed that Settlers Dunes is owned by the town until we found out it isn't so. How many others beside Martha are interested?"

"I'm not sure, but I'll bet there will be more. Of course, no one wants to see the land sold. After all, Settlers Dunes has great historic value to all of us. Be that as it may, we don't want it falling into the wrong hands, do we?"

"No, we don't."

"Smart girl. The way I see it, the appropriate project done right could be super for this town. It could draw some high-end people, increase our tax base and breathe new life into the art scene. You must admit Granite Cove could use new blood."

So could vampires, I thought. "Will the town at least make an offer?"

"Let's hope so." He wagged his finger at me. "You should be asking Mayor Froggett these questions. He's in charge."

"I'd like to, but I can't get through to him," I said. "What do you think are the chances Dwayne Frost will donate the land to the town?"

"Ah, that would be lovely, wouldn't it? Unfortunately, I'm under the impression he's got a cash flow problem."

I nodded. "I understand Mr. Frost was in town. I wish someone had tipped me off earlier. I'd have loved to interview the last family member of our town's founder."

"He was only here a little while. The Chamber asked Martha and me to put him up. We were happy to do it. After all, you can't expect a member of the founding family bunking at the YMCA, can you?"

"No, I suppose you can't," I said, picturing Martha tucking her guest in at night.

Perhaps sensing my disappointment, Spencer put an arm around my shoulders. "Just between the two of us, you didn't miss much. Mr. Frost is a little rough around the edges. When I suggested a tour of the ancestral home, he couldn't care less."

"You can't blame him. The ancestral home is now a funeral parlor."

He ignored the remark. "Dwayne was more interested in spending time at the Sacred Cod bar." He rattled the ice in his empty glass. "Which reminds me, I'm ready for a refill. Can I get you one, Rose? Remember you're a guest tonight, not a journalist. Put away the notebook and have fun."

"I'm going to look for Kevin," I said. "Nice talking to you, Spencer."

I found him on the terrace. Together we gazed out at the moon. It cast a silvery path upon the ocean, where nearby the Phipps's yacht Rhapsody rocked gently back and forth. "You know what this feels like—you, me and the moon?" Kevin asked.

"What?"

"Feels like we're on our honeymoon."

I glanced at him. Kevin is rarely given to romantic sentiments, let alone intimations of marriage. Before I could respond, we were again interrupted by Myrna Phipps. "So this is where you lovebirds are hiding. Are you enjoying the party?"

"Love it," I assured her. "By the way, where's Raul?"

"He's resting upstairs. Meeting everyone has worn the little darling out. By the way, did you get a chance to see his bed? It's a miniature replica of Marie Antoinette's." With that, she clamped a jeweled hand on Kevin's arm. "If you don't mind, I'd like to borrow your young man for a moment. A light in the pantry has burned out, and he's the tallest person here tonight."

"I'm sure Kevin would love to assist," I said.

"At your service," he said, nodding.

"Come with me, my dear," Mrs. Phipps said, slipping her arm through his. "My husband makes an excellent martini, but he cannot change a light bulb."

Watching her lead Kevin away, I recalled Yvonne's fear that he wouldn't fit in. Au contraire.

On my own, I wandered to the end of the terrace where the buffet was being set up on linen-covered tables. Waiters rushed back and forth from the kitchen bearing silver platters and large chafing dishes My attention was drawn to a young staff person. Her pale hair was worn in a single braid. There was something familiar about the slim build and straight-backed posture. When she turned, I gasped.

"Brandi!"

"Rosc! I didn't know you were here tonight."

"Because I'm too poor for this crowd?" I said, teasing.

"No," she said, lowering her voice, "because you're too nice."

"How long have you worked for Cassandra's Catering?" Even in the simple uniform of black skirt, white blouse and tie, Brandi looked elegant.

"A couple of months. It's just a couple nights a week."

"And you're at Stella's every day? That's a tough schedule."

"I'm saving for a car." She cast a quick glance behind her. "Let's move to the hors d'oeuvres table. I've got something to tell you." When we approached the table, she picked up a tray laden with treats. "Seafood puff pastries," she said. "Help yourself, and take your time. I want the manager to think I'm working."

"You are," I said, studying the array and popping a miniature tart into my mouth. I hoped it wasn't eel or something raw, but it was delicious, a creamy lobster filling inside a flaky, buttery crust.

"Take another," she said. "Keep eating."

I hadn't had dinner, so stuffing my face with seafood savories was no hardship. "Go ahead," I mumbled, spraying crumbs. "Tell me."

"Rusty told me something that might be important. The night Dr. Klinger was killed, he saw someone sleeping in a car in the Harbour Building parking lot, someone who shouldn't have been there at that hour. "

"Someone he knows?"

She nodded. "He's reluctant to talk about it, though he told me. I'm one of the few he trusts."

"Who did he see?" I said, eyeing a fat pink shrimp perched atop a toast point.

She glanced over my shoulder. "I have to go. My boss is looking this way."

She was right. A stately woman in a flowered smock eyed us like a Brinks guard. I grabbed a toothpick, saying loudly, "Just one more, miss," and stabbed a tiny salmon mousse turnover, which I crammed into my mouth. "Who did Rusty see?" I mumbled.

"Spencer Farley," she said, brushing pastry crumbs from her hair.

I gasped, and at the same time, inhaled a bit of crust. This resulted in a coughing fit. When I didn't stop, Brandi got alarmed. "I'll get water," she said, shoving the tray at me and rushing off to the bar.

Seconds later she returned with a glass, saying, "Drink it slowly."

I did as I was told. "I thought you'd have to do the Heimlich," I said, blotting my mouth with a napkin.

"Are you okay?"

I nodded. "Why was Spencer Farley sleeping in his car, and what time was it?"

"It was getting dark, probably around eight-thirty. Rusty doesn't pay attention to time. He rapped on the window, thinking maybe the guy was dead. He was snoring, like he was passed out, and he didn't wake up. When Rusty checked the parking lot an hour later, Spencer's Mercedes was gone." She touched my arm. "Don't mention this to anyone. Rusty doesn't want any trouble."

"You know I won't." Even if I did, few would give credence to claims made by Rusty Favazza.

As if reading my thoughts, Brandi said, "Rusty's not crazy, you know. I got to know him when I stayed at the shelter. He's a decent person. He looked out for me, made me feel safe. Other guys were just looking to use me. "

Brandi didn't have to convince me. Before the booze and drugs had taken their toll, Rusty had a natural charisma. He was someone who, in the words of my dad, could charm a dog off a meat wagon. Thus, it was no surprise that a young Vivian Klinger had fallen for him. And, judging by Rusty's recent reminiscings in my car, the attraction was mutual:

Gripping the soggy Dunkin' Donuts cup filled with scotch, Rusty said, "Vivian had balls, you know? That chick was afraid of nothing."

I took a tiny sip from my cup. "Were you in love with her?"

He stretched his legs, wincing. "At the time I was nuts about her. I never knew anyone like Vivian. Her old man was a multi-millionaire. They were into culture big time: Museum of Fine Arts, Huntington Theatre, lectures. All that shit. You knew she had class just listening to her. She talked like that actress in that weepy movie, Love Story. Come to think of it, Vivian looked like her, too.

"Me? I was a typical college jock, going to bars, frat parties, getting wasted and passing out. Waking up God knows where. Sometimes I'd make morning class, sometimes not. At the rate I was going, I wouldn't be at BC long. Truthfully, I didn't really care. I wasn't cut out for college. I just wanted to party and play football."

He grinned. "Then I met Vivian. It was at a party at Wellesley College. Normally I wouldn't go there—bunch of tight-asses. But my roommate was dating a Wellesley girl and invited me. Hell, I'd go anywhere for free booze. Anyway, at this party they only served beer and wine, so I went outside to have a pull from my flask.

"I was standing there drinking Jack and listening to the bullfrogs when I heard this voice behind me go, 'Do you always bring your own alcohol to parties?' I nearly pissed my pants. I thought I was alone. I turned and said, 'Yeah, want some?' I was thinking it was some smart ass bitch, but she surprised me by taking a couple swigs." He laughed. "That got my attention. I got a look at her. She was pretty, kinda skinny but like a model. Classy. We stayed outside and finished the pint."

He stopped to gaze out at the wharf where the hulk of an old steel trawler clanked and shuddered with each roll of the sea. "Vivian was always trying to improve me. I loved Chuck Norris movies, but there I was in Cambridge, watching French films with subtitles." He shook his head in wonder. "Going out to dinner was a goddamn etiquette lesson. 'Don't use the dinner fork with dessert,'" she'd instruct me.

"Did you mind?" I asked.

"Nah. I gotta admit those lessons stuck with me. For instance, the other night I was at the Sacred Cod, passing through the restaurant section to the john. I saw some guy eating a steak, holding his knife like a friggin' spear. I stopped and said, 'Were you raised by pit bulls?'" Then I showed him how it's done. He wasn't too happy, but I'll bet he remembers."

"What caused the eventual break-up?"

"It was the parents, mostly the old man. She insisted on me meeting them. I was dead against it. We'd been going out a couple months when she asked me to dinner at her house. That's probably the reason for the etiquette lessons, preparation for meeting the parents. At the time, Vivian made it sound casual, like it would be hot dogs and beans on TV trays. Was that ever wrong."

I unscrewed the cap and poured more scotch into his cup. "What was it like, meeting the Klingers?"

"What was it like?" He took a sip and sighed. "In the first place, their house was a mansion straight out of Gone with the Wind. Red brick with big white columns, an acre of lawn in front. Seeing it for the first time, I was scared shitless. It didn't help that a maid answered the door. If I hadn't had a couple drinks in the car on the way over, I would have turned and run away." He wiped his mouth. "Maybe I should have."

"Go on."

"The maid took me to this big room with a fireplace where Vivian and her parents were sitting, all three on a little sofa. Right away I figured the old man was trouble. He was a little guy, and he looked at me like I had fish scales stuck in my hair. That whole friggin' night he watched me like I was gonna steal the silverware."

I laughed at his description of Lawrence Klinger. "What about Mrs. Klinger?"

He whistled. "She was quietly wasted. All through dinner everyone pretended not to notice she was sliding out of her chair. Vivian and her father were at one end of the table arguing about politics, while the old lady sat across from me playing footsie under the table."

"No! Mrs. Klinger?"

"Uh huh. Three nights later she called my dorm, wanted to meet me at the Colonnade Hotel for a drink."

"Did you go?"

He gave me a withering look. "I might be crazy, but I'm not stupid."

"Did Vivian know about her mother calling you?"

"I never told her. The way I see it, the mother was jealous. Vivian was daddy's girl. Vivian was brilliant, going to take over the family business. The old lady felt neglected."

I remembered Mrs. Klinger's empty eyes and felt a renewed pity. "Why do you think Vivian moved to Granite Cove?"

"She loved it the minute she saw it. One day we borrowed the old man's boat. He kept it moored in Weymouth. When we sailed into Granite Cove harbor, Vivian said, 'This is where I'm going to live someday.'"

I waited a beat and asked, "How did it end between you?"

Instead of answering, he turned his empty cup upside down. I poured more scotch. The bottle was a third empty. Rusty closed his eyes and continued. "What happened was, the old man went on a campaign to get rid of me. He wanted his darling to marry someone from Harvard or his alma mater, MIT, not some loser from the wharves of Granite Cove.

"He threatened to cut off her tuition payments unless she saw a shrink. I guess he figured she must be crazy or on drugs, going out with me. To keep the old man happy, Vivian saw a shrink."

I sat up straight. "Do you remember the doctor's name?"

He shrugged. "Some guy with an office on Newbury Street. According to the old man, the shrink was smarter than Freud himself."

"Was it Dr. Bingham? Chandler Bingham?"

"Yeah, that sounds right. He was a friend of the family. I heard him once on her answering machine. He talked like bloody Prince Charles. Anyway, to get daddy off her ass, Vivian made an appointment to see the shrink." Rusty laughed out loud and slapped his knee.

"What's so funny?"

"Just thought of something. Gee, this stuff sure improves my memory."

I got the hint and poured more. "What do you remember?"

"One day I met Vivian after her appointment with Dr. Bing Bing, or whatever he's called. We met at a little French restaurant near his office on Newbury Street. Vivian was upset and wouldn't tell me what was wrong at first. After a couple glasses of wine, she talked.

"She said that during therapy she always sat in a leather recliner while Bing Bing sat to the side, taking notes. On that day he was awfully quiet, so she turned around and caught him with his hand down his pants.

"That was it. She got out of the chair and marched out the door. At the same time she asked herself what in hell was she doing talking to some creep just to please her father. She wasn't gonna pay the price anymore. She didn't need the old man's money, and she didn't want to run the family business. She wanted to help women learn to stand up for themselves."

"Did her father cut her off?"

He nodded. "He's tough, her old man. Vivian applied for scholarships and got a research job. She did it all herself." He sighed. "It's funny how things work out. The old man sent her to therapy to straighten out her head, which she did, but not in the way he expected."

Now, while Brandi and I talked, I watched her boss approach, a pained smile upon her face. "Brandi, the shrimp bowls need more ice," she announced. Before the woman could whisk the hors d'oeuvres tray from Brandi's hands, I made a seagull dive for the remaining pastries.

"I'll take care of it," Brandi said, giving me a wink.

I grabbed her wrist before she headed to the kitchen. "Call me if you learn anything, and keep that information to yourself." She nodded and followed her boss into the kitchen. I watched her go. Brandi was an odd combination of street smarts and childlike idealism. Although she was convinced of Rusty's innate goodness, I remained skeptical. His tale about Spencer Farley asleep in the Harbour Building parking lot sounded far-fetched. Moreover, if Rusty had been at the park that night, he was drinking. What kind of witness is that?

Clutching a glass of champagne, I wandered through the rooms downstairs, searching for Kevin. Many of the guests had moved to the buffet. I longed to join them but didn't want to get in line alone. I decided to check upstairs and at the same time take a peek at Raul's famous bed.

I crept up the narrow back stairs to the second floor. A long corridor ran the length of the house with four bedrooms on either side. It was so quiet you could have heard a tick fall. I tiptoed down the dim hallway, passing over-decorated bedrooms. The wallpaper and curtains were covered with billowy roses and peonies.

At the end of the hall I stopped at what appeared to be the master bedroom. A king-size bed with a canopy looked sumptuous. In a corner of the room was a pink satin lounge chair straight out of Sunset Boulevard.

I was drawn to a wide window where, out on the horizon, pinpoints of light—ships at sea—bobbed on an ocean of black. As I gazed at the view, I became aware of a strange sound coming from across the room.

I turned on a small bedside lamp and searched until I found the source of the peculiar noise. On the floor next to the master bed sat a miniature ornately carved wooden bed. Lying upon it and snoring like a Rottweiler was Raul. I watched until a voice startled me:

"Rose! I've been looking everywhere for you."

It was Kevin, standing in the doorway and looking as if he'd been mugged. His hair jutted in all directions and his shirt hung out; his bow tie was askew. I stared at him. "What happened to you?" He put a finger to his lips and motioned me to follow, disappearing down the dark hallway. I turned out the light and stood in the doorway; he was nowhere to be seen. I stared down the long corridor. "Kevin, where are you?"

"Here!" A beckoning hand emerged from the gloom. I walked to the end of the hall. He was in a small room, undoubtedly once a maid's. He pulled me inside and locked the door behind me. We stood nose to nose in the dark.

"What's going on?" I whispered.

"Mrs. Phipps attacked me."

"She what?"

"We've got to get out of here. The woman's insane."

I took his hand, guiding him to the single narrow bed. "Sit and tell me from the beginning."

He sat, hunched. Light from a window illuminated his face. "You know how she asked me to fix the pantry light? As soon as I followed her into this tiny dark room, she was all over me like a pit bull. It was pitch black and I kept banging into pots and knocking into things. The whole time I was scared stiff the husband would open the door. He's probably got a gun to go with that cowboy hat."

"Kevin, I can't believe it." I held his hand. "What did you do?"

"It's true. I was struggling for my life, holding her off with one hand and with the other, searching for the doorknob. All the while she was going,'Take me now.'" He stopped to let out a shuddering breath. Silently, I contemplated the vivid scene he'd described. Although the story was outlandish, his distress was real. He broke the silence. "Aren't you going to say something?"

I opened my mouth to speak, and a giggle emerged. It turned into wild, hysterical laughter. When I couldn't stop, he covered my mouth with his hand and pulled me down on the bed. "Please, be quiet," he whispered in my ear. "She'll hear us. She's stalking me."

I giggled again and finally stopped. We listened, straining our ears for sounds outside the door, but all was quiet. Downstairs, the piano played "Over the Rainbow." The music mingled with laughter from the terrace and the clinking of glassware. Remembering the platters of food warming on the buffet table, I turned to Kevin. "I'm starved. Let's go down and eat."

"In a minute. What's that perfume you're wearing?"

"It's called Kenzo."

"It's wonderful. "

"It smells like fresh mown grass, don't you think?"

"It smells sexy."

I stared at him in the dim light. His face got closer. Soon he pressed his lips to mine. We kissed, each one lasting longer until I felt his hand tug at the zipper of my dress. I opened my eyes. "Kevin, not here."

"Shh. The door's locked. No one's coming."

"But they expect us for dinner. I'm the guest of honor."

"Hush," he whispered, brushing the hair from my forehead. "Hush."

A gentle breeze stirred the window curtain, carrying in the achingly familiar smell of the sea. Outside, gentle waves lapped the rocks below. Down the hall in another darkened room, a little dog slept. Beneath us on the terrace, music and laughter floated out across the water. But in the little room at the end of the hall, Kevin and I drifted away in a world of our own...

Nine

"Rose, you've created quite a buzz with this pig story, but what will Stella say?" Yvonne was hunched at her desk, in the process of giving our latest issue a quick preview.

"She'll approve," I said, grabbing a copy from the stack. I immediately flipped to my story: "Do they Dare? Seniors Vow to Honor Prank Night." After laboring over a feature, I still get a kick out of seeing the printed results. When I no longer feel that sense of excitement, it's time to look for another job.

Yvonne pointed to the picture of Stella brandishing her spatula. "She looks positively menacing." Underneath was Stella's quote: "Whoever lays a hand on my pigs will end up in the sausage."

I studied the layout, the work of a small Midwestern printing company. The bigger commercial presses had gotten too expensive for our small town paper. We keeps expenses down by hiring college interns and other money-saving measures.

"What do you think of Cal's picture?" I asked. Behind the mirrored sunglasses his expression was inscrutable. However, the set of his jaw said don't screw with me.

"He can put those handcuffs on me any day," Yvonne said with a roll of her eyes. When I turned to stare in shock, she looked up, annoyed. "Don't give me that look. Just because I'm a widow doesn't mean I lack... feelings."

"Of course not."

She folded the issue. "All in all, I think it's effective. Maybe the young people will read it and forget about this prank nonsense." She peered at me over the top of her glasses. "Your tone was somewhat taunting, Rose. Was that your intention?"

"I guess you could say I'm torn. Prank Night comes once in a kid's life. I'm all for letting them have a little fun before joining the real world."

"That's all well and good, but it won't do to antagonize Stella. She's a tough cookie. I once took Mother to her restaurant. When I inquired about the sodium content of an entree, Stella indicated we could leave."

"Stella's not into the healthy eating craze, but in answer to your question, she doesn't mind publicity. It's good for business. And regardless of what happens, Cal will be guarding the pigs during Prank Night. He claims that violators will spend the night in jail, courtesy of the Granite Cove Police Department."

Yvonne shook her head. "I don't understand young people today. Don't they have anything constructive to do?"

"Yvonne, don't you remember that period in your life right before high school graduation? You knew things would change. Nothing would ever be the same again. Friends you'd spent every moment with would soon go their separate ways. Didn't it make you want to go out and do something crazy, if only for one night?"

She gave me a blank look and I realized it was a foolish question to ask of someone who wears lavender espadrilles. "Don't forget I went to Catholic schools," she said, "where we got probation for swearing. If you think Stella is tough, you should have met Sister Florene. She once spotted a hickey on Sherry Moscarelli's neck and made that girl scrub it with holy water in front of the entire parish."

"My mother tried sending me to Catholic school," I said. "It was the only time my dad stood up to her."

"That's too bad. It would have benefitted you in many ways."

Before I could ask which ways, she said, "By the way, did I thank you for being such a good sport about attending the Phipps's party?"

In my opinion, enjoying champagne and lobster at a seaside mansion did not add up to heavy lifting. "Somebody's gotta do it," I said. "Speaking of the party, I had a talk with Spencer Farley that night."

"A most attractive man, n'est pas?"

"Right. We talked about Settlers Dunes. Maybe you don't know, but things are moving fast. The land could slip right through the town's hands."

She shook her head. "I'm not surprised. This town bungles everything. For instance, when I looked into home health services for Mother, I learned they'd cut back on senior care. Now I scrimp just to have a PCA a few evenings a week."

"Every department is feeling pinched," I said, "but can we talk about Settlers Dunes for a minute? It's our heritage. It's where the original Granite Cove immigrants built their homes. It's also where the Native Americans put up their fishing shacks. On this sacred land Martha Farley intends to build a bunch of high-end villas called Cormorant Cove."

"I told you we would cover the hearings, which I understand are starting next week."

"Good, at last we'll get things out in the open."

"I've asked Coral to cover it."

I stared at her. "What? Coral's a gardening columnist. Not only that, you said she's afraid to go out at night."

"Stewart's going with her."

I stood up. "Yvonne, I don't understand. You've been avoiding the Settlers Dunes issue. Now you're trying to keep me out of it. Are you afraid I'll ruffle Martha Farley's feathers?"

"Don't be so dramatic," she said.

"Don't you trust me to behave civilly?"

"I trust you, Rose." She studied her bitten nails. After a moment she continued. "Maybe I'm too old for this job. I worry about things. Right now I'm Mother's sole caregiver. If something were to happen to me, she'd have to go to a... home. "

Her voice trailed off. It was the second time Yvonne had expressed that particular fear. "If what happened to you?" I asked. When she didn't look at me, I said, "Does it have anything to do with Bunny Alfano?"

She closed her eyes. "A despicable man."

"He told me you two go way back."

"Unfortunately, we've had dealings in the past, newspaper related. Today I go out of my way to avoid him." She glanced at me. "You don't know what he's capable of. Did you hear about the call girl ring in Peabody? Bunny was involved in that. Some people claim he set up the whole operation. It got national attention because the women were local housewives earning extra money while their kids were in school. One even drove a big yellow school bus, parked in front of the house. They were your typical suburban soccer moms with car pools and mortgages.

"What happened to Bunny?"

"They had nothing on him that would stick. He's cagey and totally immoral."

"How do you know him?"

"Years ago I lived in Dudley and was women's editor at the Dudley Daily. Bunny owned a bar downtown. It was a nice little suburb, not particularly prosperous. When the YMCA needed a new swimming pool and the high school needed bleachers for the stadium, guess who offered to raise the funds? Of course they welcomed Bunny's generosity

"His bar was called the Nite Owl. It attracted a bad crowd and was frequently written up in the police notes for fighting and underage drinking. Weekends, I'm told, were like Dodge City. One night when the mayor's son got beaten up outside the bar, the mayor pressured the licensing board to do something. They scheduled a hearing. The head of the licensing board was a man named Clarence Nutting, a lovely man. He used to play Santa Claus at the nursing home's Christmas party.

"A few days before the hearing, Clarence appeared in town wearing a sling. He claimed he'd fallen off a ladder at home; as a result, he quit the licensing board. After that, he and his wife took a long cruise. He didn't even come back for his retirement party." She looked at me. "Do you see why I'm reluctant to interfere in anything involving Bunny Alfano?"

"But you're friends with his brother, the police chief."

Her face flushed. "That's a professional relationship. Not only that, Victor barely acknowledges Bunny."

The way Yvonne said "Victor" told me her feelings were more than professional. And come to think of it, they made the perfect geeky pair. Too bad there was a Mrs. Alfano in the picture.

I left work early to get ready for the double date with Betty Ann and Tiny. Before leaving the office, I left a message on Kevin's answering machine saying we'd pick him up at six thirty. I refrained from telling him to behave.

When Chester didn't greet me at the door, I hurried inside and searched the downstairs. I finally found him upstairs on my bed, looking guilty. I've banned him from the bed. Like many old dogs—and old folks—he leaks. I kissed the top of his head. "If you really like sleeping here, I'll put the old comforter back on."

In response, he wagged his stubby tail. Chester's hearing was worsening; likewise his aging joints. Eleven in Lab years is comparable to a man in his eighties. I wondered what I'd do when Chester no longer greeted me at the door. The thought made me so depressed, I decided to fix myself a drink.

Before heading to the kitchen, I checked my messages on the answering machine. I pressed the play button and was surprised to hear the booming voice of Frank, my landlord:

"Rose, you won't believe this. I was sitting at my bar last night talking to a nice couple from Wickford, Rhode Island. When I mentioned living in Granite Cove, they became quite animated about a murder. I confessed that the only news I read on the island is the local rag. The handful of TV stations here play nothing but reruns.

"That's why I was shocked to hear about Dr. Klinger, of all people. She used to speak at our Rotary meetings." He paused. "I hope they find the killer. Make sure you lock the doors and windows at night, and don't go out alone. On the other hand, knowing you, you're probably right in the middle of it."

Frank knew me pretty well, although his implication that I was in the middle of it was just that, an implication. My quasi-investigation could be compared to the act of kayaking on the salt marsh. There's no central route to follow, just bogs that veer off. Some bogs take you nowhere. Yet unless you're familiar with the marsh, you have to navigate each until you find the one that eventually leads you to the source.

I knew it was going to be one of those nights: Kevin appeared outside his house wearing the chicken hat. As if that wasn't enough, the weather was dismal. A cold drizzle oozed from the sky when B.A. and Tiny picked me up at precisely six-fifteen.

"Hello, lovebirds," I said, climbing into the back seat.

They muttered a response I couldn't hear. When Betty Ann turned to me, a telltale crease was etched between her brows. Tiny backed down the driveway and shifted into drive, glumly staring straight ahead.

The atmosphere inside was so tense I would have opened a window if not for the weather. I searched for something to say and then noticed B.A.'s hair. The curls were tighter than a showdog poodle's."Did you get a perm?"

She groaned. "Uh huh. My regular stylist was out, so a newcomer offered to take her place. She looked like a professional, wearing a white jacket and all. I figured, what harm could she do?"

"It'll loosen up," I said, patting the tight waves. "Just you wait."

She grunted and we lapsed into silence. Kevin will lift the mood, I thought, eager to reach his house. But one glimpse of the chicken hat, and I knew it wouldn't happen. The hat is an orange and yellow knitted affair. The chicken's legs hang in long flaps over his ears. It's a novelty item he wears whenever he sings a particular barnyard song. The hat and song always get a laugh from the crowd. Unfortunately, it wasn't having that effect tonight.

He opened the passenger door, holding a bottle of Sam Adams beer. "Anyone want a roader?"

"No, thanks," Tiny said, "I'm driving."

"I'll drive," he offered.

"Kevin, just get in the car," I said, yanking his sleeve.

He climbed into the back seat of the tiny car, folded his long legs and put an arm around me. "Hi, babe. You look nice"

"Thanks."

As we headed out, Kevin turned to me, a questioning look on his face. I shook my head. Finally Betty Ann broke the silence. "You were a big hit Monday at the nursing home, Kevin. The residents were still singing 'Galway Bay' when they got back to their rooms."

"Thanks, Betty Ann. I appreciate the support"

"In fact," she said, "you're the only entertainer who keeps them awake."

"Maybe I could use that on my brochure: Kevin Healey, the Irish Fiddler. He'll keep you awake."

"You keep the nurses awake, too," she said.

"They like my music, do they?"

"They like *you,* darlin.' The only time they show their faces in the activities room is when you're featured."

"Tell me more, Betty Ann," I said.

Kevin turned to me. "Are you jealous, babe?"

"It's true," Betty Ann said. "Sometimes a resident will needs nursing assistance. Say they're delusional and disruptive. We call their floor, requesting a nurse to come down and check on the patient. They always say they'll send someone down, yet they rarely do. When Kevin is entertaining, the nurses not only show up, they hang around until the program's over. "

"They always request something tough, like 'Danny Boy,'" Kevin said.

I nudged him. "You're getting off the subject. Betty Ann was talking about the nurses' interest in you."

He grinned. "You've got to get up before the rooster gets his pants on to fool ol' Rosie."

"Speaking of roosters," I said. "I hope you're not planning to wear that hat inside the restaurant."

"I thought you liked it," he said.

"I've got my reputation to consider."

Betty Ann stole a glance at Tiny hunched over the steering wheel. "Are you okay?" she asked.

He didn't answer at first. Then he glanced at us in the rear view mirror, "I wanted to say something, but you're all talking a mile a minute. I couldn't get a word in."

"You've got the floor, man," Kevin said.

"I wanted to comment on the nurses," he said.

"What about them?" B.A. asked.

"They're a horny bunch." With that, Betty Ann jabbed him with her elbow. "Easy, honey," he said, laughing, "I'm talking about the ones I see when I tend bar at the Sacred Cod. A group from the hospital rents the banquet room for retirement parties. I always warn the bus boys to watch out. After a couple drinks those nurses start playing grab ass. The married ones are the worst."

"Do you know Cal's wife, Marcie Devine?" I asked. "She works at the hospital."

"I know Marcie. She studies the bill at the end of the night, making sure we didn't screw them."

"Sounds like Marcie," I said. "She doesn't play grab ass, does she?"

"No way," he said. "Marcie's as much fun as a whoopee cushion at a funeral."

"Hey, I like that," Kevin said, pulling me closer. "Promise you'll bring a whoopee cushion to my funeral?"

"What makes you think you'll go first? You're younger than me."

Tiny spoke up. "Trust me, Rose. He'll go first."

We laughed, more from relief that Tiny had come out of his funk. When the laughter died, Betty

Ann added, "Unless the town murderer gets to us first."

"Lighten up, honey," Tiny said. "You sound ghoulish."

"I'm sorry. I guess I have a hard time accepting what's happened. All my life I felt safe in this town. Growing up, it was one big playground. Everyone knew each other, watched out for each other. My dad used to say he didn't need to use his car's directional signals because people knew where he was heading.

"Now the downtown's full of strangers. Newcomers arrive, stay a couple years and move on. They don't care about saving the old granite buildings, the ones our great grandfathers built. The city council wants to knock 'em down. Bringing them up to code isn't cost-effective, they claim. Settlers Dunes is just another sign of the times, the last nail in the coffin."

"That'd be a shame," Tiny said. "All my old friends have stories about the place. In high school, we hung out at the Dunes during Senior Week. We drank beer, got naked and ran screaming into the water." He chuckled. "Man, it was cold in early June. Now when I bump into those guys they tell me their kids visit the Dunes. Nothing's changed, they say, except there's more condoms in the parking lot and the empty beer cans are imported."

"Tell those guys to come back in a couple of years," Betty Ann said, "when Settlers Dunes becomes Cormorant Cove. On second thought, they'd better stay away unless they strike it rich. The common folk will not be welcome."

"It hasn't happened yet," Tiny said. "Maybe it won't."

"It will," she said. "Money talks and the city council listens. We just have to get used to it. Seems like there's a lot we have to get used to lately, including a murderer in our midst."

From the outside, the Sacred Cod resembles the seamen's tavern it once was at the turn of the century. Although the parking lot has been enlarged, it's changed little over the years and thus oozes authenticity. While the day-tripping tourists may not appreciate this, the purists do. They're not fooled by seafood restaurants that overdo the nautical theme and seal everything in polyurethane. No, the Sacred Cod is as realistic as a Winslow Homer painting. For those reasons and more, the place is unique and upright without being upscale.

Betty Ann, Kevin and I waited outside while Tiny parked the car. I looked out at the gray and forbidding water. Offshore gusts rattled the plastic tarps covering the boats nearby. Seagulls huddled together on the wooden railing bordering the lot. Kevin zipped his jacket and bounced to keep warm. Earlier I'd convinced him to leave the chicken hat behind.

I turned to Betty Ann. "What was up with you two earlier? I felt a chill the minute I got into the car."

"We had a fight," she said. "Tiny learned that Judy may need back surgery following rehab. That means Jonah will be with us indefinitely. In that case, why not drop the custody fight, I said. Why go through the aggravation and expense?"

"What did he say?"

She shrugged. "He won't discuss it with me."

"How long will Judy be recuperating?"

"They don't know; it's complicated. If she has surgery, she'll be given pain medication afterward. In other words, the very thing she got addicted to. In that case, more rehab could likely follow back surgery."

"How long are they talking about?"

"Her therapist wants her to transfer to a halfway house after rehab, since Jonah's staying with us."

"Maybe rehab will straighten her out," I said.

Kevin piped up. "I once had a roommate in Boston who ended up putting vodka in his morning orange juice. He went into rehab and they're still waiting for him to get out."

"Kevin, that was years ago," I said, stepping down on the toe of his shoe.

"Ouch! Listen Betty Ann, look at it this way. If Jonah is as bad as you say he is, Tiny may voluntarily drop the custody business."

B.A. shook her head, looking grim. "Tiny is committed. He's talked to Spencer Farley about representing him." Her voice shook. "Here I am trying to give up smoking, and he won't even discuss the suit with me. Everything is done behind my back. He even visited Jonah's teachers alone.

They said his grades are the worst in the class. All this makes Tiny feels guilty for not stepping in earlier. He blames himself for Jonah's problems."

Kevin whistled. "Sounds like you're in the shit can."

I turned on him. "Kevin Healey, that's not being helpful. Betty Ann needs our support now. She's going through a rough time."

He looked contrite. "I'm sorry. Don't listen to me, Betty Ann. What do I know about kids? Maybe after you and Jonah get to know each other, he'll think of you as the mother he never had."

She groaned. "Cut the crap, Kevin. You're right, I am in the shit can. I married Tiny for better or for worse but not for Jonah. If my husband doesn't care that the custody issue is destroying his marriage, I have to rethink our relationship." Having said that, she lowered her head and sobbed.

Moments later, when Tiny arrived, he found Kevin and I, our arms protectively wrapped around Betty Ann. "Can I join the lovefest?" he asked.

We're comforting your wife," Kevin said, prim as a schoolmarm. If I hadn't been embracing Betty Ann, I'd have given him a big fat kiss.

Tiny stuck his hands in his pockets. "Okay, any time you're ready to go inside."

Betty Ann produced a tissue and blew her nose. "I'm ready now. Thanks, Kevin and Rose. You're the best."

Tiny skipped ahead and held the door for us. "What about me, honey?" he asked Betty Ann as she approached. Instead of a response, she raised her chin and walked past him. I followed, averting my eyes while Kevin brought up the rear. Before scooting inside, he gave Tiny a shrug.

Walter, the Sacred Cod's manager, greeted us. "We'll take a booth in the bar," Betty Ann said. At that hour the dining room was busy and the bar quiet. Walter led the way, stopping at a high wooden booth whose window overlooked the harbor. After distributing menus, he mentioned that night's special, Finnan Haddie.

I sat next to B.A. Tiny and Kevin were across from us. As we studied the menu, Kevin broke the silence: "What in heck is Finnan Haddie, anyway?"

"It's Scottish smoked fish," Tiny said, "that tastes like crap."

We mulled our choices as a waitress arrived to take our drink order. When it was his turn, Kevin requested a Beefeater martini with two olives. "It's your liver," Tiny muttered.

His remark was not lost on Betty Ann. "Have five martinis, if that's what you want, Kevin. Ignore Eagle Scout over there. Just because he's cleaned up his act he expects everybody to do the same."

"If you're referring to the custody case, honey, I'm only doing what my lawyer advised," Tiny said. "Judy's lawyer will do anything to discredit me." He gave her a hurt look. "I was hoping you'd be more supportive."

"At the moment Judy is wearing paper slippers at a detox," Betty Ann retorted. "How can her lawyer justify that?"

"You don't understand how the courts operate. People 'in recovery' are goddamn saints, regardless of their former record."

Betty Ann turned to Kevin. "Judy is a drug addict, yet I'm the one who has to quit smoking for his damn custody case."

Tiny leaned forward. "Not just for that reason. I want you to do it for your health as well. Remember, I'm not enforcing the law, the court is. They won't place a child in a home where he's exposed to cigarette smoke. It's considered abuse."

"Give me a break," Betty Ann said, slapping the table with her palm. "Do you mean a mother who murders guinea pigs is preferable to a smoker?"

"Murders what?" Kevin asked.

"Cut the drama, Betty Ann," Tiny said. "Judy might be an airhead, but she's not cruel. She didn't do it on purpose."

"What didn't she do?" Kevin said, even though I'd kicked him under the table.

Tiny ran a hand through his short, bristly hair. "One night Judy had a few too many and decided to give the guinea pig a bath. It slipped out of her hands and somehow got outside. She claims she searched for hours in the snow. She even called 911. She never found it. Unfortunately, it was Jonah's classroom's guinea pig. "

"She called 911 for a guinea pig?" Kevin asked.

Tiny nodded. "My ex-wife might be a technical wizard, but when it comes to common sense she doesn't have two brain cells to rub together. That's why I want Jonah with us. I can't undo the past, but I can try making it up to him."

"Mea culpa," Betty Ann whispered, tapping her chest.

Fortunately, at that moment the waiter arrived with our drinks. After we were served, I raised my glass. "I'd like to make a toast to Tiny and Betty Ann. May their problems dissolve in time. They deserve it."

When the toastees showed little interest in responding, Kevin piped up, "You got that right."

Dinner progressed mostly in silence as Betty Ann and I focused on our scallop plates and Kevin on his fried clams. Tiny, dousing his meat loaf and mashed potatoes in gravy, said nothing. I was caught off guard when he suddenly spoke. "Rusty, how ya doing?"

I looked up to see Rusty Favazza, his long hair hanging in his eyes, leaning over our booth. He nodded at me. "I see you're still robbing the cradle, Rose." Before I could respond, he waved a hand. "Don't worry, I'm not going to join you."

"We didn't ask," Tiny said. At that, Rusty laughed, causing him to lurch forward. He grabbed the edge of our table, spilling the drinks. Tiny stood up. "Okay, time to go. I'm getting Walter to call a cab."

"Don't bother, I'm leaving," Rusty said. He straightened and took a last look around the room. Something caught his attention because all at once he said in a voice that could be heard all over the restaurant, "Look who's slumming tonight. Whats'a matter, The Four Seasons closed?"

Along with everyone in the place, we turned to see who he was addressing. A grim-looking Spencer and Martha Farley stood at the bar's entrance. Behind them stood Granite Cove Bank's president, Sanford "Sandy" Singleton and wife Bitsy. Both couples wore tennis outfits. Martha's white pleated skirt peeked out from under a long navy cardigan. Her legs looked as sturdy as they had in high school when she was girls' field hockey captain.

Now she nudged Spencer, who hesitated. In his path stood his tormentor. He moved forward, shoulders squared like a gladiator going into the arena. Behind the Farleys, the Singletons cowered like scared rabbits. The room became quiet. All eyes were on Rusty, leaning against the booth and grinning.

Turning to me, he said in the same mocking voice, "Did ol' Spencer ever talk about his friendship with Vivian?"

I gasped. At the same time Spencer was finally nose-to-nose with Rusty. "You're drunk," he said, his voice flat.

"You're an ass wipe," Rusty said.

"Don't talk to him!" Martha hissed.

While we anxiously waited for Rusty's next move, Tiny got to his feet. In a split second he was out of the booth and at Rusty's side. "I'll show you to the door," he said, grabbing the man's arm.

Before Tiny could escort Rusty out, Walter appeared, pushing his way through the crowd that had materialized at the first hint of trouble. "What's the problem?" Walter said, sizing up the situation. "Show's over, folks," he announced. "Mr. Favazza is going home." With that, he dragged an unprotesting Rusty away.

When Tiny sat down, Kevin raised his glass. "Nice going, captain."

Tiny shrugged. "I deal with drunks all the time. Part of the job."

Betty Ann, gazing at him like a lovestruck teen, reached for his hand. "Honey, you were wonderful. I don't know what would have happened if you hadn't stepped in."

In response he leaned across the table and gave her a long kiss. It was interrupted by a clap of thunder that shook the room, causing several diners to shriek. Outside, lightening flashed, illuminating the harbor. Inside, the candles flickered in a rising wind that battered the panes. I shivered and pulled my sweater around me.

It looked like we were in for some stormy weather.

Auntie Pearl's Helpful Housekeeping Hints

Dear Auntie Pearl:

I'm an adult student enrolled in the evening division of our local college. This semester I developed a huge crush on my distinguished looking literature professor. After our last class, I invited him out for a drink.

One thing led to another, and he ended up spending the night. The next morning I found his argyle vest under a sofa cushion. Since then, I've e-mailed him and left messages on his voice mail. Yet he doesn't respond. This is no schoolgirl's infatuation, Auntie Pearl. I think I'm in love with the man. What should I do?

Signed,
Poe no mo'

Dear Poe:

You didn't mention whether the vest was wool or cashmere. It makes a difference. Cashmere can be dressed up with a silk blouse and pearls, but wool calls for a more casual look. Worn with a flannel skirt or tailored slacks and low-heeled pumps, you have a stylish, professional looking outfit.

Auntie Pearl

Ten

When Betty Ann and Tiny dropped me off, I sensed something was amiss the minute I got out of their car. As I walked up the driveway, I soon discovered the source of my unease. The Jetta's rear window sported a hole the size of a cantaloupe.

I carefully opened the door. In the back seat the contents of my basket that held coupons, parking tickets, Kleenex, dog biscuits and old lipstick were scattered about. Sitting on the left floor mat was a rock wrapped in paper and secured with an elastic band. I unwrapped it with trembling hands. Written in block letters were the words: STAY AWAY IF YOU VALU YOUR LIFE.

Five minutes after my frantic phone call to Cal, I heard the squeal of tires in the driveway. When I went outside, Cal was there, aiming a high-beam flashlight all over my car. With no word of greeting, he said, "Did you ask your neighbors if they heard anything?"

"No."

"Why not?"

"I don't know them. They're young guys, and when they're at home, they've got the stereo cranked."

"Neighbors should be notified regarding acts of vandalism."

"For your information it is not vandalism, it's... personal."

He moved the flashlight beam to my face. "What do you mean?"

"I read the note."

"What note?"

"The one wrapped around the rock that broke my car window."

"Where might that be?"

"On my kitchen table."

"You touched it?"

"Cal, how could I read it without touching it?"

He turned the flashlight off with a sigh. "Let's have a look."

In the kitchen I heated up the morning's coffee while Cal, wearing latex gloves, deposited the evidence into a plastic bag. "We'll see what the lab can make of it. No doubt your fingerprints are all over this."

"I'm sorry. I was in a state of shock. I came home and discovered my car was a victim of violence. When I found the rock, I automatically read the note." I poured two mugs of coffee and brought them to the table where, underneath, Chester slept on.

Cal eyed him critically. "I don't think that dog offers much protection. I'll bet he never even barked tonight."

"Chester's a great watchdog," I said, "when he's awake."

Cal sat back, crossed his arms over his chest and stared at me. "What do you plan to do?"

"About what?"

"About the fact that someone's made threats. Any known enemies?"

"Well, there's Mayor Froggett. I've been on his case ever since he bought that SUV from Buster Moles."

"It's not the mayor's style to creep around at night breaking car windows."

"What about Buster, his brother-in-law? What's his style?"

"Buster wouldn't break windows. He'd steal the car and chop it up for parts."

"Okay, that rules them out. Hmm, lately I've been interviewing people about the murder. I wonder if it has anything to do with that."

Cal looked stricken. "Rosie, you're a great gal, but you walk into situations with your eyes closed. What about the lowlife you've been associating with?"

"Who are you calling lowlife?"

Cal set his mug on the table and looked at me. "I'm talking about Rusty Favazza, for one. The other night you were drinking outside his house for at least an hour."

My face flushed. "I wasn't drinking. Well, maybe I had a sip or two in order to be companionable. How do you know that, Cal Devine? Are you spying on me?"

"Not you, honey, him. Rusty's a former drug dealer, an ex-con. You're keeping bad company, and I'm worried about you."

"Don't worry, I know Rusty. I trust him. Sure, he looks scruffy, and he drinks too much, but he's no murderer."

"Have you looked at his rap sheet? You're a babe in the woods when it comes to guys like Rusty Favazza."

"I've known him since high school. He's had some bad breaks, but he's trying to stay clean."

"I've known him since high school, too. Remember, we were on the football team together. Back then he was using amphetamines, steroids, pot."

"Then you know Rusty's childhood. It's right out of Dickens. He's basically a decent guy who screwed up, and the cops have it in for him, maybe because he was such a big star." Cal's amused expression fueled the flames. "While we're on the subject, let me remind you that you're not perfect. Remember senior year, the night before final exams? Who cut the fan belts on the school buses?"

His smug expression changed to alarm. "Don't ever mention that."

"Relax, the statute of limitations has run out on that crime."

"So I was a punk, so sue me."

"As I recall, you were a hero for that act—no school and finals postponed."

Now his smile was genuine. "This time of year always reminds me of Senior Week. Remember that day we skipped school and went to Settlers Dunes, just the two of us?"

I nodded. "We wore bathing suits under our clothes to fool our mothers."

"We were the only people at the beach. The ocean was wild with lots of whitecaps. Fortunately, I had an old blanket in my trunk."

"So thoughtful of you."

He continued. "I spread it out in the dunes, out of the wind. I'll always remember taking my shoes off, how warm the sand felt. I was afraid to take my pants off because my legs were so white. You wore a yellow bikini, the same color as the buttercups sprouting in the sand."

I nodded, blushing in spite of myself. Cal's vivid description took me back twenty years. I felt I was again lying on his scratchy wool blanket that smelled of motor oil under a brilliant May sun. When we finally got the courage to go in the water, we held hands running to the surf. Cal's grip was strong. The soles of our feet stung from running on the hard sand. Then after taking a plunge in the water, we raced back, shivering, and wrapped ourselves in the sun-warmed blanket. I don't think we spoke five words the rest of the day.

"My mother knew something was up when she saw my sunburned nose," I said.

"At that point I don't think we cared." He looked at me. "Know what?'

"What?"

"That was the best day of my life."

"I know what you mean," I said.

We were silent for a long time. When I looked over at him, he was watching me. I didn't look away. As we smiled at each other, the years slipped away. I don't know what would have happened if Chester hadn't gotten to his feet and stumbled to the door, whining to be let out.

I resignedly stood and went to the door. When I returned to the table, Cal was on his feet, zipping his jacket. "At least promise me you'll stay out of Harbor Heights, Rusty's neighborhood. It's not a safe place for a lady."

"For your information, I'm no lady. And I've no further need to return. I've already interviewed Rusty."

"Just between us, he's become a person of interest to the department. Not only that, Chief Alfano's being pressured by Mayor Froggett, who's taking heat from the Chamber of Commerce."

"Why's the Chamber involved?" I asked.

"Tourist season starts soon. They want closure on the murder."

"Right," I said. "Murder's bad for business."

That night I dreamed I was being chased by wild pigs down a lonely stretch of beach. Too tired to maintain my pace, I slowed. Soon I felt sharp bristles poking my bare legs. I tried running faster, my heart ready to burst, but it was no use. Eventually the pigs closed in, their hot breath searing my skin...

I woke with a yelp and discovered Chester's prickly snout in my face. The clock read eight-fifteen. Chester may not be the greatest watchdog, but he's a damn good alarm clock.

Upon reaching the office, I called the insurance agent to report the broken car window. He gave me the name of a glass company that would visit my "place of employment" and install the replacement.

Overhearing my conversation, Yvonne said, "I worry about you all alone in that big house with a madman on the loose."

"My landlord's coming back next month," I told her.

"A lot can happen in a month," she said. "You're welcome to stay with me in the meantime."

Her generosity was touching. "That's very nice of you, Yvonne, but I'm not afraid. Cal promised to increase the police patrol in my neighborhood."

"The police can only do so much. If you ever feel unsafe, don't hesitate to call. You'd be no trouble, and it would be a treat for Mother. You two could do fun things. She's always looking for Scrabble partners."

"She's pretty good, is she?"

"Oh, yes. She's number two Scrabble player at the senior center."

"All modesty aside, I'm not bad myself," I confided. "Maybe I'll come over some night."

"Excellent. Once you feel comfortable, you could help with Mother's ADLs."

"What's ADLs?"

"It means activities of daily living and involves food preparation, bathing, toileting. No heavy lifting, in other words."

"I see. Well, I'll give it some thought."

"Speaking of food preparation," she said, rummaging through a wire basket on her desk, "there's a new advertiser I'd like you to interview."

I got up and took a brightly colored flyer, obviously the work of an amateur. "Marilyn's Pie Palace, Pies to Die for," I read and noted the unfamiliar address. "Where's Reservoir Road?"

"It's on Route 128. You might be familiar with the former business, a tourist place called Our Native Arts."

"I know the place," I said. "They sold stuff made out of fishing nets like place mats, hanging plant holders, string bikinis. Before that, it was a bait and tackle shop my dad used to frequent."

"It's not the best location, that stretch of road. That's why Marilyn is hoping people will hear about her homemade pies through word of mouth. She's staying open all night through the summer."

Putting the flyer in my To Do file, I promised to visit Marilyn's Pie Palace, interview the proprietor, and perhaps sample the wares.

At noon, I watched Yvonne stand up and wrap a long silk scarf around her neck, tossing one fringed end over her shoulder. "Going out to lunch?" I asked.

"Uh huh. I'm meeting with the program coordinator at the Senior Center. She wants me to direct their next play, a production of *Guys and Dolls*. The pay's not much to speak of, but it might be fun."

My enthusiastic response was not entirely related to Yvonne's new undertaking. It was the fact she'd be out of the office, allowing me to leave for my appointment with Veronica Klinger. I wouldn't have to tell a lie, which I hate almost as much as community theater musicals.

Boston's Back Bay stretches roughly from the State House atop Beacon Hill along to Kenmore Square. The area is what tourists mean when they speak of the city's Old World charm. Not surprisingly, it is the most upscale address in the city proper. However, not far outside the city limits, Chestnut Hill is equally as chi chi.

I approached via the busy, narrow Jamaica Way. Cars bombarded me, passing on both sides. No matter how often I visit the city, the impatience and aggressiveness of Boston drivers scares me to death. I dare not hesitate before making a turn. The resulting blast from the horn behind me can stop my heart.

As a result, I've developed the Granite Cover's aversion to crossing the bridge, both metaphorically and physically. As much as I enjoy the city and its arts, I still prefer the cry of seagulls to the screech of tires.

Newton, the city in which Chestnut Hill is located, recently won the distinction of being rated the safest town in the U.S., as reported in The Boston Globe. Judging by the impressive houses set far apart and away from the road, it's obviously one of the wealthiest, as well.

Too soon I came to number 1141, the Klinger manse. I slowed, as the narrow, two-way street running in front of the house discouraged parking. This left me no choice but to pull into their big circular driveway where I parked as far away as possible from the entrance. Although the Jetta's duct-taped window was temporary, it was hardly a reassuring sight.

I turned off the ignition and sat back, taking in the imposing red brick house. As Rusty had claimed, it was like something out of Gone with the Wind. I understood his intimidation. I, too, was reluctant to enter. Finally, I got out, marched across the driveway, and knocked on the black, lacquered door.

A somber, slight woman in a maid's uniform appeared. I gave her my name, and she beckoned me to follow. We passed a long expanse of stark, white wall interrupted by abstract paintings in muted, muddy colors. My footsteps echoed on the bare hardwood floors. I was reminded of my visit to Mrs. Phipps, where I also trailed behind the maid. Nonetheless, the two homes were vastly different. The Phipps' Hemlock Point estate was elaborately overdone with marble busts on pedestals at every turn. The Klinger's was austere, the furnishings minimal.

Soon we came to a room the size of a bus terminal. Tall palladium windows looked out on an expanse of evergreens. The ceilings were high and the furniture sparse. The only color came from brightly woven area rugs. All in all, the room resembled an upscale lounge in an outré Back Bay hotel.

Mrs. Klinger sat at a desk near a window. She stood and approached. Dressed in black silk pajamas, she resembled a licorice stick. Her hair was worn in a loose silver braid that hung down her back. "Good afternoon. Did you have any trouble finding the house?" she asked. Although her eyes were on my face, I got the impression she was taking in every detail of my appearance.

I shook her cool hand. "None at all, thanks"

"Janitza, you can bring the tea in now," she said, addressing the maid who stood silent at the door. My hostess then gestured to a sofa near the far windows. "Shall we sit over there?" I noted that, unfortunately, the sofa was white; I made a quick decision not to eat anything, lest I spill. For that same reason I wore a navy skirt and paisley blouse.

I sank into the sumptuous cushions and glanced around me. On an end table was a silver-framed photo of a smiling, young and tanned Vivian Klinger. "That's a wonderful picture," I said. "When was it taken?"

"I believe that was taken when Vivian was at Dana Hall, my alma mater as well. She thrived there as she did everywhere." Resting a hand on my arm, she said, "Tell me again the name of your magazine. It slipped my mind."

When I told her, she said, "Yes, I think I saw that at the dentist's office." I countered with my pitch, how *Bay State Living* tackles important political issues and champions women's causes. She gazed at me, her eyelids half shut. "Yes, I see."

Quickly I rummaged in my bag for my notebook. "I'd like you to know how much I appreciate your seeing me at a time like this."

She dismissed my words with a wave. "I've always found comfort and strength in literature. Are you familiar with Samuel Beckett?"

"I was an English major in college."

"Then you must know these lines." She closed her eyes, resting her head against the sofa. Although the window's harsh light emphasized the wrinkles around her eyes and mouth, her cheekbones were sharp enough to break open a clam. In a husky voice she recited, "You must go on; I can't go on; you must go on. I'll go on."

Before I could utter a response, Janitza entered carrying a tray.

"Ah, our tea has arrived," Mrs. Klinger said, her face brightening.

We waited as the maid placed the tray on the coffee table and deftly removed the contents: a silver ice bucket, a pitcher filled with what looked like tomato juice, a bottle of Finlandia vodka, two china cups and saucers, two tall glasses, a teapot and a small bowl of lime wedges.

"Do you take horseradish with your Bloody Mary, Ms. McNichols?" she asked, digging into the ice bucket with silver tongs.

"If you don't mind, I might try a little tea first. And please call me Rose."

"Rose, how evocative." She poured tea and handed me a cup. Although I didn't see any sugar or cream on the tray, it was just as well, as there were no teaspoons.

I sipped from the dainty cup and tried not to watch Mrs. Klinger liberally pour vodka into her glass and as an afterthought, add a splash of tomato juice. She squeezed a lime wedge, dropping it into the glass. "I learned to appreciate afternoon tea when we lived in London." She took a long swallow. "A most civilized pastime." Then she leaned back against the cushions. "Don't wait for an opening, Ms. McNichols. Fire away with your questions."

I glanced at my notes. "I'll start by asking if Dr. Klinger ever mentioned having difficulties with anyone while she lived in Granite Cove. A nemesis, if you will."

"You sound more like a policeman than a reporter," she said. "Of course there were those who resented Vivian. She had a driving ambition, much like Hillary Clinton, another Wellesley grad, by the way. Women like that attract critics."

"Did she mention anyone in particular?" I hesitated and added, "Please understand this isn't for the story."

"Then why ask?"

I looked down into my cup. "I ask because I grew up in Granite Cove. I know the town, and I know its people. Every day I wonder how Dr. Klinger, a young and vibrant woman, could be cut down in the prime of her life. How is this possible in Granite Cove? "I felt my face grow warm under her critical gaze. "I can't explain it adequately. All I know is I can't let go."

"If you were older, my age for instance, I'd say you were facing your own mortality." She sighed. "But you're too young for that." She took another long swallow. "Frankly, if it's an in-depth story you're planning to write, you're wasting your time talking to me. Vivian and I weren't close in the way mothers and daughters often are. She didn't share intimate details of her life. Vivian and her father, on the other hand, were cut from the same cloth." She leaned forward to pour more vodka into her glass. "Unfortunately, you'll never interview him."

"Why is that?"

"Because he's never at home. Right now he's in Japan, checking on the company's new laboratory. Since Vivian's death he's always gone, as if thousands of miles could distance him from his pain."

"I'm sorry. Did the two have their differences?"

"Differences? From the time Vivian was old enough to talk, they argued." She stared into her glass. "Yet he adored her. She was the light of his life, his shining star. Like King Midas, whatever she touched turned to gold. Her father assumed she'd join him in the family business, eventually taking over when he retired."

When she lapsed into a brooding silence, I asked, "And she had other plans, is that right?"

She closed her eyes and handed me her glass. "Do they teach you to make decent Bloody Marys at that newspaper of yours?"

"No," I said. "I learned that in journalism school."

When I handed her a fresh drink, she said, "What was it you asked me?"

"I asked how father and daughter became estranged."

"It was at Wellesley that Vivian began asserting her independence. Her father is very traditional. In his family, the parents' wishes are sacrosanct. Therefore, he expected her to follow his rules." She turned to me. "You don't happen to have a cigarette, do you?"

When I shook my head, she said, "It's just as well. Chandler wants me to quit. Now I've lost my train of thought. Oh, yes, it was at Wellesley where Vivian rebelled, changing her major from chemistry to psychology. It absolutely crushed her father, though he'd be the last to admit it. My husband is one of those proud individuals who will take their regrets to the grave."

"What brought about the rebellion?"

"I think she realized there was more to life than attaining a Phi Beta Kappa key, which she did, of course. It was in her junior year that she began to resent her father's control. Of course any act of resistance on her part resulted in heavier demands on his. The final blow was when she changed her major. That was the ultimate break as far as he was concerned."

"What did he do?"

"He cut her off financially. He'd warned her, but Vivian could be just as stubborn as he. I'll give her credit for going it alone. She applied for scholarships, got a loan and a research position. For the first time in her life she was independent and determined not to crawl back to her father."

"All this because she changed her major?"

"There were other provocations," she said. "Academics had always come first with Vivian. She'd gone to girls' schools all her life. Boys hadn't entered the picture until college. Now that she was exposed to the wider world, she began meeting inappropriate types.

"I chalked it up to the fact she'd led a sheltered life of country clubs, sailing and tennis. Although Wellesley's environment is outstanding, it can't always protect its students from the city's undesirables. And Vivian has always been a champion of the underdog, you know. Consequently, she became acquainted with an unsuitable young man, obviously a gold digger." She laughed, the sound harsh. "In fact, he came here to dinner. Afterward, the maid reported some missing silver. I wasn't surprised."

I leaned toward her. "Mrs. Klinger, the young man you're referring to... was his name Rusty?"

She closed her eyes. "Please, it was so long ago. I don't remember."

Eleven

In the middle of the night, in the middle of the dream, my phone rang. My heart lurched, pounding with an adrenaline rush. I fumbled in the dark. "Hello?"

"Mother of God, you're there."

I glanced at the clock. "Where else would I be at two-fifteen in the morning, Betty Ann? This better be good."

"I'm sorry I woke you. I wanted to say goodbye before I left."

"What? Where are you going?"

"Home Suite Homes on Route 1."

"Betty Ann, you can't do that. Not at this hour."

"I can't take the stress anymore. I'm saving my life"

I kicked off the covers and dragged myself to a sitting position. "What are you doing right now?"

"I just put a turkey tetrazzini casserole in the freezer with instructions to heat it. I'm standing in the kitchen ready to leave."

"Where's Tiny?"

"Sleeping."

"Okay, now do me a favor."

"Another time," she said. "I'm going."

"Meet me for a cup of coffee—just one cup."

"There's nothing to discuss, Rose, and nothing's open at this hour anyway."

"I know a place that's open all night. It's called Marilyn's Pie Palace, and it's on 128 South. It's got an orange roof. Do you know what I'm talking about?"

"Yeah, that's where Tiny buys worms."

"They don't sell worms anymore, they sell pies. All night long. I'll meet you there in twenty minutes."

"Okay, but it won't change anything. I'm still taking my suitcases."

The building that housed Marilyn's Pie Palace had undergone various incarnations over the years. In the '50s it was a Howard Johnson's with the requisite orange plastic roof, still intact. Later it became a motorcycle repair shop. Its last metamorphosis, before pie emporium, was a bait and tackle shop. Under the cracked plastic roof, hope sprung eternal.

B.A. was waiting when I pulled in next to her Thunderbird. A suitcases sat in the back seat. She got out and together we stared at the low-slung building where a sign on the roof read Marilyn's Pie Palace. "Is she nuts?" B.A. said. "Who's gonna drive way out here for pies?"

"Let's give her a break. She's only been open a month."

I guided her to the entrance. A bell over the door tinkled when we entered. Inside, fluorescent lights illuminated freshly painted aqua walls. A long Formica counter held a row of pies under clear plastic domes. Facing them was a row of plastic-covered stools. It was like stepping into a time capsule circa 1955.

"How about this booth by the window?" Betty Ann said.

"I gotta wipe it down first." A waitress, vigorously sponging a table at the end of the room, spoke up. We waited while she attacked our table with antiseptic spray. When we were seated she distributed menus and stood back. A plastic name tag on her shirt read Donna: Happy to serve you!

"Would you like to hear our specials tonight?" she asked, whipping out an order pad from an apron pocket.

"Just coffee for me," Betty Ann said, handing back her menu.

"It's a five-dollar minimum after midnight to sit in the booths," she said, "but not at the counter."

"I'd like to hear the specials," I said. "By the way, how's business?"

She shrugged. "It's okay. A lot of people still come in looking for worms." She read from her pad. "Tonight's pies are pineapple custard, key lime, butterscotch parfait and prune whip."

"How about plain old apple?" Betty Ann said.

Donna shook her head. "Don't have that. You want time to think it over?"

"What the hell," B. A. said. "I'll have the butterscotch whatever and black coffee."

"Butterscotch parfait," Donna said, writing on her pad.

"I'll have the key lime," I said, "and coffee with milk."

Donna slipped the pad into her pocket and headed for the counter. Betty Ann watched her go. "Is this the diner from hell? How'd you hear about this place?"

"Yvonne and Marilyn attend the same church."

"Well, they'd better pray hard. This place won't last the summer."

We stared around at the empty booths and row of pies on display. I tried to think of something positive to say. "You've got to admit it's clean."

"Seriously, the only people who'll come here are drunks after the bars close."

"Not so loud," I whispered as Donna appeared with a tray.

She placed our pie and coffee on the table. "Anything else I can get you?"

"This is fine, thanks," I said.

Betty Ann dug into a mound of fluff atop her pie. "Mmm, this is good. Cream tastes fresh."

"Of course it's fresh. Do you think Marilyn would serve canned whipped cream?" We ate in companionable silence. I watched Betty Ann scoop up every bit. When she leaned back, I asked, "How long since your last cigarette?"

"A whole week."

"You should be proud of yourself. You're saving your lungs."

"Saving my lungs and losing my mind."

"It won't always be like this," I added.

"No, it'll get worse. Jonah will become a teenager, the kind in the tabloids who stab their parents in their sleep."

"Things still lousy between you?"

She shrugged. "I've stopped trying. Yesterday when I got home from work, I smelled smoke. Sure enough, Jonah was in his room with another juvenile delinquent smoking cigarettes. I think he did it on purpose, to tempt me. He was mad I hadn't knocked first. We fought and he said, 'You're not my mother.'"

"I'm sorry," I said.

Don't be. At least I have *something* to be happy about."

"What's that?"

"I'm not his mother."

"Summer's coming. Can't you send Jonah off to camp?"

"Tiny wouldn't allow it. He says Jonah needs nurturing, not discipline."

I put my hand over hers. "Hang in there, buddy."

"I left Tiny a note. I said he's gotta choose. It's either Jonah or me. He can't have both, not in the same house." She blinked back tears." You have no idea what hell it is, quitting smoking." I handed her a napkin from the dispenser. She blew her nose and said, "Why oh why didn't I follow Father Brendan to Pawtucket?"

"Father who?"

She stared at me. "I never told you about Father Brendan?" She smiled crookedly. "He was an interim priest from Ireland, just out of the seminary. I was a senior in high school, immediately in love. I started attending Mass every day. That summer, I spent so much time in church my mother thought I'd become a nun."

"Somehow I can't imagine that," I said.

"Everyone loved Father Brendan... kids, parents. To me it was a spiritual experience to sit in church and watch him say Mass. His shoulders were broad and h is hair was thick and black. When I knelt at the altar for Communion, he seemed to pause while standing over me. Once, his hand brushed my face, sending thrills through my body." She glanced at me, her cheeks flushed. "I sound like one of those true love magazines, don't I?"

"Go on."

"One day, Father Brendan chaperoned our CYO trip to Canobie Lake Park. It was a hot summer day and I wore shorts. My legs were slim then, and tanned. During the bus ride, I felt Father Brendan's eyes on me. Later, I don't remember how it came about, but we found ourselves sharing a car on the roller coaster. Father Brendan's arm rested on the back of the seat. We didn't look at each other.

"At the top of the ride, kids were screaming like crazy, but we never made a sound. Sitting next to him, I wasn't the least bit scared, even though I'm petrified of heights. After hovering for the longest time at the top, we plunged straight down into a dark tunnel. For one moment there, Father Brendan put his arm around me and pressed his leg against mine."

"Are you sure?"

"Oh, I'm sure."

"So, what happened?"

"Nothing. The ride ended."

"He didn't say anything?"

"No, and I didn't expect it. Back then priests lived by the rules, the good ones."

"That was the end of it?"

She shook her head. "About three weeks later, I went to confession. I'd been staying away from church. My feelings for Father Brendan were intense, confusing. That afternoon, when I stepped into the confessional booth, I felt he was expecting me. When he slid open the screened panel, my heart pounded. Seeing his profile, I wanted to cry. Instead, I mumbled something about my sins... you know, the usual stuff about arguing with my parents, lying to them.

"He listened, absolutely still. Then he asked if that was all. I said, 'No, Father. I've had impure thoughts.' I closed my eyes. All I could hear was his breathing and the faint sounds of traffic outside. When I opened my eyes, his palm was flat against the screen."

"He put his hand on the screen?"

She nodded. "I didn't hesitate. I put mine flat against his. For a few seconds our palms touched. I felt like we were joined. He was first to slide his hand away. He gave me my penance, which I immediately forgot." She sighed. "I loved him. It was as simple and as complicated as that."

"What happened then?" I said.

"A week later my mother came home and said she'd heard that Father Brendan was being transferred to a parish in Pawtucket, Rhode Island."

"No! Did you see him before he left?"

The night before he was to leave for Rhode Island, around midnight, I snuck out of the house. I walked two miles to the rectory. I stood in the shadows under a tree. I didn't have long to wait. Father Brendan appeared at an upstairs window, as if he'd been expecting me. He wore a white tee shirt. I'd never seen him in anything other than his collar.

"I moved from the shadows and stood under his window. The moon was full that night. We looked at each other for a long time. It was like being in a trance. If he'd asked me in, I would have flown up the stairs. Eventually, he lowered the shade, and I went home."

"You've never told me that story," I said.

"I guess I was afraid to sound silly. Not long after Father Brendan left, I went off to college. During the next couple years I wanted to drive to Pawtucket but never got the courage. I've always wondered: does he remember me?"

Before leaving Marilyn's, we left a nice tip for Donna, who stopped scrubbing long enough to wave goodbye. Outside, a bright moon lit up the parking lot, illuminating the cars. "What happened to your window?" Betty Ann said when we reached the Jetta.

I told her about the warning note. "And you didn't tell me? That's it, you're coming home with me."

"I thought you had a reservation at Home Suite Homes. I wouldn't want to bump into Cal. He's living there, you know."

She grinned. "Have you visited him?"

"You know I wouldn't—"

"Well I would. Matter of fact, this might be my chance. Does Cal like turkey tetrazzini?"

"You're forgetting Mrs. Devine."

She smirked. "Marcie, the barracuda. She knows Cal's carried a torch for you since fifth grade. Marcie got him on the rebound after you got cold feet."

"I had cold feet long before that. It didn't have anything to do with Cal."

"Why did you lead him on, pretending you'd marry him?"

"I thought I could go through with it. I was wrong."

She leaned against my car. "The guy's a certified hunk. You make marrying him sound like gall bladder surgery. When exactly did you bow out?"

"A couple months before the wedding."

"You just woke up one morning and thought, 'I can't do this?'"

"I never felt the excitement that brides are supposed to feel. Sure, I showed off the ring and talked wedding plans, but my heart wasn't in it. Meanwhile, it was tearing me up because I loved Cal. He was my best friend. Maybe if we could have run off to a remote island...

"The awakening came at Elegant Interiors, the shop where I'd gone with my mother to look at china patterns. She loved that stuff. After looking at a hundred plates, I found a pattern I could live with. My mom, however, thought it was too casual. I told her that's me, I'm not a formal person. Frankly, plastic plates would suffice.

"She lectured me on my upcoming social obligations, like hosting dinners and setting a correct table. I'll never forget her words: 'Soon you'll be a young matron.' That made me think of prison. It led to a verbal exchange, me saying I would not be entertaining unless it was in the backyard, over a grill. She told me to grow up, that marriage required maturity.

"At that moment it hit me: The only reason I was going through with a traditional wedding was because of her. I didn't want any of it. I didn't want an expensive dress I'd never wear again. I didn't want pots and pans and I didn't want to invite people I ordinarily avoided. I hated all the details. It felt like Cal and I were disappearing into a whirlpool with no choice but to go along with it. So, in the Lenox China section of Elegant Interiors, I handed my mother the plate I'd chosen. I told her she was right, the pattern was inappropriate. In fact, the upcoming wedding was inappropriate and I'd have none of it."

B.A. whistled. "What did your mom say to that?"

I fished my car keys from my bag. "I don't know. I turned and marched out of the store. I walked home. It was five miles but I could have walked twenty, I felt so good, so... unburdened. Not long after that I did the only thing I could under the circumstances: I left Granite Cove."

"And returned when your mother had a stroke," Betty Ann added.

I looked at her. "Are you connecting the two, my walking out and her illness? Didn't we get enough guilt in Sunday school?"

"I didn't connect the two, you did. It's plain to me you still feel guilty about your mother. She was devastated when you called off the wedding. You stayed away to avoid dealing with her disappointment."

I unlocked the car and slid in. "A nice theory, Dr. Zagrobski. Thanks for the free analysis."

"Rose, I'm your best friend. I'm not judging you. I just want you to see it objectively. After your mother's death, remember how you insisted your dad move in with you even though he didn't want to? It was like you were atoning for your sins. You had to make it up to everybody." When I didn't answer, she continued. "It explains your obsession with Dr. Klinger."

"My obsession?" At that, I got out of the car, slamming the door.

"Just see it my way," she said. "You're a local gal who's won awards for your writing. Meanwhile, the snooty Women's Professional League takes no notice. They choose Dr. Klinger, an outsider, as Woman of the Year. Don't tell me you didn't resent that. Remember, you never liked the woman. You referred to her as Dr. Anal."

When I protested, Betty Ann held up a hand. "Then when Dr. Klinger was murdered, you felt guilty and unworthy all over again. Can't you see? For you, Vivian Klinger is the mother figure that you can't please."

I stared at her for a moment and finally said, "I do see, Betty Ann. I see that you should have gone to Pawtucket—and stayed there."

She threw her head back and laughed. "Give me a hug." We rocked back and forth on the asphalt. "Sorry I'm such a big mouth," she said, wiping her eyes.

"I'm used to it," I said, pulling away. "Where are you headed now?"

She jiggled her keys. "It occurred to me that I'm in the parking lot of Marilyn's goddamn Pie Palace. It's two-thirty in the morning. Something is wrong with my head, but I can't fix it by running away." She got into her car. "Holy crap, I hope I get home before Tiny reads that note."

"Let him worry for a change," I said. With that, I slid into the Jetta's front seat.

She started the ignition and rolled down her window. "Rose?

I leaned out. "Yeah?"

"I just want to say thank you."

"Don't mention it."

Auntie Pearl's Helpful Housekeeping Hints

Dear Auntie Pearl:

I leave my condo building early in the morning when few tenants are up. Lately, however, I've noticed a man who occupies the ground floor unit in front of my assigned parking space. On several occasions he's been outside on his deck watering the plants. Sometimes his bathrobe falls open, revealing he is naked underneath.

When it first happened, I was in my car and thought I was mistaken. The early morning mist collects on my windshield, making it difficult to see clearly. But after repeated "exposures," I am certain he is doing it deliberately.

Now I am considering making a formal complaint to management. My roommate, meanwhile, says to notify the police. What do you think is the best course of action, Auntie Pearl?

Signed,
Grossed out in Gloucester

Dear Grossed:

I keep the niftiest item in my glove compartment—a "moisture mitt" for windshield condensation. It sounds like you have that problem as well. Here's what you do: Take an old pair of white cotton gloves (you may have to ask your mother for hers) and sprinkle with ammonia. Roll them up tightly and put inside a plastic bag, sealing it well.

Stored inside your glove compartment, this little driver's helper will provide a clear view, no matter what time of day or weather conditions!

Happy motoring!
Auntie Pearl

Twelve

On Tuesday, I was searching the archived photos from the Wellesley College yearbooks dated 1981 to 1985 when Yvonne returned from lunch. I knew she had something up her sleeve when she placed a Styrofoam cup on my desk.

"Caramel Mocha Chill. Your favorite, *n'est pas?*"

I stared at the sweating container. "Hey, thanks."

Yvonne is not in the habit of opening her purse strings unless there's something in it for her. This was one of those instances. Instead of returning to her workstation, she hefted her buttocks onto the edge of my desk. Leaning toward me in a confidential manner, she said, "I've just had the most delightful lunch with Chipper Foss."

"Who's Chipper Foss?"

"He's the theater director at the community college. He's going to work with the actors."

"For the play you're directing?"

"Guys & Dolls. I can't tell you how relieved I am. Directing is demanding enough without having to be acting coach as well."

"I imagine he's had a lot of experience."

"Are you familiar with *The Music Man?*"

"Sure, somewhat."

"Chip had the leading role at the Ogunquit Theatre in Maine. That was several years ago, of course." She patted my hand. "You must come to opening night. A percentage of the profits are going to Youth at Risk."

"What's that?"

"Instead of sentencing juvenile offenders to a locked facility, the court sends them to theater camp. Isn't that a marvelous idea?"

Shakespeare in the yard. "I'll buy a ticket," I told her. "Matter of fact, put me down for two. I'll bring Kevin."

"Kevin at the theater?" Her eyebrows rose to her hairline.

"Kevin adores the theater, particularly Ibsen. He likes dark and brooding."

She blinked. "I had no idea."

I turned back to my monitor. "Now if you'll excuse me, I've got one more yearbook to search."

The following day I forfeited lunch and instead headed for Granite Cove Community Hospital. Doc Moss had been after me to get my thyroid checked. During my last visit I'd complained of a general malaise. Life had all the appeal of a bowl of shredded wheat. I doubted my thyroid was to blame. If anything, I needed sun. Not just an hour or two, but a week in St. Lucia. Such a trip would alleviate my symptoms.

The sky was gray and threatening when I left the house. I took an umbrella. Once inside the hospital, I followed the central hallway to the lab. On the way I passed patients wearing johnnies, some ambulatory, some in wheelchairs. A thin, elderly man tethered to an IV pole shuffled past. His legs beneath the flimsy gown looked like straws. I was reminded of Yeats's line, "An aged man is but a paltry thing." Silently, I counted my blessings.

In the lab's waiting area, I took a seat on a plastic bench. A large woman in green sweatpants sat inside a cubicle at the end of the room. She grunted when the lab tech removed the IV needle from her arm. What nearly made me swoon was the bulging purple sack suspended above her. While I can watch slice 'n dice movies without cringing, when faced with real blood, I'm weak kneed.

Before long a young woman in a white lab jacket called my name. Reluctantly, I followed her to the cubicle next to Green Sweatpants. "Roll up your sleeve and hold out your arm," she said. Running a finger over my inner arm, she said, "Mmm hmm. Please make a fist."

"They always use a pediatric needle on me," I reminded her. "My veins are small."

"I'll do that," she said, "soon as I locate one."

"I'm having a bad vein day."

It's my lame joke for those occasions when I have to give blood. Eventually, after fruitless poking and probing, the lab tech will call in the top gun, a phlebotomist who's been there for decades. These individuals can find an elusive vein while wearing oven mitts.

That was how the session played out: after the fifth needle poke, I got to my feet and threatened to leave. "Sit tight," the young tech said. "I'm calling my supervisor."

"Finally," I muttered as she fled the room.

Seconds later, a frizzy-haired woman in a white coat swept into the room. "You the troublemaker?" she asked, peering at me. I nodded meekly, and before you could say "Type A Negative," she slid a needle into the vein.

I peeked at the free-flowing blood filling the syringe. "Piece of cake."

After that ordeal, my hemoglobin needed fortification, so I took the elevator to the basement cafeteria. It was after lunch, and most of the tables were empty. I grabbed a tray and headed for the salad bar. The offerings were impressive: everything from deviled eggs to marinated chick peas. I filled a large plastic bowl with everything but lettuce and stopped at the frozen drink dispenser for a mocha iced coffee with cream.

At the register, the cashier was nowhere in sight. "Excuse me," I called.

A young woman who'd been chatting behind the soup tureens approached. "Sorry," she said, sliding my hefty salad onto a scale. "That's seven dollars and eighty-five cents."

I handed her a ten dollar bill and glanced at the plastic name tag on her breast pocket: Sunnie: Food Services Associate. "Sunnie's a pretty name," I said. The remark is often an icebreaker, I've found. People generally like talking about themselves. Of course it helps if the name really is pretty and not something like, well, Bertha.

"Thanks. It's not a nickname. Sunnie's my real name."

"Have you worked here long?"

"Three years this June," she said, "part time. I'm taking classes to be a licensed massage therapist." The row of brass hoop bracelets lining her arm clanged when she handed me my change.

"Then you must have been familiar with Dr. Klinger."

She made a sad face. "She came in here a couple days a week. She saw the in-patients on Bigsby, the hospital's mental health unit."

"Did you talk to her?"

She pursed her lips. "Dr. Klinger wasn't what you'd call friendly. She came in alone, always bought the same lunch and always ate it over there by the window."

I had to ask. "Do you remember what she ordered?"

"Uh huh. A plain salad, slice of lemon on the side."

I glanced down at my salad mountain smothered in a puddle of blue cheese dressing. "So she never talked to anyone?"

"Not really, though she got to know the kitchen staff. Dr. Klinger helped them out with an employees' issue."

"How is that?"

She glanced around before speaking. "It's not confidential. After all, it was written up in our newsletter, The Dietary Digest. See, the hospital had a policy that women working in the kitchen had to wear hair nets, but not the men. It wasn't a problem until they hired some high school girls who squawked. They wanted to know how come the cook has a ponytail and doesn't have to wear a hair net. They got a petition going, but before they could get enough signatures, my boss fired them."

"Sounds like they had a grievance," I said.

"That's what Dr. Klinger said."

"How did she happen to get involved?"

"One of the girls saw her on that cable TV show, Speak Up, Citizens, and got in touch. Dr. Klinger contacted the Attorney General's office." She giggled. "My boss was written up for violations. After that, you better believe she hated Dr. Klinger." Sunnie leaned closer, lowering her voice. "She said she hoped there was an E. coli outbreak the day Dr. Klinger came in for lunch."

"Your boss said this to you?"

"She said it to the cook."

"The ponytail guy?"

"No, the head chef. He's older. They're always chit-chatting." She rolled her eyes.

"I take it your boss isn't here today?"

"She works three afternoons a week for her sister's catering company, thank God. Soon as I'm licensed, I'm quitting this place."

"Good luck," I said. "By the way, do you know the name of the catering company?" When she shot me a suspicious look, I added, "My boyfriend and I are marrying next year. We're looking into caterers and bands, all that stuff."

"Awesome," she said. "It's called Clarissa's Catering, and between you and me, they're a rip-off."

I thanked her and asked, "By the way, did the kitchen workers get their jobs back?"

"Yup. Now everyone in food prep has to wear a hair net, guys included."

"How'd they like that?"

She shrugged. "Most of them ended up shaving their heads."

Normally, I eat breakfast at home, except when I oversleep. That's what happened the next morning. The thick towel I placed over the alarm clock to muffle the sound had worked too well; I didn't even hear the buzz. Chester likewise hadn't awakened me, no doubt in retaliation for leaving him behind the night before.

In the bathroom I did an abbreviated version of my routine. Instead of foundation, powder and blush, I slapped on bronzer. The mascara and lip gloss I could apply while driving. There was no time to make coffee. I decided to kill two birds with one stone and get an egg sandwich and coffee at Stella's and have a quick chat with Brandi.

I got the last space in the parking lot, pulling in next to Spencer Farley's regal Mercedes. I peeked in the window. The car, inside and out, was immaculate. Even the tennis racket on the back seat had a nice suede cover. I hoped he didn't spot my car. I wouldn't want any neatnik seeing the rubble inside my car. On the other hand, Spencer Farley doesn't strike me as the peeping type. Some people are born nosy. Thank God I'm one of them.

A man in a fluorescent vest had just vacated a stool at the end of the counter when I walked in. I grabbed it and glanced around. It was the usual early morning mix of office workers, tradespeople and retirees. The latter sat at their customary table wearing sweatshirts with the group's name, The Gab & Gaiters, printed across the front. Their morning walks always end with Stella's blueberry pancakes.

At the far end of the counter, Spencer sipped coffee and read *The Wall Street Journal*. Without being asked, Brandi put a steaming cup in front of me. "One Sweet 'n Low, one Equal and one teaspoon of sugar, right?"

"You're a wiz," I said. "By the way, can I talk to you for a second?"

She drew an order pad out of the pocket of her jeans. "First tell me what you want. I'll put it in and be right back." She glanced at the wall clock over my head. "The next wave doesn't arrive until after nine."

I rattled off my order: egg sandwich on a grilled English muffin with sausage and cheese, honey mustard on the side. Brandi nodded and scooted off to the grill where Stella flipped eggs and pancakes. Ten seconds later she appeared before me. "Okay, what's up?"

I kept my voice low. "It's about Cassandra, the caterer you work for. Do you know her sister, who also works for her?"

"Mary Lou? She works afternoons, three days a week. I don't really know her because I work nights."

"Do you know of any instance, while catering, where she might have interacted with Dr. Klinger?"

"Hmm. Now that I think of it, there was one, a luncheon. It was called Hooray for Healers, given in appreciation for those who make a difference in the community. Dr. Klinger was one of those honored."

"Did you ever hear Mary Lou say anything about Dr. Klinger?"

"Like I said, our hours don't overlap. The only time I spoke to her was when I went to Cassandra's house to pick up my check. Mary Lou was kind of snippy. "

"Okay. The next time you work for Cassandra, ask the staff what they know about Mary Lou. See what you can find out."

"You're saying she didn't like Dr. Klinger?"

"It seems she didn't care for her at all."

Thirteen

The next morning I found myself trapped in the recurring dream of being pursued by pigs while slogging through knee-deep sludge. I awoke when the phone rang, yanking me back to reality. In the tangle of blankets I struggled to reach out and croak a greeting. "Yeah?"

"Rose? It's me, Brandi." She was crying.

I sat up. "Brandi, what's wrong?"

"He's dead!"

"Who's dead?"

"Rusty. They said he drowned."

I kicked the blankets off. "Who said he drowned? Start from the beginning."

She let out a shaky sigh. "This morning I was listening to Stella's police scanner. They mentioned a forty-two year-old man found that morning in the park, drowned in the fish pond. I was afraid it was Rusty. I borrowed Stella's car and got there as the ambulance was leaving. They wouldn't let me get close or say who it was until they'd made a positive

ID. Then I spoke to Cal, and he admitted it was Rusty."

"But that's a kiddie pond, not more than two feet deep."

"Cal said Rusty had been drinking. He must have fallen and hit his head on the concrete embankment."

"How do they know he was drinking?"

"They found a bottle near his body."

The news was too much so early in the morning. I needed coffee and time to think. "Brandi, I'll stop by later today, okay?"

Her voice was subdued. "I'll be at Stella's."

I raised the shade. The sky was a dirty bowl overhead. Rain coursed down the window panes. It was the kind of morning that made you wish you were retired... or a dog. After letting Chester out, I rifled through the freezer among the unidentified frozen objects and found a fossilized bagel. I put it in the toaster oven and dialed Cal's cell phone. He answered right away.

"Hi, Rosie. Change your mind about dinner at my place?"

"Cal, Brandi Slocum called me earlier."

"Uh huh. It's a shame about Rusty. The guy had talent. I got the impression Brandi doesn't think his death was accidental."

"I said I'd get back to her when I learned more."

"There's not much to learn. The toxicology report will be more specific, but it's pretty obvious. Rusty was in the park. He got drunk and fell, hitting his head on the cement apron of the kiddie pond. Around six-thirty this morning, a senior citizens' walking group called the Gab and Gaiters came upon the body. Not long after that the EMTs verified his death."

"You don't suspect foul play?"

"Rosie, you've been reading too many Robert Parker novels."

"Cal, I'm in no mood for smart-ass comments. I just want to know the official cause of death."

"Don't get your undies in a twist. Doc Moss says it's a subdural hematoma. Rusty fell hard, as drunks do. They lack the involuntary protective response: raising your hands to break the fall."

"Is it possible he was hit?"

"Everything's possible, and everyone's a suspect, including Brandi. Maybe they had a lover's quarrel."

"They weren't lovers. Rusty was like a big brother to her." Cal snorted into the phone. I ignored it and asked, "How about the street people who hang around the park? Will you question them?"

"In due time. Remember, Rusty pissed off a lot of people. There's a group of skinheads, tough guys who ride skateboards near the Homer Frost statue. We get complaints about them all the time. They pee on the petunias and scare the squirrels. One day Rusty kicked their ass. Someone heard them threatening him."

"Please follow up on that, Cal. Now before I let you go, do you know if there's going to be an autopsy?"

"Rose, the chief is satisfied. We'll interview people, but basically this is considered an accidental death."

"But an autopsy would reveal more about the head wound."

"It might, had we found him earlier. His head was in the water for several hours and, well, the fish did a thorough job of cleaning the wound."

An image of big orange carp surfaced in my mind. I put the bagel down. "You're saying the department won't pursue the issue?"

"What do you want me to do, request an autopsy just to satisfy you and Brandi? I don't mean to sound heartless, because I liked Rusty. He was a great athlete at one time. He was also a drunk, an ex-con and a murder suspect."

"So that's how it works. Justice is meted out according to one's standing in the community. One set of rules for the Rotarians, another for the riffraff."

"Rose, honey, you're letting Brandi influence you. I was there. I saw the body. I smelled the booze. Many nights I'd see Rusty staggering around in the park. What's amazing is that he lasted so long."

"I guess there's no point in continuing this conversation. The chief's got his loose ends all tied up in a nice bow. Mayor Froggett and the Chamber will be pleased that Dr. Klinger's murder is solved.

Now there's no need for a trial. Good riddance to bad rubbish, eh?"

There was no response for so long, I thought Cal had hung up. Finally, he said, "I'm not the enemy, Rose. I just do my best. In any case, after I'm done guarding Stella's pigs, I won't be working the streets anymore. I put in for a transfer, mostly to satisfy Marcie. I'll be Director of Roads and Highways. So, if you find a dozen bodies in the fish pond, don't call me, because I won't give a damn."

I sucked in my breath. "I never thought I'd hear you say something like that, Cal Devine."

"That makes two of us. Goodbye, Rose."

By the time I reached the office, my mood matched the weather. Stewart was working on a story about Rusty, searching the archives for pictures and clips taken during his football years. "The guy was phenomenal," Stew said. "I saw all his games—as a kid, of course."

"Were you with your nanny?" I asked and immediately felt bad. Stewart didn't deserve the fallout from my black mood. "Don't mind me," I said. "It's been a rough morning."

I got up to get coffee in the break room. A sign tacked to the wall announced that coffee had risen to seventy cents a cup. Stew is in charge of buying and making the coffee. While he claims it's Blue Mountain, I suspect generic. Why else would he volunteer for the coffee job if not to make a few bucks to augment his trust fund checks?

I carried the mug back to my desk and listened to my voice mail. The first message got my attention. The voice was young and guarded. She said she was calling in response to my story about Stella's pigs and what she perceived as the high school administration's heavy-handedness toward the seniors. "I just want you to know we're fighting back." Before hanging up, she left a number.

I sat back in my chair, a genuine smile on my face. This was what I'd hoped for, a response from the seniors, a sign proving they weren't all main-streamers, that their spirit was alive and well.

I dialed the number. A young man answered. His voice, too, was guarded. After he'd determined my identity, we made a date to meet at the high school parking lot, near the bleachers, in an hour. "Look for a red van," he said.

After hanging up, I let out a whoop. It startled Yvonne, who'd just arrived, wearing a metallic rain poncho. "Yvonne, the pig story is catching fire. I'm meeting with some high school seniors in an hour. They want to speak anonymously. "

She shook out her umbrella. "Under the circumstances, an anonymous source is fine. Not only that, we have to pay attention to our young people. They're our future readers."

Stew piped up. "Was that the only response you got?"

"So far," I said. "I haven't listened to all my messages."

I booted up my computer, determined not to let Stewart's remark destroy my excitement. While the

Gazette readers hadn't responded as passionately as I'd hoped, I had reached someone. One must work with the raw materials at one's disposal, or as my dad is fond of saying, "You can't make chicken salad out of chicken shit."

Before long I found myself in the back seat of a red van parked in the high school lot. The two kids sitting across from me, Meggie and Seth, made me smile. I was reminded of myself at that age.

"They're incapable of independent thought, "Meggie said, referring to the faculty. "There's no flexibility, no thinking outside the box. Every week they make up new rules just to keep us in line. It's senseless."

"Do the students have any input regarding the rules?" I asked.

Seth, who wore a single skull earring, said, "If you're involved in school citizenship projects, you can participate in weekly community meetings. Whoopee."

"And the ones who are involved are dweebs who are only looking to build an impressive résumé," Meggie said.

"Old people forget what it's like to be young," Seth said. "They're afraid to be spontaneous. They might lose control. We're not talking about a drug orgy, we're talking about kidnapping a plastic pig. It's a prank, for God's sake. Now the principal has blown it all out of proportion."

"As always," Meggie said, resting her elbows on her knees. "Two days ago his car was stolen. Now he blames our group. He says anyone taking part in Prank Night won't graduate with the class." She rolled his eyes. "Who cares? I've already been accepted to college anyway."

"Where are you going?" I asked, curious.

"MIT."

Seth turned to me. "What's ironic is, in the beginning we were like, okay, maybe we'll do something for Prank Night, and maybe we won't. Then when Mr. Sheedy, the principal, banned it, we had no choice but to get involved."

"It's just the two of you?" I asked.

"There's a couple others," Seth said. "They used to be apathetic like the majority of students. Now they're psyched for Prank Night."

The school bell rang in the distance, too long and too loudly, as it had twenty years ago. Outside the van we shook hands. "Whatever you kids decide, be careful," I said.

"Thanks," Meggie said. "Want to hear our cheer?"

"Sure," I said.

They stood back and shouted "Prank Night, it's our right!" while at the same time leaping into the air and pumping their fists.

I liked their spirit.

Heading back to the Jetta, I noticed the number of students' cars in the lot. I wondered how they paid their insurance, considering the state's high premiums for teenage drivers. I didn't envy today's young people. Life had changed in the decades since I'd been a student. Back then, misbehavior was often chalked up to youthful indiscretion. Today, the consequences were harsh, with more to lose. I wondered if in future years Prank Night would be regarded as an anachronism, a pointless pursuit. Thus was keeping it alive a doomed mission?

I didn't know the answer, but I knew whose side I was on: *Prank Night, it's our right!*

On my way back to the office, I stopped at Stella's. In the parking lot, a photographer crouched below the pigs. I hoped he was a hobbyist and not with the media. If word got out about Prank Night, it would spoil everything. So many good ideas are ruined by over-exposure. Look what happened to Yoga.

The little bell over the door tinkled when I walked in. Distracted, I was stunned when Stella yelled my name, adding, "I wanna talk to you!" With her jowls quivering, she looked like an enraged bulldog.

"Me?" I squeaked.

She laughed heartily and pointed her spatula at me. "You should see the look on your face. Just like my husband when I caught him sneaking out the window one night."

"Really? What happened there?"

"He broke his neck. Drunker than a mule." She grabbed a newspaper on the counter, opened it and pointed to her photo. "My brother says I look like a junk yard dog."

I relaxed. "Then you're not mad at me?"

"Nah. I know you gotta sell papers. I just want kids to get the message that my pigs are off limits. Touch them, and I assault their asses."

"Don't worry, they got the message." I looked around. "Is Brandi here?"

Stella went to the back door and yelled for Brandi. Moments later she arrived, wearing jeans and a candy pink tee shirt. "Can we talk for a minute?" I asked.

She nodded and led me to a window table. The minute we sat down she asked, "Did you talk to Cal?"

"I did." I hesitated, wondering how much I should say about Cal's indifference to her murder theory.

"Let me guess. He thinks I'm crazy."

"He didn't exactly say that."

"He didn't have to. None of the cops take me seriously, especially Chief Alfano. When he didn't return my calls, I decided to visit the police station, talk to him in person. I had something important to tell him about the bottle found next to Rusty's body." She leaned toward me. "Rose, it was Jack Daniel's."

"Pretty good stuff."

"Too good," she said, sitting back. "Rusty couldn't afford Jack Daniel's. He bought the cheap stuff. 'Whatever works,' he used to say."

"What are you saying?"

"Someone must have given it to him."

"Or he stole it."

She shook her head. "It was from the Liquor Chest downtown. The receipt was still in the bag. Paid for with cash, a hundred dollar bill. Where would Rusty get a hundred dollars?"

"Do you have the receipt?"

She nodded. "I showed it to Chief Alfano, told him Rusty not only didn't have the money, he was banned from the Liquor Chest."

"Are you sure?"

"A couple of weeks ago he had a fight with the clerk, an old guy who works there. The clerk tried to stiff him, said Rusty had given him a ten dollar bill when it was a twenty."

"Did you tell this to the chief?"

She nodded. "He wasn't impressed. I asked if they were performing an autopsy. He said they're following protocol, that Doc Moss has over thirty years' experience. The whole time, he didn't once look at me." She stared at her hands. "It got worse. Maybe I had it coming, trying to stand up for myself. "

"Had what coming? What happened?"

She hesitated. "When I didn't appear satisfied with the chief's explanation, he took a folder out of a file cabinet. Then he slapped a photo down in front of me." She closed her eyes. "It was a picture of Rusty, underwater. His eyes... they stared right at me."

I grabbed her hand. "Don't worry, Brandi, he won't get away with that."

She got to her feet. "It doesn't matter. I'm used to it."

Fifteen minutes later I sat in Stella's parking lot recalling Brandi's story. Chief Alfano had known what he was doing. His brand of shock therapy had had the desired effect of silencing Brandi. It was the Golden Rule in action: Those with the gold shall rule. In this case, the chief had something more valuable than gold. He had power.

I vowed to bring his sleazy tactics to light. Still agitated, I switched on the ignition, shifted into reverse, and stepped on the gas. Behind me, a horn blared. I glanced in the rearview mirror. I'd narrowly missed hitting a police cruiser.

Cal Devine, shaking his head, pulled in next to me. We lowered our windows at the same time. "What's the rush?" he asked.

"Sorry, Cal. I wasn't paying attention. Have you heard anything from the coroner?"

"No, but I heard there'll be a memorial service for Rusty. Donations go to the high school athletic fund."

"Thank you for that information. Would you mind telling me what the department has learned? Any tests results?"

"The blood alcohol was three-point-five with a hefty dose of Valium that would have put me in a coma."

"Rusty's death was timely, wasn't it? The chief has an answer to the murder. Forget an autopsy. Get the body into the ground, and get on with our lives. "

"Rose, it's not homicide. You've been talking to Brandi, haven't you?"

"What of it? She raised some serious issues, and no one's taking her seriously, certainly not the chief."

"The department isn't perfect, but it functions. Doc Moss has been coroner a long time. If he thought there was just cause, he'd perform an autopsy. In any case, don't complain to me, tell the chief."

"You tell him, Cal. Tell him he's through pushing women around. If he asks what I'm talking about, he can read about it in the *Granite Cove Gazette.*" With that, I stepped on the gas and roared back. Shifting into drive, I fishtailed out of the parking lot. I hadn't felt so alive since high school Prank Night.

Up your exhaust pipe, Chief!

That night I got into bed to write my column, cushioning the laptop with a pillow. The wind shook the casings on the drafty, old windows. Outside, a car drove by, sloshing through potholes. Was it my imagination, or did it slow down? If it did, I hoped it was a police cruiser. Cal assured me my road was being patrolled regularly. Although I believed him, how often was regularly? Hourly? Daily?

While waiting for the ancient computer to boot, I reached for the TV remote. Maybe the local cable news had more on Rusty's death. Setting the laptop aside, I clicked on the power.

News anchor Myranda Trowt appeared onscreen standing in front of a tall stockade fence. Occupying the upper left portion of the screen was a familiar face, pale and sullen. It was a young face that begged to be slapped. I reached for my glasses to read the name underneath and almost lost control of my bladder. The face belonged to Jonah Zagrobski.

The news anchor continued her report: "The thirteen-year-old, an honor student at Granite Cove Middle School, apparently wandered into Moles Used Car lot where he was bitten by the dog."

Honor student? According to Betty Ann, Jonah was flunking every subject.

Now a new face appeared opposite Jonah's, that of a pit bull, its ears pressed tight to its head. Black beady eyes glared at the viewer. The camera moved in for a close-up of Myranda Trowt's concerned face. "The dog is believed to be owned by Buster Moles, who at this time cannot be located. Unless Mr. Moles provides authorities with a current rabies certificate, the dog will be euthanized, and young Jonah will undergo a series of painful, precautionary inoculations. In the meantime, Granite Cove Police continue their search. If anyone has information regarding Buster Moles's whereabouts, notify police immediately."

I clicked off the TV and grabbed the phone, punching in B.A.'s number. It was late, but I knew I wouldn't sleep unless I spoke to her. After six rings the call was routed to her voice mail. I left a message: "Betty Ann, I just saw the news on TV. I'll call you tomorrow." I hung up and sank back into the pillows, the image of Jonah's face stuck in my mind. The situation certainly didn't bode well for Tiny's custody fight.

Finally, I sat up and began typing. The crisis would have to wait until tomorrow. Tonight I had a column to write.

Auntie Pearl's Helpful Housekeeping Hints

Dear Auntie Pearl:

My friends all warned me about Warren. They said a man of forty still living at home with his mother had issues. But instead of listening to them, I married him. Five years later I'm considering divorce.

Why? Because every Sunday and holiday is spent with Mother, who ignores me and dotes on her son. The last straw was his birthday. I'd invited our friends for a party, and Warren showed up two hours later. He'd been at Mother's, enjoying her triple-layer buttercream frosting cake.

Auntie Pearl, do you think I'd be better off alone?

Signed,
Disrespected in Danvers

Dear Disrespected:

My first thought was: Did your mother-in-law augment the butter in the frosting? While it's fine to use butter along with powdered sugar when making frosting in the winter, it won't work in the summer. It could wilt, and become rancid. Furthermore, a butter-heavy frosting is too rich for today's calorie-counting guests.

Let me tell you my little secret: marshmallow! That's right, simply add a few spoonfuls of the sticky white stuff from a jar. Set your blender /mixer to its highest setting and whirl away. The marshmallow adds sweetness and stability to the mixture. You're less likely to have a meltdown in an overheated room.

Send a stamped, self-addressed envelope along with a $5 check made out to Auntie Pearl, c/o this newspaper. You'll receive a fabulous collection of my family's favorite cake recipes. I guarantee your husband will stick around on his next birthday!

Bon appétit!
Auntie Pearl

Fourteen

The next morning, as I was leaving a message on the Zagrobskis' answering machine, a breathless Betty Ann picked up: "Rose! I've turned off this phone—too many calls. I'm also taking a sick day to bring Jonah to Doc Moss's office. He wants to check the stitches." "

"Jonah had stitches?"

"Seven on his right buttock. I'll give the little bugger credit, he didn't even cry."

"How did it happen?"

She let out a long breath. "From what he's told us, around seven o'clock last night Jonah and a friend climbed over the fence at Moles Used Motors. He claims they wanted to look at the junk. Once inside, they were charged by a pit bull that guards the lot.

"The other kid made it back over the fence, but not Jonah. The dog leaped up and bit him." She lowered her voice. "He had some deep puncture wounds. Doc Moss said the buttocks are a particularly painful area. To make matters worse, along with the antibiotic injections, he needed anti-rabies shots because no one knows if the dog's been vaccinated."

"I guess that means they didn't find Buster."

"That sleaze-bag took off leaving nobody in charge. "

"How's Tiny holding up?"

Doc Moss made him lie on a cot in the emergency room. He feared Tiny would pass out."

"How's Jonah?"

"He hates having to drop his pants so I can change the dressing, but he's got no choice."

"What happens now?"

"If the police don't locate Buster in the next twelve hours, the dog will be put down." She let out a sigh. "This morning while Jonah was watching the local news, he asked Tiny what euthanize meant. When Tiny told him, he started blubbering. He said it wasn't the dog's fault, he was only doing his job. Now if the dog dies, Jonah's gonna feel terrible. He's in his room crying his eyes out. Tell you the truth, I feel sorry for the kid."

"Let's hope Buster will be found," I said. "Call me as soon as you hear something." Before hanging up, I added, "Remember, B.A., you don't have to smoke over this."

"Are you kidding? Between the cops and visits to the doctor's office, I don't have time to pee."

Later that afternoon I stood outside the door to my dad's apartment. His TV was so loud I felt the vibrations through the floor. After I pounded on the door, he finally appeared. "Rose, it's you."

"I've been knocking on your door for five minutes."

"Didn't I give you a key?"

"You did. It's in my glove compartment."

"You're the one who told me to lock my door," he said. "I don't care about my stuff. Let 'em have it."

"Never mind, Dad. I brought your favorite, an egg and sausage sandwich."

He glanced at his watch. "I can't have it now. Doris Zack is coming any minute. If I start eating, she might show. I always leave when she arrives."

"Okay, have it when you get back."

He shook his head. "That'll be close to supper, and I took a macaroni and cheese from the freezer."

I threw up my hands. "In that case I'll give it to Chester."

"Don't do that," he said, taking the bag from me. "I'll have it tomorrow."

"Why didn't you say that in the first place?"

He headed for the kitchen. "You didn't give me time."

Like many elders, my dad is set in his ways. It was one of the reasons our earlier attempt at living together failed. Another reason was the fact we're too much alike. I had an epiphany one evening about a month after he'd moved in. Dad had gone to bed, and I was looking forward to being alone with a glass of wine and the latest issue of Yankee. Stretched out on the sofa, I opened the magazine. A tiny pile of toenail clippings fell onto my chest. I knew our roommate days were numbered.

And yet, as Betty Ann pointed out to me in the parking lot of Marilyn's Pie Palace, I'd been the one who'd insisted he move in with me. "Dad, can I ask you something?"

"Ask me anything."

"After Mom died, did you think I was trying to take her place?"

He was in the process of wrapping a scarf around his neck. "You could never be as neat as your mother. Few could."

"Would you say I suffered from guilt?"

"If you did, you had nothing to feel guilty about."

"Mom was disappointed that I didn't marry Cal and have a storybook wedding."

He stuffed the ends of the scarf inside his cardigan. "That was your mother's way. If she found a stray sock in the washing machine, she'd turn the house upside down searching for its mate. She hated loose ends."

A brisk knocking interrupted us. I opened the door and found Doris Zack in the hallway, an upright vacuum cleaner at her side and bucket of cleaning supplies at her feet. The plastic name tag on her pocket read: Doris, Granite Cove Elderly Services. I grabbed the vacuum cleaner and dragged it inside.

"Put it over there, Rose. I use the outlet behind the sofa." She turned to my dad. "I'm doing the bathroom first, Mr. McNichols. If you've got any business in there, you better go now."

"I already went," he said. "Are you coming, Rose?"

"I want to talk to Doris, Dad. I'll see you later."

I watched her removing supplies from the plastic bucket and setting them on the kitchen counter. "How are things at the Harbour Building?" I said. "Has anyone moved into Dr. Klinger's office?"

"You wouldn't think anyone would want it, but a young fella's moved in, a stockbroker. First thing he did was hire one of those cleaning teams. If you ask me, they do a crummy job."

"You're still working for Mr. Farley?"

"Uh huh. I don't mind saying it gives me the chills. The connecting door's locked now. It's sad to see his mug all alone on the shelf." She shook her head. "I don't suppose he'll be doing any drinking with the new fella."

At the mention of Spencer Farley's mug, a thought formed in the back of my mind. "Doris, the morning you discovered Dr. Klinger's body, do you remember if Mr. Farley's mug was still on the tray with hers?"

She stopped and scratched her head. "Hmm, it's been a while, but I got a good head for details. My Harold says I can remember every lottery number I've played, including the new one that's all the rage in New Hampshire. "

"Think back for a minute," I said. "Think back to that morning. Did you see both mugs on the cart?"

She put her hands on her hips and peered at the ceiling, as if the answer was encoded there. "Let me go back and remember what I did that day. One thing that was different, I deodorized the Oriental runner in the reception area. I used to do it every week, but folks complained about how the smell lingers. Another thing I remember was how Mr. Farley's secretary left a plant on her desk. When I picked it up there was a white ring on the wood. What I did was, I brought some olive oil from home and some ash from Harold's cigar. You mix the two together and rub it into the wood with a cloth. Let it set overnight. The next day the stain's gone. I never waste money on that commercial stuff."

Getting back to that morning, if you will..."

She snapped her fingers. "Now I remember. His mug wasn't on the tray. It was back in his office, on the shelf. At first I figured maybe they hadn't had their cocktails, but they had. The liquor bottle was there and a silver bowl of almonds, almost empty. It was just her mug sitting there, yet Dr. Klinger wasn't the type to drink alone. Now that you mention it, I thought it was a little odd at the time."

"And Mr. Farley told the police they'd had a drink together that night," I said. "Could she have returned the mug to his office?"

She shook her head. "Mr. Farley locked the connecting door behind him when he left. It locks from the inside. Even if she wanted to return it, she'd have to go outside to the corridor and use his main door, which would be locked."

"You think that's unlikely?"

"Why go to all that trouble to return a cup? Remember, those two were used to people cleaning up after them."

"If that's the case, someone must have returned his mug," I said." Did you mention this discrepancy to the police?"

"I told them only what they asked me. My clients' business is none of their business."

"So the coffee mugs were never mentioned?"

"Not by me."

"Doris, I can't tell you how helpful you've been. I've got a lot of work to do right now." I got up, my head whirling with ideas.

"Tell your dad I'll wash his shower curtain next week."

"Thanks, Doris, thanks a lot." The nagging thought in the back of my head was expanding, pushing out all extraneous matters. Most likely it had been building while I, distracted by life's minutia, hadn't paid attention. This time I wouldn't shut it out.

At the office I let myself in without bothering to turn on the main light. After switching on my gooseneck desk lamp, I booted up the computer. From a zippered case, I removed the stack of photo CDs, flipping through them until I found what I hoped was the right one. Seconds later the monitor bloomed with photos of the Professional Women's League awards luncheon. The photos advanced in a slide show as I studied each. After repeating it, I began to think the image I was seeking had been a figment of my imagination, a snippet from a dream.

Until a face in the background caught my attention.

I clicked on the photo to enlarge it, peering at the results. The intensity of raw emotion on the features made me shiver. I sat back, awed, as everything fell into place. I hadn't imagined it after all. I'd been on the right track. Most likely my unconscious mind had stored the image. Now, six weeks later, it sent me a reminder.

I switched off the lamp. For a little while I sat in the darkened newsroom. Outside, people passing by cast long shadows across the wall. Soon the street lights would go on. In the meantime, I would wait. What I had in mind required the cover of darkness.

The sunset was fading when I finally locked up. Streaks of lavender colored the horizon. In my car, I joined the line of late commuters inching along Main Street. Then, leaving the traffic, I got onto Route 62, passing Stella's restaurant. The waning light bathed the pigs in a soft glow.

Prank Night had finally arrived. Would the seniors cave in to pressure from authorities, or would they uphold decades of tradition? Although I felt protective of Stella's pigs, I was rooting for the kids. Now more than ever, the world needed pranks.

My first stop was Kevin's house. I pulled in behind his Mustang, noting that his trunk was open. An assortment of speakers, cables and lights was neatly arranged inside. It was a far cry from the interior of Kevin's house.

Walter was in his vegetable patch, pants rolled to his knees, revealing the whitest legs I'd ever seen. He stood. "Rose, I want you to have some of my bean salad. I'll get it inside."

"Thanks, Walter," I said, rapping on Kevin's front door. "I'll be right out."

Seeing me at his door, Kevin looked surprised. "Rosie, what's up?"

"Just thought I'd stop by to borrow something."

He cocked his head. "You look like a kid at the carnival. Your eyes are like pinwheels." He pulled me inside and wrapped me in an embrace. But soon he pulled back, saying "What's wrong? Do I have B.O. or something?"

"Sorry, Kevin. I've got a lot on my mind. I wanted to ask if I could borrow your button-down black shirt."

His eyes narrowed. "You're not involved in Prank Night, are you?"

For a moment I considered telling him my plans until I realized how much he'd worry. Although his manner is irreverent, Kevin is not a risk taker. "I'll tell you about it tomorrow, okay? I've got to go now."

He slipped into his bedroom, plucking the shirt from his closet. "I don't know what you're up to, but I don't approve."

"How do you know I'm up to something?"

"I can tell. You're humming on all burners. "He pulled me to him again, resting his chin on the top of my head. "Rosie?"

"Yes?"

"Will you come over tonight afterward?"

"You won't be through until two a.m. How about Friday night instead?"

"Good. I'll make us breakfast."

"Uh huh. Captain Crunch and Mountain Dew."

"Nope. Eggs and bacon, the real thing."

I looked up at the ginger-colored freckles sprinkled across his cheeks. This time when he kissed me, I responded. The events of the day vanished. Everything was centered on the present. It was blissful until a voice outside shattered the silence. "Rose, I've got your beans!"

Kevin groaned, and I laughed. "It's Walter. I've got to go."

He held my face in his hands. "Be careful."

"I always am." Even to my ears, I didn't sound convincing.

It was dusk when I headed for Shore Road. The sea was silvery calm. In the distance, a lobster boat headed for home trailing an entourage of seagulls.

I slowed as I approached the entrance to Settlers Dunes. A half-dozen blue and gold balloons were tied to the sign: Coming Soon! Cormorant Cove! I drove past the entrance, pulling into a narrow dirt path further down the road. It was a seldom used turnaround, overgrown with tall pampas grass and stubby shad trees. It would conceal the Jetta. I shut off the engine. Outside, the tree frogs were in full chorus while above, an early moon appeared in the darkening sky. The air smelled of wild beach roses and seaweed.

I got out and put on Kevin's shirt. The sleeves were long; the cuffs hid my hands. I locked my pocketbook in the trunk, pocketing the keys. Muttering a quick prayer to St. Theresa, I set out, pushing through the tall grass and down the road toward Settlers Dunes.

Fifteen

I kept to the edge of the road, ready to leap into the bushes should a car approach. In the event I was spotted, my excuse would be that I'm a reporter covering Settlers Dunes. I had every right to be there, I reminded myself.

Upon reaching the entrance, I ducked inside and scurried over the sandy, rocky road until I reached the clearing. The sight of the pale, shimmering dunes and the sea beyond filled me with awe. According to the history books, the individuals who settled the area preferred living by the open sea rather than in town with the others. They were a small intrepid band whose shelters were clustered together against the Atlantic gales. Despite their first harsh winter, the group survived. They were on good terms with the Indians who fished nearby. Early drawings show the wooden fish shacks alongside the Indians' weathered canoes. The sea provided for all, the bluefish so plentiful, reports claim the settlers scooped them from the surf with bare hands.

I hid behind the giant boulders at the entrance. Just as I expected, a dusty black Mercedes station wagon was parked in the clearing near the eel grass. Business as usual. I approached in a crouch, circumnavigating the gravel parking lot. When I got closer to the car, I stopped, waiting for my heart beat to slow.

Still crouching, I scurried to the opposite side of the car and waited, my chin resting on my knees. When I was sure all was quiet, I raised my head and peeked inside the car's window. In the front seat a crumpled blazer lay across a brief case. In the back, a half dozen signs lay stacked on the seat. The station wagon's rear door was open; I crawled to the back.

A wooden tool box was covered by a blanket. I yanked it off, finding jars of nails, a collection of paint brushes and two cans of paint inside. I continued peering into the dark recesses of the trunk, finally pushing the tool box aside to lean in.

Too late, I heard a crunch of gravel behind me. I turned, felt a whir of motion, and thunk. Lights exploded in my head while a buzzing like soda water filled my ears. It grew louder, the vibrations traveling in waves through my body until everything faded to black.

Time passed. I came out of the blackness aware of movement. At first I thought Chester was pulling at my blankets. I opened my mouth to scold him, and an all-encompassing pain gripped my head, radiating from the back. When I reached to touch it, I discovered my hands were tied.

I longed to sink back into the fog of oblivion. Instead, I reluctantly turned my attention to my body; it was in motion. In fact, it was being dragged over slippery, wet grass. The grass gave way to smooth, cool sand. I liked the coolness, despite the clumps of dried seaweed that scoured my exposed skin.

Finally, I opened an eye to squint at the night sky and the clouds covering the moon. Against this panorama, a bent figure pulled me across the sand. The strong, bowed back reminded me of a character from the painting, "The Peasants Wedding," by Brueghel.

The clouds scurried by. The moon appeared, and the pulling stopped. The figure turned and spoke: "For a skinny bitch you're awfully heavy." Although the voice lacked its usual Hemlock Point diction, it was one I knew, the voice of a high school field hockey captain.

My voice was a croak. "Martha, let me go."

She dropped her end of the coarse rope that bound my ankles and rubbed her hands. "What were you doing snooping in my car?"

"Your car?" Confusion increased the pain in my head. Tonight I'd visited the Dunes, but why? Through the fog of pain, an image appeared of a young Martha Muldoon running down the athletic field in a short, plaid skirt and waving a stick. I squeezed my eyes shut. No, it wasn't a stick, it was a mallet, like the one she used to pound in her real estate signs.

That night, on the way to the Phipps' party, when Kevin yelled to Martha, her angry face had remained stuck in my mind. For good reason. The expression was identical to the one she wore in the photo of the Professional Women's luncheon. As Dr. Klinger received her award, those around her smiled—all except Martha, who wore a murderous look.

Her voice interrupted my reverie. "Forget it, McNichols. I don't care what you were looking for. You've caused too much trouble already."

I tried to raise myself up despite the throbbing in my head. "Martha, I understand what you went through. You felt threatened by Vivian Klinger."

She snorted. "People were stupid not to see what a phony she was."

"Did you hit her?"

"Ask anything you want, McNichols. This isn't TV where you get a last-minute confession."

I tried another angle. "It must have hurt, knowing she was having an affair with your husband."

She shrugged. "I wasn't impressed with her Ivy League degrees. She was a high class tramp who'd do anything to make a name for herself."

"You were smart," I said. "You slipped Valium into the bottle of scotch. That's why Spencer was sleeping in his car the night she died." When she said nothing, I continued. "It's common knowledge the scotch was drugged. The police are onto it."

Her laugh was harsh. "You're the one tied up, yet you expect a confession from me?"

"I know everything that happened, Martha. Not only me, but others, including Cal Devine. Chief Alfano suspects you also put Valium in the Jack Daniel's you bought for Rusty. Your fingerprints are all over the receipt you carelessly left in the bag."

"Rusty." She spat the word. "The town's better off without that parasite. He was a loser and a snoop just like you. You know what happens to snoops? They learn their lesson the hard way."

"Rusty was in the park the night Dr. Klinger died," I said, "and he saw you."

"That scumbag dug his own grave when he demanded money from me." She turned and scanned the shoreline. "Okay, the tide's just about to turn. Let's get this over with."

"Martha, use your head. The note you threw in my car window? It's now at the state police lab. If anything happens to me, that note will lead straight to you."

"I don't know what note you're talking about, McNichols. That whack I gave you must have scrambled your brains."

She yanked on the rope. Soon I was being dragged over wet sand. In desperation I looked around the deserted beach. No one, not even a lone seagull to witness my plight. Finally, I spoke, my mouth dry, my throat constricted. "Cal Devine knows I'm here tonight. He's looking for me right now."

"Nice try," she said. "Cal's at Stella's keeping an eye on those pigs." Finally we reached the water's edge. She peered at her watch. "One more minute and the tide turns. With any luck your body will wash up in the Azores."

I struggled to raise myself up. "You're jeopardizing everything, Martha. It's not too late to let me go. On my father's life, I promise this will stay between us."

Instead of responding, she looked all around, turning in a full circle. "You see this stretch of beach? It's going to be mine someday." She gestured toward the dunes. "Cormorant Cove villas will sit over there. Right here I'm thinking of building a pier for the residents' yachts." She looked down at me on the ground. "Do you have any idea how much money we're talking about? Of course you don't. You're a townie who's content to write about other townies."

One second later, her tone was conversational. "McNichols, do you know what my grandfather did for a living?" When I shook my head, she said, "At the turn of the century he drove a wagon around Hemlock Point. He cleaned the residents' out houses." She chuckled. "Imagine Mickey Muldoon's granddaughter becoming the richest woman on Hemlock Point. "

"It's an amazing story," I said, frantically attempting to work my hands free, "and I'd love to write it."

My efforts weren't lost on her. "Don't bother struggling with those ropes. I made sailor's knots.

You'll never get out." She checked her watch again and said, "Tide's perfect. Let's do it." With that, she yanked the rope, causing me to fall back. Frigid sea water seeped into my clothes. Lying flat on my back, I looked up at the stars, my eyes filling with tears. The night had never looked more lovely. I thought about my dad and Chester, Betty Ann and Kevin.

With my last reserve of strength, I cried out, "Please, Martha! Please!"

She gave the rope a savage tug. Currents of pain shot up my legs as I was being dragged through the shallows. Waves lapped my chin. One splashed full in my face. "Help me! Somebody help me!"

Martha stopped, breathing heavily. She looked up and down the shore. "This is a good spot. "She lifted her foot and placed it on my chest. I thrashed in the water, fighting the ropes that bit into my wrists. "It's nothing personal, McNichols," she said. "You chose the wrong cause when you came after me. You ought to know I stop at nothing."

The pressure of her foot increased, forcing me deeper into the water. An incoming wave washed over my face. I gulped sea water, coughing and gagging and gasping for air. Still the unrelenting waves continued. Water ran into my nose and ears.

Just as the surf washed over my head, the pressure suddenly lifted from my chest. I managed to scramble to a sitting position before an incoming wave hit me full force. I rolled over and over, yet somehow managed to get to my knees.

I looked around, gulping air, the salt water stinging my eyes. Martha was flying down the beach as fast as she'd run back in high school as captain of the girls' field hockey team. If that wasn't cause enough for rejoicing, another amazing spectacle was unfolding up in the dunes. A giant pig, his body gleaming in the moonlight, slid down the sands. The pig was followed by leaping, tumbling and rolling bodies.

Some took off after Martha. One ran straight toward me.

For the second time that night I came to on the sands. This time it wasn't Martha Farley hovering over me, but Cal Devine. He straddled my body, pressing strong, warm fingers into my neck. When I tried to speak he said, "Quiet. I'm checking your pulse." I didn't protest. It was heaven lying on dry sand. "Let's get you to the hospital," Cal said, crouching to pick me up. When he got to his feet, he staggered. "You're heavier than you look, kid."

"Someone else mentioned that tonight," I said, glancing around. "Where is everybody?"

"If you mean the students, they're chasing Martha Farley."

He carried me across the sand. On the way we passed the pig lying on its side. "Cal?" My voice was weak.

"Don't worry, I'll get someone to pick it up," he said. "And don't talk. You've got a head wound."

In the clearing, the cruiser was parked behind the red van. "How'd they steal it?" I asked as he lowered me into the front seat.

"It's a long story. I'll tell you when we reach the hospital."

I leaned my head gingerly against the seat. "Don't be hard on the kids. If they hadn't shown up here, I'd be rolling out with the tide right now." En route to the Azores, I thought, remembering the helpless feeling of being bound in the water. I shivered, and seconds later my body shook uncontrollably.

Immediately, Cal stopped the car and leaped out. He appeared at my side with a blanket. "Hypothermia. Let's get you out of those wet clothes."

"Cal, you're a married man," I said, closing my eyes.

"Don't worry," he said, unbuttoning my blouse, "I'd never take advantage of a women covered in sand."

Sixteen

Fortunately, Doc Moss was on duty when Cal carried me into the emergency room. Immediately, a gurney arrived to whisk me off to X-ray. After that, I found myself back in the emergency unit lying on a table inside a curtained enclosure. Someone shook my shoulder. I looked up into the face of Marcie Devine.

"Sorry, Rose. You can't sleep yet. I have to shave your head."

"My whole head?"

"Just in the back."

Doc Moss entered, pushing aside the curtains. "We checked your x-rays, Rose. Your skull's intact, but you need a couple of stitches. Because it's a head wound, I'm admitting you overnight to keep an eye on you."

Marcie vanished and soon reappeared, rolling a cart. On it was a tray containing an assortment of sharp, gleaming instruments that caused me to look away. She helped me to a sitting position and stood behind me. Soon I felt her clipping my hair.

"How many stitches?" I asked, my voice sounding like an eight year old's.

Doc Moss patted my knee. "Four or five. Be thankful for that thick Irish skull."

As Marcie silently clipped, I wondered if she'd seen Cal carry me into the emergency room. When she finished with the scissors, she dabbed the area with cold antiseptic. Then Doc Moss took her place. "This might sting a bit," he said, brandishing a hypodermic needle.

"Owww!" I squeaked, drumming my fists on my knees. Marcie slipped a hand into mine. I squeezed it until the injections stopped and the Novocain started taking effect. At some point while Doc Moss sewed me up, Marcie left the cubicle. By then I barely felt the needle, outside of a little tugging.

"Good girl," he said when the last bandage was in place. "Someone will take you to your floor. In the meantime, a police officer outside wants to talk to you."

He opened the curtain and Cal entered. "You've got five minutes," Doc Moss warned him. "This young lady's had a rough night."

Cal nodded and yanked the curtains shut. "I like your headdress," he said, pulling up a chair.

I touched my head. It felt like a padded gourd. "What's going on?"

"I just talked to the chief. The kids caught up with Martha. They tackled her, even brought her in. First thing she did was call Spencer. The chief wants a statement from you tomorrow morning."

"I hope you told him how Martha tried to drown me. If you hadn't come along, she would have succeeded. Not only that, she's responsible for the deaths of Rusty and Dr. Klinger."

His eyebrows shot up. "She admitted that?"

"Not in so many words, but she didn't deny it, either. Martha put Valium in the bottle in Dr. Klinger's office. It was easy for her; she must have used her husband's keys. She drugged Rusty's bottle of Jack Daniel's as well. That was the easiest: she'd bought it for him. Then she whacked both of them with the same wooden mallet she used on me. Can you locate it?"

"Easy, girl. How'd she happen to club you?"

"She caught me looking in her car at the Dunes."

"You realize that Spencer will hire the best criminal lawyers in Boston. They'll probably claim that it was dusk and Martha mistook you for an intruder... which you were."

"I was peeking in her car. That's no reason to club and drown a person."

He held a finger to his lips. "Let's talk about it later, okay? Doc Moss wants you to stay quiet."

"What about the mallet? Can they do DNA testing?"

"I seriously doubt she'd keep a weapon lying around. My guess is she went sailing and tossed it overboard. Your theory will be tough to prove."

"It's no theory, it's a fact. Dr. Klinger was a threat," I said, "not only to Martha's marriage but to Cormorant Cove, her upscale development."

"Dr. Klinger was more a threat to Bunny Alfano, who was running for the same office," he said.

"But Cal, I have proof it was Martha."

"What do you mean?"

"Doris Zack confirmed it. The night Vivian Klinger was killed, she'd had a drink with Spencer. Following that, his mug was mysteriously returned to his office. Now, Spencer never returned his own mug, and Dr. Klinger wouldn't have returned it— his office door was locked. Then who returned the mug to Spencer's office? Obviously Martha. She'd reacted instinctively, putting it back to protect her husband. She wasn't aware that was Doris Zack's job."

"Mug?" He scratched his head. "What are you talking about?"

"I'll go into the details later, but first, what about the rock thrown in my car window? Martha's prints will be on that note."

Cal got to his feet. "Honey, Doc Moss said five minutes. You need to rest."

I grabbed his sleeve. "Cal, you turned the note over to the lab, right?"

"I meant to tell you about that."

"About what?"

"That note wasn't from Martha."

I stared at him open-mouthed. "What? Who was it from?"

He placed a finger to his lips and whispered, "Marcie."

"Marcie!"

"Not so loud. I suspected Marcie all along. For one thing, the spelling on the note. The word 'value' had no E. That's just the way Marcie writes, in a rush, always abbreviating words."

"Marcie admitted it?"

He nodded. "I confronted her."

"So that's why she was nice to me tonight."

"We had a long talk, something we haven't done in years. Neither of us wants to end the marriage and hurt the kids. We're getting back together."

"That's very unprofessional, Cal Devine, withholding evidence."

He winced. "I know, but it was a domestic issue. No sense wasting the state's money on unnecessary testing."

"Before you go, tell me how the high school kids managed to outsmart you tonight."

He groaned. "Someone called the station to say there's a body lying alongside Brightside. Since the dispatcher knew I was in the area, he called me. I left Stella's for a quick check, long enough to check the area and determine there was no body. When I got back, sure enough, the pig was gone. Punks used a blowtorch on the chains."

"Well, you don't have to worry about Stella's backlash now that you're transferring to a new department."

"It's not official yet. It might never happen."

"Really? What made you change your mind?"

He shrugged. "For one thing, chasing the kids at the beach tonight, I got a little winded. Can you imagine what shape I'd be in if I took a desk job?"

I looked up into his face. "I'm glad you were on duty tonight, Cal. You saved my life. Will you do me a favor before you go?"

"Anything, honey."

"Will you call Betty Ann and ask her to let Chester out in the morning? I don't know what time they're releasing me."

"She'll be happy to do it. Did you know that Tiny's kid Jonah is a hero?"

"Jonah?"

"When we couldn't locate Buster Moles, we got a search warrant to go inside and try to find the dog's records. We found them, all right, along with a few other things, such as the high school principal's car. The serial number had been filed off. It was ready to be shipped off to the islands. Behind that tall fence Buster was running a busy chop shop."

"I wouldn't be surprised if the mayor's SUV was stolen, too," I said. "As for Jonah, does this mean the dog won't be put down?"

He nodded. "He's at the shelter, and guess who wants to adopt him?"

"Don't tell me."

He nodded. "Jonah."

"Betty Ann doesn't need a pit bull at this point in her life."

"Apparently the dog's a big teddy bear off duty. Jonah's naming him Sparky."

"It'll make a great story for the paper," I said, yawning.

"And I know just the person to write it," he said, leaning down to kiss my cheek.

After Cal left, I listened to the hospital's night sounds: the hurried footsteps, the muted voices and the unceasing intercom's announcements. In another cubicle, a child cried and in response, someone sang a song. It was a lullaby about the moon, the stars, and a silver comet come to Earth. I pulled the flannel blanket to my chin and before long drifted off to sleep.

Epilogue

"Rose, you finally got rid of that nest."

I turned in my chair to face Stewart. "What nest?"

"The one you've been wearing these past weeks."

"If you're referring to my hairpiece, I no longer need it, thank you. My hair's grown back."

"I know why you got rid of it," he said.

"Why's that?"

"Ever since the Women's Professional League named you Woman of the Year, you've had a swollen head."

Yvonne spoke up. "Don't tease Rose. This newspaper shares her honor as well."

"Thanks, Yvonne," I said, although I wondered how honored she'd feel had Martha Farley pulled her ads. Incredibly enough, Ask Martha! Real Estate is still conducting business, although Martha keeps a low profile while out on bail. Judging by the way her lawyers keep continuing the court date, we'll all be in nursing homes by the time the case goes to trial.

In any event, it's out of my hands. Although Martha wasn't implicated in the murder of Dr. Klinger, she's no longer involved in Settlers Dunes. Neither is Bunny, who immediately distanced himself from "Mad Martha," as the tabloids called her.

In a heaven-sent development, the Klingers stepped up to the plate. After my story, "An Unimagined Death," appeared in *Bay State Living*, the TV show New England Ventures got into the act. The Martha scandal helped create a buzz. They did a feature on Granite Cove, touching on the plight of Settlers Dunes.

That's when the Klingers got involved. Soon the site will be home to the Vivian Klinger Marine Preserve. The plans call for an environmental educational center complete with museum, research lab, classrooms and scholarships for budding marine scientists.

For me, being named Woman of the Year was frosting on the cake. Recently, I bought a small recorder to practice my acceptance speech while driving. Not only that, Brandi's promised to tape the awards luncheon. She's majoring in film studies at the community college. By all accounts, she's something of a tech whiz.

Occasionally, I have to pinch myself to make sure I'm not dreaming. Life is funny. Sometimes it seems intent on breaking you; other times it hands you a break. When the latter happens, don't get in your way. As my dad is fond of saying, "When your ship comes in, don't be in the bathroom with your pants down."

Auntie Pearl's Helpful Housekeeping Hints

Dear Auntie Pearl:

I play bridge once a month with a group of retired women from my neighborhood. We take turns hosting, and each member brings dessert. Last week, when Loretta hosted at her house, I brought prune squares. The next day, realizing I'd left the platter behind, I asked my husband to pick it up on the way back from his walk.

He returned two hours later, saying he'd helped Loretta install a grab bar on her tub. (Loretta's husband died last year.) Not long after that, he greased and tightened the coils on her overhead garage door. I didn't think much about it until my husband began going over there more and more. He put a washer in a bathroom faucet, put new batteries in her cable remote, transplanted a large jade tree, etc. When I put my foot down and forbade him to go to Loretta's house, he stormed out. The next day he vanished—along with Loretta.

I am crushed, Auntie Pearl. Should I consult a lawyer or a private investigator?

Sleepless in Salem

Dear Sleepless:

Here's a tip: Check the newspaper and bulletin boards for notices of church fairs and yard sales. When you arrive, make a beeline for the housewares table where you will find attractive plates at dirt cheap prices. It doesn't matter if they don't match your dishes at home. They will be used for those occasions when you bring a dessert, such as your prune squares.

(By the way, check out my website: AuntiePearlBakes.com for exciting alternatives to fruit squares.)

Best of all, should you leave a dish behind, it won't matter. And who knows, you might even come upon your lost platter. Don't hold your breath waiting for your husband.

Auntie Pearl

Meet the Author

Sharon Love Cook has an MFA in Writing and has written for magazines, newspapers and anthologies. She is also an art school grad who illustrates her book covers. *A Nose for Hanky Panky* is Cook's first Granite Cove Mystery, followed by *A Deadly Christmas Carol*. Sharon and her husband live north of Boston in Beverly Farms with a herd of rescued cats. Contact her at cookie978@comcast.net.